GHOULSLAYER
A GOTREK GURNISSON NOVEL

Collections

The Realmgate Wars: Volume 1
Various authors
Contains the novels *The Gates of Azyr, War Storm, Ghal Maraz, Hammers of Sigmar, Wardens of the Everqueen* and *Black Rift*

The Realmgate Wars: Volume 2
Various authors
Contains the novels *Call of Archaon, Warbeast, Fury of Gork, Bladestorm, Mortarch of Night* and *Lord of Undeath*

Legends of the Age of Sigmar
Various authors
An anthology of short stories

Rulers of the Dead
David Annandale & Josh Reynolds
Contains the novels *Neferata: Mortarch of Blood*
and *Nagash: The Undying King*

Warcry
Various authors
An anthology of short stories

Champions of the Mortal Realms
Various authors
Contains the novellas *Warqueen, The Red Hours, Heart of Winter* and *The Bone Desert*

Gods & Mortals
Various authors
An anthology of short stories

Myths & Revenants
Various authors
An anthology of short stories

Oaths & Conquests
Various authors
An anthology of short stories

Novels

• HALLOWED KNIGHTS •
Josh Reynolds
BOOK ONE: Plague Garden
BOOK TWO: Black Pyramid

Eight Lamentations: Spear of Shadows
Josh Reynolds

• KHARADRON OVERLORDS •
C L Werner
BOOK ONE: Overlords of the Iron Dragon
BOOK TWO: Profit's Ruin

Soul Wars
Josh Reynolds

Callis & Toll: The Silver Shard
Nick Horth

The Tainted Heart
C L Werner

Shadespire: The Mirrored City
Josh Reynolds

Blacktalon: First Mark
Andy Clark

Hamilcar: Champion of the Gods
David Guymer

Scourge of Fate
Robbie MacNiven

The Red Feast
Gav Thorpe

Gloomspite
Andy Clark

Ghoulslayer
Darius Hinks

Beastgrave
C L Werner

Neferata: The Dominion of Bones
David Annandale

The Court of the Blind King
David Guymer

Novellas

City of Secrets
Nick Horth

Thieves' Paradise
Nick Horth

Code of the Skies
Graeme Lyon

The Measure of Iron
Jamie Crisalli

Audio Dramas

• REALMSLAYER: A GOTREK GURNISSON SERIES •
David Guymer
BOXED SET ONE: Realmslayer
BOXED SET TWO: Blood of the Old World

The Beasts of Cartha
David Guymer

Fist of Mork, Fist of Gork
David Guymer

Great Red
David Guymer

Only the Faithful
David Guymer

The Prisoner of the Black Sun
Josh Reynolds

Sands of Blood
Josh Reynolds

The Lords of Helstone
Josh Reynolds

The Bridge of Seven Sorrows
Josh Reynolds

War-Claw
Josh Reynolds

Shadespire: The Darkness in the Glass
Various authors

The Imprecations of Daemons
Nick Kyme

The Palace of Memory and Other Stories
Various authors

Also available

Realmslayer: The Script Book
David Guymer

GHOULSLAYER
A GOTREK GURNISSON NOVEL

DARIUS HINKS

BLACK LIBRARY

A BLACK LIBRARY PUBLICATION

First published in 2019.
This edition published in Great Britain in 2021 by
Black Library, Games Workshop Ltd., Willow Road,
Nottingham, NG7 2WS, UK.

Represented by: Games Workshop Limited – Irish branch,
Unit 3, Lower Liffey Street, Dublin 1,
D01 K199, Ireland.

10 9 8 7 6 5 4 3 2

Produced by Games Workshop in Nottingham.
Cover illustration by Johan Grenier.

Ghoulslayer © Copyright Games Workshop Limited 2021. Ghoulslayer, GW, Games Workshop, Black Library, Warhammer, Warhammer Age of Sigmar, Stormcast Eternals, and all associated logos, illustrations, images, names, creatures, races, vehicles, locations, weapons, characters, and the distinctive likenesses thereof, are either ® or TM, and/or © Games Workshop Limited, variably registered around the world.
All Rights Reserved.

A CIP record for this book is available from the British Library.

ISBN 13: 978-1-78999-055-3

No part of this publication may be reproduced, stored in a retrieval system, or transmitted in any form or by any means, electronic, mechanical, photocopying, recording or otherwise, without the prior permission of the publishers.

This is a work of fiction. All the characters and events portrayed in this book are fictional, and any resemblance to real people or incidents is purely coincidental.

See Black Library on the internet at

blacklibrary.com

Find out more about Games Workshop
and the worlds of Warhammer at

games-workshop.com

Printed and bound by CPI Group (UK) Ltd, Croydon, CR0 4YY

For the Ancestor Gods: William King, Nathan Long, Josh Reynolds and David Guymer.

From the maelstrom of a sundered world, the Eight Realms were born. The formless and the divine exploded into life.

Strange, new worlds appeared in the firmament, each one gilded with spirits, gods and men. Noblest of the gods was Sigmar. For years beyond reckoning he illuminated the realms, wreathed in light and majesty as he carved out his reign. His strength was the power of thunder. His wisdom was infinite. Mortal and immortal alike kneeled before his lofty throne. Great empires rose and, for a while, treachery was banished. Sigmar claimed the land and sky as his own and ruled over a glorious age of myth.

But cruelty is tenacious. As had been foreseen, the great alliance of gods and men tore itself apart. Myth and legend crumbled into Chaos. Darkness flooded the realms. Torture, slavery and fear replaced the glory that came before. Sigmar turned his back on the mortal kingdoms, disgusted by their fate. He fixed his gaze instead on the remains of the world he had lost long ago, brooding over its charred core, searching endlessly for a sign of hope. And then, in the dark heat of his rage, he caught a glimpse of something magnificent. He pictured a weapon born of the heavens. A beacon powerful enough to pierce the endless night. An army hewn from everything he had lost.

Sigmar set his artisans to work and for long ages they toiled, striving to harness the power of the stars. As Sigmar's great work neared completion, he turned back to the realms and saw that the dominion of Chaos was almost complete. The hour for vengeance had come. Finally, with lightning blazing across his brow, he stepped forth to unleash his creations.

The Age of Sigmar had begun.

PROLOGUE

One by one, the lights began to fade. They burned brighter for a moment, like votives kindled by a breath, then blinked into oblivion. All across the Eventide they slipped from view, and a shroud spread over the sea, mobile and impenetrable, consuming everything.

'What is it?' whispered Veliger. He was at the uppermost rib of the Twelfth Prominent, resting his elbow on the head of his scythe, leaning out from the battlements. He had manned the walls for decades, but he had never seen anything like this. 'There's Lord Samorin,' he whispered as, several leagues away, the Sixth Prominent pulsed brighter, its shell-like whirl illuminating the waves before the fortress sank from view, adding another pool of darkness to the growing void. Before the light faded something shimmered over the Eventide. It looked like gossamer caught in the breeze. 'Rain?' said Veliger, but there was something odd about how it flashed and banked.

Veliger wore the uniform of the Gravesward – a thick cloak of glossy white feathers clasped at the neck with an iron skull brooch and draped over lacquered black armour. He pulled the cloak closer as a breeze whipped through the shadows, even colder than usual, tightening around his chest and snatching his breath.

'And there goes Lord Ophion,' replied the figure next to him as another temple grew suddenly brighter. Meraspis wore the same uniform as Veliger. He was also carrying a scythe and a tall white shield designed to resemble a wing. Like Veliger, his head was gaunt, pale and hairless, but he was older, his forehead networked by lines and locked in a permanent frown.

They watched in silence as the fortress blazed then sank into the sea.

Veliger turned to look at the walls behind them, half expecting the light of their own temple to be fading. The Twelfth Prominent was unchanged. It was a mountainous edifice – a crumbling, spiral curve of bone, perched at the crest of an ancient, dusty wave. Souls burned at its heart like purple fire, bleeding through its walls, spilling amethyst over the peaks and troughs of the Eventide, and the fortress' outline was clouded by white moths, circling in their millions like sea spray crashing over a hull. Light shimmered across the moths, radiated through the walls and flashed in Veliger's eyes as he looked at Meraspis.

'What's happening?'

Meraspis did not seem to hear. He kept his gaze on the horizon. 'What if they *all* vanish?'

Veliger looked up at the heavens, imagining a world without light. The stars would not help – they were ghosts, echoes of the living realms, with no interest in illuminating the underworlds of Shyish. Without the light of the prominents, the Eventide would be in darkness.

As he stared into the growing darkness, Veliger heard an unfamiliar sound. It was like pebbles clattering across a table. At first it was distant and gentle, but as the minutes passed it grew louder, becoming a roar.

The two men looked at each other in confusion as millions of white shards rattled across the Eventide. The sea that had never moved suddenly looked storm-tossed, and as the downpour moved closer it crashed violently against the fortress walls, filling the night with a deafening roar.

Meraspis stepped forwards and reached out from the embrasure. 'Is that hail?'

Then he cursed and whirled away from Veliger, hissing in pain and clutching his hand.

'What?' cried Veliger, rushing over to him.

Meraspis shook his head, hunched over and gripping his hand. 'By the Shroud,' he muttered.

Veliger helped him stand, then gasped. Meraspis' flesh had been torn apart. The rain had punched through his skin and bone, tearing the ligaments so badly that his hand looked like a scrap of bloody meat.

Meraspis cradled his butchered hand in his good one, groaning, cursing and staring at the rain.

Most of the shards had punched straight through his palm, but one of them was still wedged between his knuckles, gleaming white against the dark, exposed flesh.

Veliger gently plucked it from the wound and peered at it. 'Bone?'

They both looked out at the storm, baffled.

Veliger dropped the shard and quickly bandaged Meraspis' hand. The cuts were deep. He doubted the hand could be saved. But he could at least stem the bleeding.

Meraspis grimaced as Veliger worked, but did not cry out, despite the terrible pain he must be in.

'We should go to Lord Aurun,' he said hoarsely.

Veliger looked south to their nearest neighbour, the Barren Points. It was still smouldering with a steady, unruffled light.

'Yes,' he agreed. 'Lord Aurun will know what to do. He'll know what this is.'

Meraspis straightened up and clutched his broken hand to his chest. 'Look,' he said, nodding out across the battlements. 'It's stopping.'

The storm was already fading, the bone shards hitting the walls with less violence as the clouds rushed off to the south.

They watched the storm move away across the Eventide, still shocked by what had happened, then Veliger fastened his helmet and checked that the rest of his armour was fully attached, turning on his heel and heading for the stairs. 'Aurun will know what this means. It will only take a couple of hours to get there.'

Meraspis shook his head. 'We can't leave the Unburied unattended. You go. I would slow you down anyway. I will wait here and tend to my wounds.'

Veliger hesitated, looking at Meraspis' hand, then nodded. 'Very well. I'll find a Cerement priest. I'll bring him back with me.'

Meraspis waved to the stairs. 'Just go. And go quickly.' He looked up at the clouds. 'Even your armour might not protect you for long if that storm comes back.'

Each fortress was linked to its neighbour by a bridge, miles-long walkways slung from the gates like iron tendrils. The bridges were called wynds, and they stretched over the Eventide in graceful arcs. Some were only wide enough for five men to pass down them side by side, others were vast highways, and all of them were illuminated by the light of the temples at each end. As Veliger sprinted down the south wynd, his boots clanged against the ancient metal, scattering dust and moths. It was a long time since anyone had passed this way. Each fortress was almost self-sufficient, able to feed its garrison for months before requiring new supplies from the capital. The guards at the Barren Points would be shocked to see him rushing towards them. No, he realised, correcting himself, they would not. They must have seen the lights fading too. They would know exactly why he was coming.

As he ran, Veliger could not stop thinking about Meraspis' ruined hand. How could weather do such a thing? Where had that storm come from?

Veliger had not gone far down the wynd when he heard the sound he had been dreading – the same ominous hiss he had heard earlier. Bones were falling across the Eventide again, filling the darkness with noise. He staggered to a halt, shaking his head and cursing. There was no way he could reach the Barren Points without the storm overtaking him. And what if his armour did not hold?

As he looked back at the fortress, he let out a horrified cry. A shadow had engulfed his home. The vast, curved surface of the Twelfth Prominent looked stained – as though someone had poured ink over its battlements.

Veliger stared harder and saw that the darkness was a heaving mass of smaller shapes – men, robed in shadow, flooding over the Eventide and climbing up the walls of the fortress like vermin. It was an attack. The idea was even more shocking than the bone rain. The prominents had not been attacked within living memory. The invaders were crossing the surface of the Eventide as though it were harmless. How could that be? The dead waves were lethal. No one could touch them and keep their sanity intact. Who were these people?

Veliger stumbled back the way he had come, dazed and muttering as the bone storm rushed towards him through the darkness.

He broke into a run, but it seemed agonisingly slow. With every step, the rain rushed towards him, crashing over the Eventide and rattling across the wynd.

He reached the end of the bridge and raced up the steps and through the fortress gates, dashing under the first roof he came to.

As he stood there, trying to catch his breath, the light blazed brighter, dazzling him. His eyes adjusted to the glare after a few seconds, and he saw a familiar figure sprinting towards him across the square.

'Meraspis!' he cried out, lowering his scythe.

The man crashed into him, sending them both toppling back down the steps.

Veliger rolled clear and leapt back onto his feet, moving with an agility borne of years of training.

'What are you doing, Meraspis, have you–?' His words died in his mouth as the man turned to face him. It was not Meraspis. It was a hunched, slavering wretch, a stooped horror with wild, staring eyes, whipcord limbs and flesh sagging from its bones. It looked like an animated cadaver. It was trembling and palsied, and its flesh was a dark, mottled grey, but it lunged at Veliger with shocking speed.

Veliger stepped back, moving without thought, led by the precepts of his training. His scythe flashed twice, slicing through the creature's torso, and it slapped to the floor in two halves.

Veliger staggered away, shaking his head, staring at the butchered corpse. 'What was that?'

With a shuddering groan, the corpse's upper half jerked into motion and began crawling towards Veliger, dragging itself with its hands, trailing innards, its eyes still rolling.

'Shroud!' cried Veliger, hacking furiously at the thing until it collapsed and finally lay still.

Veliger's relief was quickly replaced by a rush of horror. When he had looked back from the wynd, he had seen dozens of figures. What if they were all like this?

He gripped his scythe tighter and ran on, muttering in confusion.

Before he was halfway up the steps, the shadows began to shift and roll, rising up and gathering to block his way. Dozens of figures lurched towards him, their heads twitching and their breath coming in ragged gasps. They all resembled age-blackened corpses, shivering and frantic as they locked their blank, yellow gazes on him. Some clutched splinters of bone or fragments of broken weapons.

'Mordants,' whispered Veliger, feeling as though he were in a dream. He had heard tales of corpse-eaters but had never seen them first-hand. One or two occasionally sniffed their way into the prominents, but he had never heard of them attacking in these kinds of numbers. As Veliger looked at the tide of darkness gathering around him, he guessed that there must be hundreds of them clambering over the walls.

The mordants rushed towards him without a sound, twitching and juddering. They were like dumb animals that had taken human form.

Veliger staggered backwards, unbalanced by the ferocity of the assault, trying to stay calm, scything through the throng, filling the air with dark, treacly blood.

He charged up the steps, hacking and lunging and trying to break through the crush, but it was useless. The flesh-eaters forced him back until he lost his footing, nearly beheading himself in the process.

He leapt to his feet, hacked down more of the mordants and backed away, crying out in shock and anger.

The walls of the fortress burned brighter, scattering shadows across the square.

Several mordants broke from the main group and loped towards the wynd, their mindless gaze locked on the distant lights of Lord Aurun's fortress.

'No!' shouted Veliger, backing towards the bridge. 'You will not taint the Barren Points!'

The crowd rushed towards him. The prominent was now shining so brightly he could barely see.

He turned on his heel and raced back towards the bridge, barring the entrance to the wynd. He would not let the mordants go any further into the princedom.

Then the light of the fortress failed, plunging him into darkness.

Veliger could see nothing but an after-image of the walls, burned across his vision.

He heard breathing all around him in the dark – ragged, hoarse gasps, approaching from every direction.

There was a drum of rushing feet as the mordants attacked.

Veliger hefted his scythe back and forth, cutting down shapes he could not see, thudding the blade into thrashing limbs.

Hands clawed at his back and face, tearing at his armour, pulling him down.

Pain erupted across his body, and he heard the storm wash across the square, punching bones through his armour and skin.

Blood rushed into his eyes and he fell, crushed by the weight of bodies, howling in agony.

Your Celestial Highnesses,

I doubt very much that these missives will get further than the next ditch, but I feel duty-bound to make the attempt. Besides, it gives me solace to fantasise that, somewhere out there, beyond these grey doldrums, an educated soul is following my adventures and sympathising with the absurdity of my situation.

Despite the horrific nature of our departure from Slain Peak, I am still in the company of the doom-seeking Slayer. I am as surprised as anyone by this turn of events. Enduring his company is an achievement far surpassing any of the trials I endured in the Murder Temples. Forgive my self-pitying tone, your highnesses, but you cannot imagine a poorer travelling companion. He persists with his pompous claims of belonging to another, older, superior realm of existence, and the longer I spend in his company, the more I wonder if he might actually be right. It does not take a great leap of imagination to picture him crawling from some long-forgotten netherworld. He's a boor and an ignoramus, and he's prone to the most bewildering vacillations of temper.

During our passage across the Dwindlesea (see my previous report) he became infuriatingly enthused – deranged, in fact – howling at the oarsmen every time they faltered, obsessed with the idea of finding Nagash, genuinely seeming to believe he would find the God of Death waiting patiently for him on the next stretch of coast. Then, after we moored at Hopetide and found no such deity, he sank into an ale-steeped sulk, the like of which you can't imagine. So I now find myself languishing in a squalid hole called Klemp while the Slayer tries to drink himself to death. There's no sign of him dying, more's the pity, but that hasn't deterred him from making several valiant attempts. Rest assured, your highnesses, I will endure whatever indignities he throws my way and stay close to him at all times. The Rune of Blackhammer is still safe, secured on his corpulent person, and one way or another, I will bring it to you. The trust you placed in me was not misguided.

As an aside, I can report that this entire stretch of coastline is in a state of momentous uproar. The dominion of the Ruinous Powers is no longer secure, which is both good and bad news for the local populace. The underworlds are in a state of revolt. Spirits and revenants have reclaimed huge tracts of land in Nagash's name, while bands of brigands have started raiding from the north. The Realm of Death is in as much turmoil as anywhere else. Anyone who comes here expecting a peaceful afterlife will be sorely disappointed. Our journey from the coast took us past several Chaos dreadholds, and they were all ruined. And there was no sign of a counter-attack. This does not appear to be the work of Stormhosts, so I can only assume Nagash is responsible. The Klemp locals are preparing to flee, and the whole region is gripped by a kind of shared madness. Every crone and conjurer claims to have received visions concerning a terrible plague of undeath. They claim that Nagash has performed a great rite or conjuration that has given him absolute dominion over Shyish. There is much talk of levitating black pyramids and fleshless legions and the like, and it's hard to know how much – if any – of it is true, but there is definitely something afoot. It would seem the arch-necromancer has found a way to regain many of the territories he lost to Chaos.

As a second aside, I should mention that during the fight at the Neverspike, the Slayer and I gained an eccentric new travelling companion by the name of Trachos. He claims to belong to our order, and perhaps he once did, but the man is clearly insane. If he attempts any form of communication, disregard it. He does not know his own mind and he is not to be trusted. I shall make sure the rune does not fall into his hands and will leave him behind at the first opportunity.

Your most loyal and faithful votary,
Maleneth Witchblade

CHAPTER ONE

THE MUFFLED DRUM

Gotrek was snoring, attacking the night with brutal barks. Even asleep he was savage, hammering Maleneth's skull with every snort. The sound rattled through the Slayer's chest and shook the chain linking his ear to his nose. The brazier in his rune-axe was still smouldering, but the light had faded from his filthy muscles. He shifted, as though about to speak, let out a ripe belch and then lay still again. He had drunk for hours, downing ale like water, before finally collapsing next to an outhouse, surrounded by the corpses of brigands who had had the ill-conceived idea of trying to rob him. There was no dawn in this particular corner of Shyish, but even the endless gloom could not hide the rune buried in Gotrek's chest. A great slab of burnished power. The tie that bound her to him. The face of a god, glaring from his ribs, demanding that she hold her nerve.

She stepped gracefully through the dead, as though gliding through a ballroom, scattering flies and gore, a dagger held lightly in each hand. The Stormcast Eternal had gone, scouring Klemp for news of his own kind, and she was alone with the Slayer.

The heart-shaped silver amulet at her throat flickered, revealing the vial of blood at its core. *Now. This is your chance.*

Maleneth ignored the voice, creeping closer to the Slayer, wincing at his stench. He was grotesque. A graceless lump of scarred muscle, bristling with porcine hair and covered in knotted tattoos. Even by the low standards of the duardin race he was primitive – like a hog that had learned to stand and carry an axe. He was shorter than the brigands he had carved his bed from, but twice their width and built like a barn. The stale, sweet smell of beer shrouded the bodies, mixing with Gotrek's belches and stinging Maleneth's eyes. She could see the dregs glistening in his matted beard as she leant closer, keeping her eyes fixed on the rune. The rune stared back.

Despite her loathing she hesitated, knives trembling, inches from his body.

The amulet around her neck flickered again. *Coward.*

That was enough to spur her on. Her dead mistress was right. Klemp would soon be rubble, just like all the other towns they had passed through. The whole region was in uproar. And when the fighting started, who knew where the Slayer would end up? Once he was in one of his rages there was no way of predicting what he would do next. It was a miracle she had stayed with him this far. This might be her last chance. The Slayer's skin was like iron, though. She would need to punch the blade home with all her strength to get the poison into his bloodstream. She tightened her grip and leant back to strike.

'Maleneth.' The voice echoed down the alley, heavy with warning.

She whirled around, blades lowered.

Trachos' armour glimmered as he limped through the darkness, sparks flickering from his ruined leg plate. He was wearing his expressionless helmet, but she could tell by the way he moved, careful and slow, that he understood what she was planning. His head kicked to one side and light crackled from his mouth grille. He gripped the metal, holding it still, but the damage went deeper than the mask. All that god-wrought armour had done nothing to protect his mind.

He stopped near the corpses, staring at her, lights flickering behind his faceplate.

He remained silent, but the way he raised his warhammers spoke clearly enough. *That rune is mine.*

They stood like that for a long moment, glaring at each other across Gotrek's snorting bulk.

Trachos came closer, his metal boots crunching through broken weapons and shattered armour. The sky had grown paler, outlining him, and she saw how confidently he gripped the warhammers. Damaged or not, he was still a Stormcast Eternal. A scion of the thunder god. He was several feet taller than a normal man and, even broken, his plate armour made a fearsome sight.

Maleneth stepped through the pile of bodies, readying herself. She had always known this moment would come. They could not *both* claim the rune. There was a rent in Trachos' leg armour from his left knee to his left boot. It had been there when he first approached Maleneth months ago, wandering out of the hills like a deranged prophet. He was in desperate need of medicine, or repairs, or whatever help Stormcast Eternals received when they returned to the Celestial Realm. Every step he took was difficult, and his Azyrite armour sparked whenever he moved. She smiled. Usually, such a warrior would be a test for even her skills, but in this state he should be easy prey. There would be blood for Khaine this night.

Maleneth dragged one of her blades across a vial at her belt. The crystal broke in silence, but she could smell the venom as it spilled across the metal.

Trachos dropped into a crouch, hammers raised.

The two warriors tensed, preparing to strike.

'Grungni's arse beard!' cried Gotrek, lurching to his feet and grabbing his rune-axe. 'Don't you people know when you're beaten?'

He swayed, obviously confused, still drunk, piercing the night with his one, scowling eye, trying to focus, trying to spot an opponent. Seeing none, he turned to Maleneth.

'Aelf! Point me to the simpletons.'

Maleneth lowered her weapons and Trachos did the same. The chance was gone. She shook her head. 'All dead.' She backed away from Trachos with a warning glare.

Gotrek's face was locked in a thunderous scowl and his skin was as grey as the corpses. He kicked one of them. 'Lightweights. They could barely swing a sword. Even splitting skulls is no fun in your stinking realm.'

Trachos' hands trembled as he slid his hammers back into his belt. 'This is no realm of mine.'

'Nor mine,' said Maleneth, looking around at the peculiar hell Gotrek had led them to. The sky was the colour of old pewter, dull, bleak and riveted with stars. The stars did not shine but radiated a pitiless black. Points of absolute darkness surrounded by purple coronas, wounds in the sky, dripping fingers of pitch. And the town was equally grim. Crooked, ramshackle huts made of warped, colourless driftwood. There were panicked shouts in the distance and the sound of vehicles being hastily loaded. Columns of smoke stretched across the sky, signalling the approach of another army. They looked like claw marks on dead skin.

Gotrek muttered a duardin curse and picked his way through the corpses. 'Where's the ale?'

'You drank it,' replied Trachos.

The Slayer frowned and scratched his shaven head, causing his enormous, grease-slicked mohawk to tremble. Then he glared at the ground, his massive shoulders drooping and the haft of his greataxe hanging loosely in his grip. He whispered to himself, shaking his head, and Maleneth wondered what he was thinking. Was he remembering his home? The world he claimed was so superior to the Mortal Realms? She suspected most of his thoughts concerned his past. What else did he have? There was something tragic about him, she decided. He was like a fossil, revived by cruel necromancy and abandoned in a world where no one knew his face.

'You're right,' said Gotrek, looking up with a sudden smile. 'We need more ale.'

Maleneth shook her head in disbelief. She and Trachos were glaring at him. Anyone else would feel their hatred like a physical blow, but the Slayer was oblivious. He waved them back down the alley, away from the outbuilding, humming cheerfully to himself as he headed out onto the main street.

They stumbled into a chaotic scene. There were wicker cages rattling against every lintel and doorframe – hundreds of them, the size of a human head and crammed with teeth, skin and bones. Alongside the offerings to Nagash there were wooden eight-pointed stars, hastily hammered together and painted in gaudy colours. Braziers spewed clouds of blue embers across wooden icons that had been painted with the faces of daemons and saints. And all of this jostled happily against yellow hammer-shaped idols that had been scored with an approximation of Azyrite runes. Every corner revealed some desperate attempt to appease a god. And through this carnival of colours and shapes, people were rushing in every direction, hurling belongings from windows and clambering into carts. There was a cold wind whipping through the streets that seemed heavy with portent. Men and women howled at each other, arguing while their children fought in the dust, like a premonition of the violence about to be visited on the town. For weeks, seers across the region had been wracked by agonising prophecies. Some sprouted mouths in their armpits and spewed torrents of bile, others were visited by horrific, sanity-flaying visions, and some had found their voices replaced by a bestial, guttural language they could no more understand than silence. Whatever the nature of their visitation, all of them agreed on one thing – death was coming to the region. Most people had taken that as a cue to flee, but Gotrek, still furious at not finding Nagash, had decided to stay, relishing the coming fight as a distraction if nothing else.

As Gotrek swaggered onto the wind-lashed street, he almost collided with an enormous beast that was being led through the crowds – an armour-clad mammoth, draped in furs and sacks and scraping tracks through the dirt with its tusks. Dozens of fur-clad nomads were crowded into its howdah, and more were swarming round it, driving it on with sticks and insults, trying to goad more speed out of the plodding creature.

Gotrek halted, glaring at the nomads, and Maleneth guessed immediately what had annoyed him. She hated to admit it, but she was starting to understand him. He was brutal and heartless in many respects, but there were a few things that seemed to offend his primitive sensibilities. The sight of a wild creature bound into servitude was one of them. For a moment, she thought he might accost the nomads, but then he shook his head and marched on, barging through the traders and making for the largest building on the street, muttering into his beard.

Maleneth struggled to keep up as the Slayer booted the door open and plunged into the gloomy interior of the Muffled Drum. Despite the scenes of panic outside, Klemp's only inn was crowded with languorous, dazed patrons – people so far gone they lacked the sense to try to save their own skin, calling the prophecies scaremongering nonsense. There were more nomads, wearing the same filthy furs as the travellers outside, but there was also a bewildering array of other creeds and races – humans from every corner of the Amethyst Princedoms and beyond. Maleneth saw hulking savages from the east, as heavily tattooed as Gotrek and looking just as uncouth. There were waif-like pilgrims, dressed in sackcloth and wearing charcoal eye makeup that had been smeared by the beer they were lying in. In one corner there was a party of duardin, dispossessed travellers, hunched over their drinks and eyeing Gotrek from under battered crested helmets.

Gotrek made a point of ignoring the duardin and stormed straight across the room to the bar, where a tall, fierce-looking woman was looming over one of her customers, shaking him back and forth until coins fell from his grip and rattled across the bar.

'Next time,' she snarled, 'it's your *guts* I'll spill.'

The man fell away from her, collapsing in a shocked heap on the floor before scrabbling away on all fours as Gotrek strode past him and approached the woman.

'Still no good,' said the Slayer, looking up at her.

She shook her head in disbelief, then leant across the bar and stared down at him, peering at his impressive gut. 'You drank all of it?'

Gotrek pounded a fist against his stomach and belched. 'For all the good it did me.'

The woman looked at Maleneth as she reached the bar. 'He drank it all?'

Maleneth nodded, grudgingly, annoyed to notice that the landlady looked impressed.

Gotrek studied the bottles behind the woman. 'Got anything stronger?'

She stared at him. 'Are you with them?' she asked, nodding at the party of duardin.

Gotrek kept studying the drinks, ignoring the question. The only sign of a response was a slight tightening of his jaw.

She shrugged, taking a bottle from the shelf and placing it before him. It was the shape of an elongated teardrop and it was clearly ancient – a plump dollop of green, murky glass covered in dust and ash. There were fragments of something suspended in the liquid.

Gotrek grabbed the bottle and held it towards a fire that was crackling by the bar, squinting at the whirling sediment.

The woman grabbed one of his tree-trunk biceps. 'It's not cheap.'

Gotrek threw some coins at her, then continued eyeing the drink.

He jammed the cork into the bottle with his fat, dirty thumb, and a heady stink filled the room.

Maleneth coughed and put a hand to her face.

Gotrek sniffed the bottle and grimaced. 'It's not Bugman's.'

'Don't drink it then,' said Maleneth, remembering what had happened the last time the Slayer got drunk. There was no way they would leave Klemp intact if Gotrek picked a fight just as an army came over the horizon.

He gave her a warning glare.

'What about Nagash?' she said, the first thing that came to mind.

His scowl grew even more fierce, but he did not put the bottle to his lips.

'You dragged us all this way to find him.' Maleneth looked over at Trachos. He was standing a few feet away, watching the exchange, but as usual he seemed oblivious, locked in his own personal hell. Realising the Stormcast would be no help, she turned back to Gotrek. 'And now, just as his armies are about to reach us, you're going to drink yourself into a stupor. You could miss the very chance you've been looking for. The chance to face him. Or whatever it is you were hoping to achieve.'

Gotrek glowered. 'He's not here. Gods don't have the balls to lead from the front. Nagash will be hiding somewhere, like the rest of them.' He drank deeply from the bottle, holding Maleneth's gaze.

Then he paused for breath, threw more coins on the bar and took the bottle to one of the benches that lined the room. The wood groaned as he sat.

There was an elderly man sitting at the bench, and he watched with interest as Gotrek drank more of the foul-smelling stuff. He was tall and slender, sitting stiff-backed and proud, and as he sipped his drink he moved with the precise, delicate movements of an ascetic. Unlike everyone else in the Muffled Drum, he was immaculately dressed. His tunic, cloak and trousers were embroidered with golden thread, and his receding, slicked-back hair was so adorned with beads and semi-precious stones that it resembled a skullcap.

When Gotrek lowered the half-empty bottle onto the table, the man leant over and whispered, 'You have business with the necromancer?'

The drink had clearly not affected Gotrek yet. His hand shot out with surprising speed and locked around the man's scrawny neck.

'Who wants to know?'

A strange noise came from the man's chest. It might have been laughter.

Gotrek cursed. Rather than grabbing skin and bone, his hand had passed through the man's neck and was left holding a fistful of ash. The powder tumbled through his fingers as he snatched back his hand. He glared at the man.

For a fraction of a second, the old man had no neck, just a landslide of fine dust tumbling from his lower jaw onto his shoulders. It looked like sand in an hourglass. Then the dust solidified, and the man's neck reappeared. He stroked his greasy hair and looked at Gotrek, his eyes glittering and unfocused, as though he were looking into smoke.

Gotrek's cheeks flushed with rage and he gripped the haft of his greataxe. 'What are you? A spirit? In my day we burned the restless dead.'

'I'm quite well rested, thank you,' said the man, with a vague smile.

Maleneth and Trachos approached the table.

'What are you?' demanded Maleneth.

The man ignored her question, studying the rune in Gotrek's chest and the barbs on Maleneth's tight-fitting leathers. Then he looked at the shattered gilded sigmarite of Trachos' war gear. 'You don't look like servants of the Great Necromancer.'

'But you do,' said Gotrek, taking another swig from the green bottle. 'Why don't you…' He hesitated, looking at the bottle with a surprised expression, rolling his head loosely on his shoulders. 'Actually, this isn't bad.'

He looked over at the landlady and gave her a nod of approval. To Maleneth's disbelief, the ridiculous woman blushed.

'Like you, fyreslayer, I kneel to no god,' said the man, looking at Gotrek with an expression that was hard to read.

'I'm not a fyreslayer, and you're nothing like me.' Gotrek stood up and started away from the table. He stumbled and had to grip the bench to steady himself. 'This *is* good.' He sat back down, and the bench gave another groan.

'Why do you wish to reach Nagash if you don't serve him?' asked the stranger.

'What *are* you?' repeated Maleneth, gripping her knife handles. 'Are you human?'

'I'm Kurin,' he replied, holding out a hand.

Maleneth eyed it suspiciously.

Gotrek had closed his eye, leaning back against the wall, and when he opened them again, he had to blink repeatedly to focus.

'You're drunk,' muttered Maleneth.

Gotrek grinned. 'And you're ugly. But tomorrow I'll be ugly and you'll still be…' His words trailed off and he shook his head, frowning. 'No, wait… I mean, tomorrow I'll be ugly and you'll still be drunk.' He shook his head, muttering to himself, trying to remember the joke he had cracked every day for the last week.

'I belong to an order of magisters called the hush,' said the man, ignoring Gotrek's rambling. 'Shrivers, as some used to call us.'

'I've never heard of you,' replied Maleneth, eyeing the man with suspicion. There were a lot of people who would like to get their hands on the rune in Gotrek's chest. Perhaps it was no accident that Kurin was in the Muffled Drum at this particular moment.

'Not many have,' said Kurin. 'Our skills are no longer in much demand.'

'Skills?'

He held out his hand again, draping it before Maleneth in such a languid, aloof manner that she wondered if he was expecting her to kiss it. Then he flipped his hand around so it was palm up.

Maleneth, Gotrek and Trachos all leant closer, watching in surprise as the lines of his palm rose from his hand, spiralling up into the air like fine trails of smoke.

'Touch them,' he said.

Maleneth shook her head, and the other two leant back.

He shrugged. 'We're an ancient order. We ruled these kingdoms once, long before any of these ill-mannered barbarians who are currently trying to claim lordship. We are one with the dust. We share none of the failings of mankind – no doubts, no regrets, no grief, no shame. The sod is our flesh and the ground is our bed. It makes life simple. Mortal concerns do not bother us, so we have time to concentrate on more elevated matters.'

Gotrek managed to focus. 'You don't care about anything?' He picked a shred of meat from his beard, stared at it, then ate it. 'Doesn't sound particularly "elevated". Even I've managed that.'

Kurin smiled, his hand still outstretched, his skin still spinning a tiny storm. 'I sense that you care about more than you would like to admit. But I can shrive you of your crimes. We are able to see into souls, Slayer – we see their value and we see what haunts them. Take my hand, tell me what drives you to drink so eagerly, and I will take the memory from you.'

Gotrek sneered, but then hesitated and stared at the man's hand. 'Take it from me?'

The Slayer had never told Maleneth much about his former life, but she knew he wished to atone for a past deed. He sought glorious death in battle as a kind of penance. Her pulse quickened. If Gotrek was able to forget the thing he wanted to atone for, he would stop charging headlong towards his own destruction. She could simply lead him, like an offering, back home to Azyr, with Blackhammer's rune intact.

Kurin was still smiling. 'Or, if you do not wish to be rid of your painful past, I can give you a chance at reconciliation. I can rouse your ghosts, Slayer. I can drag your shadows into the light. Is there someone you would wish to accuse? Or apologise to? My reach is long.'

'A charlatan,' sneered Maleneth. 'I suppose you tell fortunes too. And how much does this all cost?'

'No money. Just honesty. Nagash has persecuted my order for countless generations.' Kurin waved vaguely, indicating the streets outside. 'And left me surrounded by people so stupid they worship all the gods when they should worship none.' He looked at the three of them in turn, with that half-smile still on his lips. 'And now I hear you three are *seeking* him. While every other wretch in Klemp is snivelling to Nagash, you want to take him on. It's a long time since I heard anything other than fear.' He looked at the rune in Gotrek's chest. 'There is something different about you.'

Maleneth nodded. 'So if we tell you why we're seeking the necromancer, you'll relieve Gotrek of his guilt?'

'If that's what he desires.'

The Slayer was still staring at Kurin's hand, but Maleneth sensed that his mind had slipped back into the past again. His usually fierce expression was gone, and robbed of its normal ferocity, his face looked brutalised rather than brutal – a shocking mess of scars and buckled bone.

'Do you?' prompted Kurin, an odd gleam in his eye.

Gotrek was staring so hard Maleneth wondered if the drink had finally made him catatonic. Then he laughed and leant back, relaxing as he took another swig. 'These realms are so damned subtle. I see what you're doing, sorcerer – you would rob me of my past and leave me beaming like an idiot. You would have me forget my oath.'

Kurin frowned, confused, shaking his head, but before he could disagree, Gotrek continued.

'There's no solace for me, wizard. No absolution. No bloody *shriving*. Not until I find my doom.' As the Slayer's anger grew, his words became more slurred. 'And, one way or another, the gods will give it to me.'

'Gotrek,' said Trachos. 'We have no idea why he wants to know your business.'

Maleneth looked up in surprise. The Stormcast Eternal hardly ever spoke, and when he did, it rarely made sense.

Gotrek laughed and leant close to Kurin, waving dismissively at Trachos. 'My friend here isn't digging with a full shovel. He thinks I need to *worry* about you. If he knew half the things I've slain, he'd know I don't need to worry about someone with brains for dust.' He shook his head. 'I mean dust for brains. You're muddling my thinking, damn you. Keep out of my head. The past is the one place I'm still happy to go. I'll thank you not to ruin it.'

Kurin nodded politely. 'Of course. I hope I have not offended you.'

Gotrek stared at the table and shook his head. 'Mind you, you've actually spoken the first sense I've heard since arriving in these realms. Gods *are* idiots. Worshipping gods is the pastime of idiots. You're right.' He waved clumsily at Maleneth and Trachos. 'This pair think they can earn a place at the head of some glorious, divine host if they make a prize of me.' He laughed. 'Look at them, dreaming of being holy footstools.'

Kurin smiled sadly. 'The curse of the devout. Praying so cheerfully to the cause of their pain.'

'Aye to that.' Gotrek's tone was grim as he clanked his bottle against the old man's drink. 'The gods are good for nothing,' he muttered. 'Apart from catching my axe.'

Maleneth shook her head, not keen on how the old man was hanging on Gotrek's every drunken word. 'Trachos is right,' she said. 'We should keep our business to ourselves.'

'*Our* business?' cried Gotrek. He scrambled up onto the table and bellowed at the room. 'It's my bloody business, and I'll share it with who I like!'

The buzz of conversation died away as everyone saw the crazed, oversized Slayer swaying on the table.

Maleneth put her head in her hands.

'I've come here for Nagash!' shouted Gotrek, brandishing his axe. 'You cowardly whelps can run and hide all you like, but I'm going to find him and bury this useless blade in his useless skull.' He slammed the axe down and it split the table in half, hurling drinks and leaving Gotrek sprawled on the floor.

There was an explosion of yells and curses as people leapt to their feet, grabbing weapons and hurling abuse at Gotrek, outraged by his accusation of cowardice.

A glowering mob formed around the Slayer as he climbed to his feet and retrieved his weapon.

Maleneth drew her knives and leapt to his side, still cursing under her breath. Trachos grabbed his hammers from his belt and stood at Gotrek's other side. The trio made an unusual, impressive sight, and the drunks hesitated.

The duardin that had been watching Gotrek since he arrived rushed to stand with him, and Gotrek glared at them furiously.

'Don't come near me, you pathetic excuse for a dwarf,' he snarled, rounding on the nearest of them.

There was a chorus of gasps as the mob staggered away from Gotrek, clutching their throats and choking. The veins beneath their skin suddenly knotted together and began writhing like serpents. Some of the men dropped to their knees, murmuring and whimpering as they tried to breathe, while others stumbled towards the door.

'Wait!' cried Kurin, wiping pieces of table from his robes as he stood and crossed the room. He was holding up one of his hands with a beneficent smile. The creases of his palm had risen up in a miniature tornado again, whirling and twisting between his fingers. 'Lower your weapons, my friends. There is no need for discord. I'll pay for any spillages.'

He closed his fist, and breath exploded from dozens of lungs as people managed to breathe again.

There were more disgruntled cries, but no one attacked. They looked at Kurin even more warily than they did Gotrek. As they crawled back to their seats, muttering and wheezing, it occurred to Maleneth that until Gotrek had sat beside him, Kurin had been completely alone at the bench. No one had dared sit near him.

'You robbed me of a fight, wizard.' Gotrek hefted his axe a little higher and gave Kurin a warning look. 'And there's precious little else to do in–'

'I can reach Nagash,' Kurin said, smiling.

Gotrek froze.

Kurin's presence unnerved even the most hardened warriors in the room. As he walked slowly towards Gotrek, they backed away into the darkest corners of the inn. Maleneth had seen the same thing countless times. Few mortals were happy to risk the ire of a sorcerer.

Kurin nodded towards the street outside. 'We can talk in my rooms.' He carefully placed some coins on the bar and went to the door, waving for Gotrek to follow him.

The Slayer eyed him suspiciously, then shrugged and headed out into the gloom, Maleneth and Trachos rushing after him.

CHAPTER TWO

THE BONE RAIN

The sorcerer paused halfway across the street, staring at something. The mammoth was gone, but there were still crowds of people dashing back and forth and loading carts. Several had done the same as Kurin, halting to look back down the road in the direction of the town gates.

'God of Murder,' said Maleneth. 'What now?'

'Another gift from the gods,' said Kurin, calm despite the abomination that was spreading across the sky.

Beyond the gates the clouds were changing – swelling and trembling and forming mountainous black thunderheads. They were clearly not normal storm clouds. They were boiling out of an empty grey sky, like smoke pluming from a wound.

As more people noticed what was happening, the crowds became even more panicked. People screamed and abandoned the luggage they were trying to lug into carts. The wind grew in ferocity and bone cages broke free from the doorways, clattering down the street, scattering fingers and feathers as they whirled through the dust.

Maleneth coughed and gagged as dust filled her nostrils. There was an awful smell on the air – the heavy, thick stink of death. It was coming from the cloud forming on the horizon.

Drinkers spilled out of the Muffled Drum, pallid and swearing as they looked up at the approaching storm.

'This way,' called Kurin, waving in the opposite direction to the clouds, at a building back down the street.

Gotrek ignored him, planting his feet firmly apart and staring at the storm.

'Gotrek!' cried Maleneth. 'Whatever that is–' Her words were cut off as the inn's sign tore free and flew through the air, almost hitting her. She leapt aside and shielded her eyes as it smashed on the road, hurling shards of wood.

Gotrek was still leaning into the wind, grinning and testing the weight of his axe.

'Don't die here,' called Kurin, 'in this tiresome little town. Don't waste your energy on a place that's already been forgotten. I can show you how to reach Nagash.'

Gotrek looked back at him as the pieces of a broken shrine bounced off him – shards of bone and wire knotted with hair. He frowned. 'Tell me again why you would want to help me?'

'I see something in you, duardin. I have a feeling that–' Kurin tried to say more, but the storm was making it hard to breathe. Whatever the sorcerer was made of, his body was not bound by the same physics as anyone else's. He began to fragment and dissipate, buffeted violently by the reeking storm. For a moment, he seemed to collapse completely, snatched away by the wind, but then he reformed, his regal features tumbling back into place. 'We don't have long!' His voice reverberated down the street, laden with unnatural power.

Maleneth's legs carried her after him, moving of their own volition. She cursed as she realised the man had bewitched her.

Trachos was at Gotrek's side, hammers raised, weighted down by his hulking sigmarite armour as everyone else was being blown back down the street. The storm was now so violent that several carts were lying overturned in the whirling dust and doors were being ripped from their hinges and hurled through the air.

Gotrek was still looking at Kurin, who was flickering in and out of view, merging with the dust clouds. Then he shrugged and began walking towards the sorcerer, with Trachos staggering after him.

A porch near Maleneth broke free, and one of the beams thudded painfully into her calves. She fell and tumbled down the street, gasping and choking as she bounced over the hard ground. She slammed against the side of a wood store and managed to grab hold.

Fool, said her mistress. ***You missed your chance. I said you would.***

Maleneth snarled, wanting to disagree, but she could barely see Gotrek now. He was just a vague, stocky silhouette in the dust, with Trachos looming over him, massive and unshakeable.

'Gotrek!' she cried, but at that moment, the cloud burst, splitting down the middle with a deafening boom and spewing rain on the road to Klemp.

No, it wasn't rain; it looked more like hail – hard, white shards that gleamed as they fell and kicked up dust as they hit the ground.

The hail rushed towards the town, and the few people still on the street dived for cover, leaping through doorways and slamming shutters.

Maleneth could see no sign of Gotrek or Trachos.

'No!' She hauled herself from the wood store and dived through a broken window into the house next to it. 'I won't lose that blessed rune! Not after all this!'

There was a man cowering in the room, hunkered down behind an overturned table. She glared at him as she crawled towards an opening where the wall had collapsed. As the wind sliced into her again, she saw that the hail had now reached the town and was tearing up the street like knives, drumming loudly across the packed earth and rushing towards her in a flashing wave.

The man gasped, staring at the hail as though it were a host of daemons.

His fear was infectious. Maleneth backed away from the opening and dropped down next to him.

'What is it?' she cried, struggling to be heard over the din.

He shook his head, not looking at her, still staring at the hail.

She pressed a blade to his throat. 'What *is* it?' she repeated with more vehemence.

He still kept looking at the storm, but this time he did at least answer. 'Bone rain!' He sounded demented. 'The death storm! Nagash's storm!'

'What do you mean?' she shouted, pressing the blade harder until blood formed at his throat.

'It means the mordants are coming!' He was about to say more when his face turned a worrying shade of purple and he fell back against the wall.

Maleneth was confused for a moment, then cursed as she remembered lacing her knife with venom when she had been about to fight Trachos.

'Idiot!' she whispered, glaring at the discoloured corpse.

She let him drop to the ground then ran through a doorway into the next room, still looking for the Slayer.

There was no sign of him, just more locals, cowering fearfully under a table as the storm lashed against the walls, sounding like waves breaking against a promontory.

Maleneth cursed when she saw there was nowhere left to go. She walked over to the barred door, but the family crouched under the table immediately began screaming.

'It's just hail,' she said, glaring at them, but she did not feel as confident as she sounded.

'It's bone rain!' gasped one of them, shaking his head furiously. 'It'll tear you apart!'

Maleneth frowned. 'What are you talking about?'

The man would say no more, wrapping his arms around his head and leaning against his family.

Maleneth hissed a curse and looked back at the door. 'This is ridiculous,' she whispered, but she did not go any further.

She began pacing around the room, flipping her knives from hand to hand, glowering at the people under the table and wondering where Trachos and Gotrek would be by now.

They will have gone with the sorcerer. Gotrek will be glad to see the back of you.

Not true, she thought. *The Slayer enjoys tormenting me. And he definitely has no love for Trachos.*

After ten minutes or so, the sound of the storm started to lessen.

'It's passing us by,' she whispered, itching to open the door.

The man under the table looked up at her, hope in his eyes. 'Wait,' he said, holding up a warning hand. 'Be sure.'

Maleneth wanted to hurl a knife into his pathetic face, but she held off from opening the door until the noise had completely died away. Then she carefully opened it a crack and peered out into the gloom.

The rain had gone, but the storm had left the street cluttered with all sorts of debris. Whole sections of houses had collapsed, leaving rooms exposed and scattering furniture through the dust.

There were people sprawled in the rubble, bleeding and crying out in pain, lacerated so badly they looked like they had survived a knife fight. There were pieces of hail everywhere, creating a brittle carpet that crunched under Maleneth's boots as she walked out into the street. She stopped to look closer and saw that rather than being cold and glistening, they were dry, dusty shards.

Kurin, Gotrek and Trachos had emerged from the house opposite, and the sorcerer waved at the people lying bleeding in the dust. 'This is just the prelude.'

She shook her head, but then saw what Kurin meant. There were figures emerging from the storm, staggering through the dust clouds.

Maleneth laughed in disbelief as the first of them stumbled into view. It was as though the man were acting out a ridiculous performance. He was standing in an awkward, hunched posture, and his face was twisted in a deranged leer. Only his eyes robbed the scene of humour – they were staring and blank.

He hobbled towards Kurin, breathing heavily and flexing his bony hands. He was dressed in tattered scraps of armour and he moved like his body had been broken and only crudely repaired. He lurched and stumbled as though struggling to stand, but as he crossed the street he gained momentum, rushing through fence posts and charging.

Kurin watched the man's approach with no sign of concern, then, at the last moment, disintegrated into a cloud of dust, his would-be attacker lunging at the space he had just occupied before falling to the floor.

The man thrashed, panting and gasping, then stood and leapt at the nearest person. Unfortunately for him, that was Gotrek.

The Slayer swung his enormous greataxe with no sign of effort, sinking the blade deep into his attacker's skull.

The man staggered under the impact but did not fall. He looked confused as he reached up to touch the blade that was embedded in his head.

'You're dead,' prompted Gotrek.

The man snarled and tried to jump at him again.

The Slayer muttered a curse, wrenched the axe free and hacked it through his neck, sending his head bouncing through the dust.

For a few seconds the man carried on, staggering towards Gotrek with blood rushing down his chest.

Then he crashed to the ground and finally lay still.

'Gotrek,' said Trachos, waving one of his hammers down the street.

Dozens more people were lurching into the town, men and women dressed in bloody rags and twitching like marionettes. Their backs were so hunched that their spines jutted through their flesh, and their long, emaciated arms hung down to the ground so that they punched the dirt as they ran simian-like into the light.

'What devilry is this?' grunted Gotrek, looking at Maleneth.

She shook her head, drawing her knives as the blank-eyed mob rushed towards them.

'They're mordants,' said Kurin. He had reappeared a few feet away. Dust was still eddying around his robes, and his face took a moment to solidify. 'Their lord sends the bone rain in first. It gives them an easy victory.'

The mob limped and hopped down the street, their hands extended and twisted, like broken claws.

'What they lack in intellect,' said the sorcerer with a smile, 'they make up for in hunger.'

'Ghouls?' Gotrek sneered. 'I've met their like before.' He reeled drunkenly down the street, collided with an overturned cart then righted himself, raised his axe and hurled himself at the mob.

He landed with a flurry of blows, scattering limbs and heads.

Trachos limped to his side and began hammering the few creatures Gotrek had missed.

Maleneth gave Kurin a despairing look, but he just shrugged, seeming amused by the carnage.

'*Can* you get him to Nagash?' she cried, yelling over the sound of the fighting.

He nodded, still watching the fight.

As Gotrek and Trachos lunged and hacked, dozens more of the mordants were emerging from the storm, all moving with the same disjointed gait. They formed a ragged circle around the pair, closing in on them.

Gotrek and Trachos were hugely outnumbered, but Maleneth made no move to help. She had seen the Slayer face much worse odds without breaking into a sweat. As the crowds tried uselessly to swamp him, she turned to Kurin.

'Why would you help him?' she shouted, struggling to raise her voice over the howling wind.

'There is a change coming, aelf. I feel it in this wind. And I can see it in your friend. Getting him to Nagash could be a piece of the puzzle.'

Maleneth shook her head. 'Servants of the God-King do not–'

'I don't serve the God-King!' cried Gotrek, striding back towards them, leaving a heap of broken bodies in his wake.

'Not directly,' said Maleneth, 'but–'

'Not in any way!'

Kurin nodded in approval, then turned to Maleneth. 'And you? How many gods do you prostrate yourself before? Is Sigmar your only keeper?'

She glared at him. 'I'm an acolyte of the Hidden Temple, the Bloody-Handed, the Widowmaker. The Lord of Murder is my soul and my heart. But I'm–'

'But you're no fool,' interrupted Kurin. 'Whatever you swore to Khaine, Sigmar's Stormhosts are your only chance of survival. So your unshakeable faith is now shared with the storm god.'

Fury boiled through Maleneth. 'My queen communed with Khaine. She is the High Oracle, and she has prophesied the destruction of Chaos. Soon everyone will see the power of the Murder God.' She laughed. 'Turn your back on the gods if you like, wizard, but it won't help you escape their wrath.'

Kurin rolled his eyes.

Gotrek glanced back at the dead ghouls and then beyond the town walls, to the storm clouds that were still whipping through the darkness. 'How would you get me to Nagash?'

'I can do nothing unless we leave Klemp.'

Maleneth was about to ask another question when Kurin held up a hand for silence, nodding down the street.

Klemp was swarming with mordants. There were now hundreds of them, tearing down doors and clambering through windows. Screams knifed through the storm as the creatures dragged people from their homes, snarling and clawing, filling the air with blood.

'Into my rooms,' said Kurin, waving casually towards one of the buildings. 'Quickly.'

CHAPTER THREE

THE LAST OF THE HUSH

Trachos had to stoop to duck under the doorframe, and Gotrek had to turn sideways to fit through the narrow opening. The Slayer had finished the bottle he had bought in the Muffled Drum, and he was now so unsteady on his feet that he ripped half the doorframe away as he entered, trailing splintered wood and alcohol fumes. Kurin quickly barred the broken door, then lit a candle and held it up. The weak light revealed a hovel cluttered with mismatched furniture and the remains of uneaten meals. It was an eight-foot-by-eight-foot square, and there was something absurd about seeing Gotrek and Trachos squeezed into such a small, prosaic space.

'A smokescreen for the curious,' said Kurin, waving vaguely at the room.

The noise of fighting grew louder outside, and Kurin shook his head. 'We will have to be quick.' He took out a key and unlocked a door in the far wall, leading them into a second room, then locked the door behind them again. He carried the candle with him, and as they entered, the light flickered over dozens of silent, impassive faces.

Maleneth grabbed her knives, unsure what she was seeing. As her eyes adjusted to the faint light, she saw that the room was square, like the first one, but devoid of furniture. There were nine frail old men standing around the walls, but they were so motionless that Maleneth wondered if they were statues. They were dressed similarly to Kurin and looked almost identical to him, with the same long, aristocratic features and gangly limbs.

'What now?' demanded Maleneth. 'You've just trapped us in here. Those creatures won't take long to kick down your door!'

Kurin ignored her.

'Who are they?' demanded Gotrek, still swaying, looking at the nine motionless figures.

'My fellow shrivers,' replied Kurin, placing his hand on one of the old men's arms. 'This is all of us that remain. The last of the hush.' Muttering under his breath, he took the men's hands and linked them, creating a circle.

'Are they asleep?' asked Maleneth, finding the whole scene vaguely distasteful.

Kurin shrugged. 'We live in fragments and snatches, prolonging our span.'

Maleneth's distaste grew. The dank, dark room felt like a grave, and the silent men looked like corpses. It appalled her to think what people had been driven to in their determination to evade Nagash. 'What kind of existence is this? What kind of life is it?'

For the first time since they had met, Kurin's veneer cracked. 'This is victory. This is how we win.' His tone was brittle. 'Not through mindless devotion to callous gods.'

The noise of battle outside swelled louder. People were screaming and howling.

'Can you hear that?' demanded Maleneth. 'What are we doing in here? We need to get out of Klemp.'

Kurin regained his composure and waved a dismissive hand.

'We have time. No one passes through that door unless I permit it.' He looked at Gotrek. 'There *is* a way to Nagash. You must travel to Morbium.'

Gotrek shook his head. 'Morbium?'

'One of the Amethyst Princedoms. Not *all* of them fell. Some have remained hidden.' Kurin reached beneath his robes and drew out a chain of nine polished padlocks, each one engraved with a different rune. They clattered as he held them up and traced his bony fingers over the markings. Then he hung them around the necks of each of the silent men. 'Morbium,' he said as he worked, 'is one of the oldest of the underworlds, ruled by royal scholars known as Morn-Princes. Their knowledge of death magic is as vast as the Great Necromancer's. When Nagash tried to conquer their realm, the reigning Morn-Prince defied him. Nagash punished him for his temerity, but even as he took his revenge, he fell into the prince's trap. The Morn-Prince sacrificed himself so that Morbium could survive. A part of Nagash's power was channelled into a rite the Morn-Prince had spent years preparing. Morbium vanished, and however Nagash tormented the prince, he could never discover the location of the princedom. The Morn-Prince had engineered the rite in such a way that he did not know where he had sent his own people, only that they would escape the predations of the gods.'

Kurin explained all this with an approving tone in his voice. 'Nagash's arrogance blinds him to the subtlety of those he tries to subjugate.'

'Good for Morbium,' slurred Gotrek. 'How does that help me?'

'Things have changed. Nagash's power has grown. He has utilised a new, more powerful form of death magic. No one knows how, but he is suddenly able to drive back even the most powerful of the Chaos hosts. But it's not just the Bloodbound and the Rotbringers that have been affected. A plague of undeath has washed through Shyish. Defences that endured for a thousand years have toppled. And Morbium is no different. The wards so cleverly woven by the prince all those years ago are toppling, and the hidden jewel of the princedoms has been exposed. Morbium is one of the first underworlds, one of the oldest, and now it seems set to fall the same way as all the others. At the moment, there is no more than a crack in its wall, but it will widen.'

'Why does that make it a route to Nagash?' asked Maleneth.

'Because the wards that hid Morbium were created with Nagash's own power. Nagash is blind to it, but Morbium is bound to him. Still part of him. In a tower, in a city, in the heart of Morbium, there are stones that still remember Nagash. I have no idea who the current prince is, but he is linked to Nagash. He has a direct route to the Great Nadir.'

Gotrek grinned, revealing a mess of broken teeth. 'So if you take me to this Morn-Prince, he can *send* me to Nagash?'

Kurin looked at the ur-gold rune in Gotrek's chest. It was flashing in the candlelight, and the same heat was burning in the Slayer's eye. 'I think you are *fated* to reach him.'

The Slayer replied with the complete certainty of the completely drunk. 'Yes. I am. You're right.'

Trachos shook his head. 'We have never met this man before.'

Gotrek laughed. 'What would you have me do instead, manling? Run back to one of your stormkeeps so you can open my chest and see how this rune works?' He tapped the head of his axe on Trachos' breastplate, his eye burning malevolently. '*I* am not one of Sigmar's playthings.'

Gotrek shrugged. 'Besides, you saw what's happening outside. Wherever I go can't be any worse than this. And if there's even a chance of getting to grips with one of the gods, I'll take it.' He looked back at Kurin. 'I agree with you, wizard. I was meant to go to this Morbium.' His habitual scowl was replaced by a confused expression, and he began debating with himself. 'I've no truck with prophecies and soothsayers, but *something* brought me to this place. I'm here for a reason. I must be.'

Maleneth gave Trachos a despairing look. Every time the Slayer got this drunk, it led to disaster.

Kurin was still staring at Gotrek, obviously intrigued by him. He waved to the silent, motionless figures. 'If you really want to know why you're here, my brothers may be able to help.'

Gotrek scowled. 'I told you. My mind is my own. I'll not have you rooting around in there.'

'That's not all we do, Slayer. Is there anyone from your past who could help you? You say you're unsure why you were brought back. Back from where? Is there someone from your home who could help? A wandering spirit, perhaps – someone who might have the answer?'

'Pah!' Gotrek laughed. 'Mystic gibberish.'

Kurin smiled, saying nothing.

Gotrek peered into his face. 'You mean you can summon ghosts from one of these absurd realms?'

Kurin shrugged. 'Or another. I can summon whichever ghost you like – from whatever realm you choose.'

Gotrek scratched at his stubbly scalp and stomped around the dingy room. 'Anyone?'

Kurin nodded.

'Gotrek,' said Maleneth, shaking her head in disbelief. 'Listen to what's going on out there. We need to *leave*. You're drunk, and he's a fraud. Why would he want to help you? There must be something he's not telling us. Look at him. He's no more than a–'

Gotrek silenced her with a warning finger. 'He's spoken more sense in the last ten minutes than you've done in three months.'

Gotrek looked back at Kurin. 'There *is* a soul. A ghost I would wish to speak to.' He carried on circling the room, not meeting anyone's eye, drumming his blocky fingers on his axe. 'A poet. Felix Jaeger. I owe him an apology. I did not end things as I should have.'

Kurin's eyes glinted in the darkness. 'Felix Jaeger.' He placed his hand on Gotrek's forearm.

The Slayer moved as if to shrug him off, but something happening to one of the figures in the shadows stopped him. It shuddered, as though waking from a deep sleep.

Gotrek staggered over to it, seeming to forget that Kurin had hold of his arm.

The temperature dropped.

Maleneth glanced around, sensing the presence of something unearthly. She stepped to Gotrek's side and grimaced as she saw what was happening to the figure. The frail old man still had his eyes closed and still looked to be dead, with a ghastly complexion and no movement in his narrow chest, but something was happening to his skin. Just like on Kurin's palm in the Muffled Drum, the creases had risen up and begun moving, coiling and twisting in a silent dance.

As the miniature storm whipped across the lifeless figure, it began to blur his features and then transform them. They all watched in surprise as a new face began to appear, scarred and handsome.

'Is that you?' whispered Gotrek, staring at the face that was moving beneath the skin, as though trying to break the surface of water. 'Felix?'

'Are you really so gullible?' cried Maleneth. 'He's a charlatan! Can't you see? He's just showing you what you want to see. This is just a cheap trick designed to–'

'Can he speak?' demanded Gotrek, ignoring her.

'Give him a moment,' said Kurin. 'He's travelled a great distance to be here.'

The younger face finally broke through the surface of the older one. The man stared around the room in confusion, until his eyes came to rest on the Slayer.

'Gotrek!' His voice sounded muffled, like it was coming through a thick wall. 'Is that really you?' As it spoke, the figure lurched into life, reaching out and stumbling forwards, like the ghouls they had fought outside.

Gotrek grabbed the man's arms. 'Can you hear me?'

He nodded. 'You survived?' he said, sounding dazed.

For a moment Gotrek was too overcome to speak. When he finally answered, his voice was husky. 'I should have stayed with you, manling. They tricked me. Grimnir tricked me. The gods lied, Felix. Everything has been lost.'

The face behind the face smiled. 'If you're alive, not *everything* has been lost.' Then he frowned and looked back into the darkness, as though someone had called him. 'I can't stay,' he said, turning back to the Slayer.

'Forgive me,' growled Gotrek, still gripping his arms.

Maleneth shook her head, still unable to believe that the Slayer could fall for such obvious deception.

Felix smiled again. 'You are unforgivable, Gotrek. You always were.' Then his expression became serious. 'Make them pay. Make them pay for their lies.'

'Aye!' Gotrek was breathing heavily. 'I'm close. Nagash is within my reach. I'm going to bring his whole bloody palace down on his–' He frowned as the face under the skin vanished, leaving the sleeping face of the old man. 'Where's he gone?' Gotrek demanded, looking at Kurin.

Kurin frowned. 'You have him so clearly pinned in your memory. There should have been no problem talking to him. Something held him back. Something is keeping him from you – guarding his soul.'

Gotrek spat into the dust. 'Nagash. Who else?' He began pacing again, swinging his axe in a way that was far from ideal in such a small space. 'No matter. The manling was clear enough. Make them pay. And I will do. Starting with Nagash.' He paused and looked back at the now motionless figure, clearly still shaken by the whole exchange. Then he turned to Kurin. 'How do we get to Morbium?'

Kurin was still frowning, staring at the sleeping figure that had just been talking to Gotrek. Then he smiled, waving them back, outside the circle. He checked the chains around the old men's necks, adjusted the padlocks, then began muttering his incantation again. As he spoke, the hard-packed earth of the floor began to spiral and twist. A miniature storm raged between the silent figures, whirling and turning and causing Gotrek and the others to shield their faces.

When the dust cleared, Kurin was still smiling. There was a circular opening at his feet, with narrow steps leading down into the darkness.

'Follow me,' he said, descending. 'The entrance to Morbium is not far.'

CHAPTER FOUR

OATHBREAKERS AND FRAUDS

They emerged from an opening in a hillside, half a mile from the town.

Kurin did not pause for breath as he left the tunnel, and they had to move fast to keep up as their guide rushed into the half-light.

'Can we trust him?' asked Maleneth, eyeing the sorcerer as he slipped and scrambled down the rocky hillside.

'*Never* trust wizards,' laughed Gotrek in disbelief. 'Or aelves, for that matter.' He scowled at Trachos. 'Which only leaves you, unfortunately.' Then he shook his head. 'It's not Kurin I trust – it's Felix.' Gotrek's words were becoming less slurred. 'Besides, he got us out of Klemp, didn't he?'

They climbed down into a narrow valley, leaving Klemp behind and entering the strange landscape they had spent weeks travelling through since arriving at the coast. It was impossible to see more than a dozen feet or so due to the mist towers – sheer-sided, curved masses that soared up into the darkness for miles. This part of Shyish was relentlessly bleak. No breeze, no birdsong, no animal calls, no trace of mortality. Only one sound punctuated the darkness – the clang of a broken bell, far in the distance. It rang out every few seconds with heartbeat regularity. Maleneth remembered hearing it on the journey to Klemp, but she was surprised to hear it again now, nearly two days later. Time seemed frozen in Shyish. The realm seemed like a single, perpetual moment, hanging ominously over some terrible, imminent catastrophe.

Kurin hurried on, pausing every now and then to make sure they were still following him. Trachos' wounds caused him to grunt and mutter as he hauled his broken armour over increasingly rocky terrain, but he was far too proud to slow down or ask for help.

They travelled this way for several hours, and Gotrek began to grumble into his beard and complain that Maleneth had not thought to bring food from the Muffled Drum. Not for the first time, Maleneth wondered what Trachos would do if she rushed past him and sank a poisoned blade into the Slayer's back. It was little more than an idle daydream. Her mistress was right – Gotrek was more than a duardin. She had no idea if any of her toxins would work. And Trachos would almost certainly try to stop her. Whatever went on in that battle-ravaged head, he maintained a rigid code of honour. He would not condone a random murder, however entertaining it might be.

The sorcerer came to a halt next to a bleached, skeletal tree and crouched low, looking at something on the ground. There was a confusing mass of footprints.

'Mordants,' he said. 'But not from Klemp. These came from the south.'

Gotrek shrugged, then nodded at some tracks leading north.

'The morons were heading somewhere with a purpose. And little morons always follow big morons.'

They marched on, following the tracks, and after a while they spotted corpses, sprawled in the dust.

As they approached the bodies, Maleneth's lip curled in distaste. There were around thirty of them, twisted and feral, all wearing contorted snarls and scraps of bloody cloth. Mixed in with them were a few dead duardin, possibly the ones they had seen in the Muffled Drum. She raised an eyebrow and looked at the Slayer. 'I see your relatives made a good account of themselves.'

Gotrek glared at her for a moment, golden sparks flickering across his eye. Then he booted one of the dead ghouls and looked at the sorcerer. 'I didn't come here to fight these pitiful things. I came for a god.'

Maleneth shook her head. 'What in Sigmar's name would you do if you actually found Nagash?'

'I'd do nothing in *Sigmar's* name, aelf. A hammer-hurler's no better than a corpse-botherer. Once I've dealt with Nagash, the God-King is next.'

Trachos tensed and gripped his warhammers. His armour clicked as his head started twitching.

Gotrek laughed and slammed his chest into Trachos' armour, knocking him backwards. 'So there *is* someone in that bloody suit! That's the spirit, manling. Did Gotrek make you think a bad thought?'

Maleneth stepped back, trying to suppress a smile.

'You know nothing of Sigmar.' Trachos sounded furious, but he lowered his hammers and backed away, his head still twitching.

'I know more than you, manling. I know what happened last time he faced the Ruinous Powers. They *trounced* him. That's why he's hiding. That's why he's up there in… Where did you say he's snivelled off to?'

Trachos was clearly struggling to stay calm. 'The God-King will reunite the Mortal Realms. That which has been riven shall be reforged. Sigmar has sent his Stormhosts to–'

'Why?' The Slayer waved his rune-axe at the grey walls and up at the black stars. 'Why does he care for any of these stinking pits? I think he's had too many knocks to the head. Maybe he sits up there hitting himself with his own hammer? Maybe he's senile? Grungni's beard! There must be *something* wrong with him. He's as much a stranger here as I am. These are not his wars – these are not his people – any more than they're mine.'

'Then why drag us down here looking for the God of Death?' asked Maleneth. In truth, she did not really care, but it was amusing to see Gotrek upsetting Trachos. 'If you care nothing for these realms or these wars, why pit yourself against Nagash?'

'Because the gods *lied,* aelf. They're oathbreakers and frauds, the lot of them. They know the doom they promised me. They know what they swore. But did they hold up their half of the bargain? No! And here they are, playing games and building empires, like they always do. I turned my back on my friends and my kin because of their lies.' His expression darkened. 'And a Slayer does not forget. Not *this* Slayer, anyhow. I hold true. I remember my bloody oaths. Even when others do not. They'll give me the doom I was promised.' He scowled. 'Or I'll give them a doom of their own.'

The sorcerer watched the exchange patiently. Then, when the trio fell quiet again, he nodded and continued, following the tracks on through the dust.

Maleneth winked at Trachos, then sauntered after Gotrek.

Kurin led them to one of the soaring mist walls, hesitated briefly, then plunged through it, disappearing from sight.

It was only when they got within a few feet of the mist that its true nature was revealed. It was a tangled vine of spirits – naked, emaciated wretches bound into vast circular prisons. Each of the chimney-like structures was miles tall. There must have been millions of spirits trapped in each one. As Gotrek approached, they screamed, thrashing and struggling, trying to reach him, but they were too tightly knotted to move. Some spoke words Maleneth understood, begging her to free them, sobbing for help.

Gotrek marched straight through the ghosts, following the sorcerer, head low and axe high, like he was shouldering his way through a snowdrift.

Trachos and Maleneth hesitated before the dead, chilled by the cries. Maleneth did not fear death any more than she feared violence, but the enormity of the torment was still overwhelming. So many lost voices. So many twisted faces. And she was going to endure it for that deluded hog, Gotrek.

Trachos stepped forwards, then halted. His head was twitching again. Every now and then, he seemed to notice who he was travelling with, as though it had never occurred to him before. This was one of those times. He stared at her.

'The Slayer is insane,' he said.

'Nothing gets past you.'

He continued staring at her.

She smiled at the irony. 'And we need to keep him alive until one of us can get that rune.'

She could see Trachos' eyes through the holes in his faceplate. They were as wild as the eyes of the ghouls. He was a taut string. She just needed to keep pushing. And when he snapped, the rune would be hers.

'Aelf!' roared Gotrek from somewhere up ahead.

She closed her eyes, then stepped into the mist with a sigh.

CHAPTER FIVE

THE IRON SHROUD

The wall of spirits was thick. As Maleneth staggered on, the cries became deafening. Deeper within, the ghosts summoned the strength to attack, their cold, waxy fingers clawing at her face.

After a few steps she was fighting, punching and kicking her way through the tangled limbs. The dead were desperate, trying to tear her skin, hungry for her warmth, craving her pulse. For a while she fought in silence, but as the attacks became more frantic she felt like she was drowning. She howled in defiance. Then, as the crush was about to overwhelm her, she burst through the other side of the wall and tumbled to the ground, gasping for breath.

The air was so thick and greasy that she gagged. It was like breathing cremation fumes. She lurched to her feet, coughing, and looked around.

They had entered another expanse of grey, encircled by another tower of mist. But there was a difference. In some places, the tower had collapsed, spilling ghosts across the ground. The spirits were trying to crawl away from the walls, but outside the mist their substance gave way, dissipating as they grasped at the air, thrashing across the ground like stranded fish. Gotrek was standing in the middle of the tower, and waves of spectral debris were crawling towards him, pleading and weeping. He seemed unaware of them. He was looking around in confusion.

'Where'd the wizard go?' he cried, glancing back at Maleneth.

Then he laughed as Trachos tumbled through the wall and landed with a clatter. 'Still with us, manling?'

Trachos did not reply.

'Get over here, *Lord Ordinator*,' said Gotrek, sneering Trachos' title.

Maleneth and Trachos hurried into the centre of the mist tower and stood next to the Slayer.

'Which way did he go?' asked Gotrek.

The spirits were whipping across the ground, kicking up dust. It was hard to see anything clearly.

Gotrek studied the astrological equipment fixed to Trachos' belt. 'Can one of your devices track him?'

Trachos staggered as ghosts whipped through the darkness, battering against his armour. 'What?' he gasped as he fended off the spectral shapes.

'Take that bloody hat off and you might hear me.' Gotrek tapped one of his slab-like fingers on Trachos' helmet. 'Where. Is. The. Wizard?'

'I am a Lord Ordinator,' replied Trachos, 'not a scout. These are instruments of Sigmar's divine will. They measure aetheonic currents. They plot the celestial spheres. They do not track conjurors.'

'The bell,' said Maleneth.

'What?' snarled Gotrek.

'I heard it earlier, and now it's louder. Do you hear?'

Gotrek looked at the ground, concentrating.

'We're getting closer to it,' Maleneth said. 'This...' She waved vaguely at the diaphanous structure that was collapsing all around them. 'This place is closer to wherever the bell is ringing. The creatures Kurin called mordants were heading towards it, so he might be too.'

Gotrek grinned and clapped her on the back so hard she staggered. He looked through the crowds of struggling spectres to the opposite side of the circular wall. It was the section that was most crumbled, and it was heaving with anguished souls. 'Of course. A bell means a building. And buildings mean civilisation.' He shrugged, grimacing at the bleak wasteland. 'Civilisation might be stretching it.'

'There's something else, too,' said Maleneth.

They all listened. Along with the bell there was a clamour – incoherent, bestial cries and a low, smashing sound, like a war engine pummelling a wall.

'Sounds like a fight!' Gotrek stomped off through the dust, waving for Maleneth to follow.

'That's a warning bell,' said Trachos, staring at the tumbling walls of mist.

Maleneth nodded.

She turned to follow Gotrek, but Trachos grabbed her arm. 'No one gets the rune if he destroys himself.'

She looked at him, her expression neutral.

'And we can't keep him alive if we don't trust each other,' he continued.

Maleneth's smile was as cold as the dust. 'Of course you can trust me.' She jogged lightly away, weaving around the tumbling ghosts as she followed Gotrek.

Each tower of mist was more ruined than the previous one, and the spirits grew more desperate the further they went, but Gotrek strode on with purpose, heading unerringly towards the clanging bell. The closer they came to the sound, the more it mingled with the din of battle and the deep, seismic thudding they had heard earlier.

Finally, after breaking through a fifth wall, they saw the source of the din. Even by the standards of Shyish it was a macabre sight. Ghouls were clambering over a shrine, dozens of them, thrashing and snarling as they fought. The shrine was a splayed, claw-like structure perched on a rocky outcrop. It was made of stone, but its limbs were as sharp and twisted as a briar, hung low to the ground and knitted together in a jumble of knuckles and thorns. There were cylindrical cages hung at the end of each bristling limb, and in each cage there was a corpse. Some were no more than dusty skeletons while others were rot-bloated husks, bruise-dark and waxy, gleaming under a low-hanging moon. The corpses were moving, lunging and hacking at the ghouls, defending the shrine with silent determination.

At the sight of the frantic battle, Gotrek halted and let out an eager growl. He gripped his axe tightly and its brazier blazed with inner fire. 'We've found the puppet master!' he roared, pointing his weapon at the centre of the shrine.

At the heart of the stone briar there was a circular block, like a crooked pulpit, and inside it there was a slender man dressed in a white gown, his face hidden in a deep hood. He was waving a scythe back and forth, and with every sweep, the briar's limbs lashed out, tearing the ghouls apart and allowing the caged corpses to attack with rusting swords. It was grotesque and surreal. The monsters fought like animals, spitting and twitching, but the briar corpses were silent, even when their cages hit the ghouls with so much force they exploded, scattering shards of bone and flesh.

'A necromancer!' cried Gotrek, charging through the dust towards the shrine. There was a worrying gleam in his eye that Maleneth had seen before. His muscles were trembling and the rune in his chest shimmered with aetheric power.

Maleneth was about to follow when she noticed another shrine a few hundred yards away. It was similar to the one Gotrek was approaching, but it had collapsed. Ghouls were swarming over it from every direction, and as they reached its summit something strange was happening – they were vanishing from view, tumbling into it as though they were falling into a well. As the shrine crumbled, the spirit mist lashed down from the towers, spiralling around the crumbling stones.

'This is a wall,' she said.

Trachos stared at her.

She pointed one of her knives at the shapes in the distance. 'There are dozens of these things. They're a barrier.'

All of the shrines were under attack. Hundreds, perhaps thousands of ghouls were spilling from the mist and tearing down the stone briars. As the shrines crumbled, the spirit winds lashed around them like sails torn from their masts.

A bellowed war cry drew Maleneth's attention back to Gotrek. He drew back his axe and hurled it into the shrine wall, creating an explosion of shattered stone. Then he strode forwards, wrenched the axe free and began laying about himself, smashing mordants from the barbed limbs and bellowing. He made such a terrifying sight that even the ghouls hesitated, seemingly taken aback by the arrival of someone more deranged than they were.

The shrine heaved and lurched like an enormous crustacean, lashing out with its cages in an attempt to batter Gotrek away.

In his berserk state the Slayer was surprisingly agile. His short, muscular legs powered him through the tumult as he hacked chunks of stone from his path, howling the whole time.

The necromancer remained motionless, head down, his face still hidden in his hood, but it was clear he had noticed Gotrek's approach. The stone briar became a storm of lashing limbs and whirling blades.

A stone branch thudded into the Slayer as if to hurl him clear, but Gotrek gripped it tightly with one hand and headbutted it.

The stone broke with an explosion of sparks, and for a moment Maleneth lost sight of the Slayer.

When the flash faded, she saw him halfway up the shrine, punching a ghoul and roaring with laughter, hauling himself through the contorted shapes.

She raced towards the shrine, dodging the mordants' grasping talons and leaping up onto the twisted mass, cutting down more of the creatures as she began to climb. When the Slayer was in the grip of a kill-fever, anything could happen. She had to get close enough to protect the rune.

Trachos lurched after her with a clatter of ruined armour. Then, absurdly, he launched into song. 'Oh, faint, deluded hearts!' he sang, his voice metallic and inhuman. 'The God-King hath descended!' Ever since Gotrek had dragged them down to the Realm of Death, the Stormcast had taken to singing hymns as he fought. Either his wounds had damaged his hearing or he had never had a musical ear. He turned every melody into a bludgeoning, tuneless dirge.

Maleneth weaved and ducked, planting kicks and dancing around lunges, but it was impossible to keep pace with Gotrek. Her blades flashed through necks and wrists, slicing the ghouls apart with calm efficiency. They tried to swarm over her, but she was too light on her feet, dancing away from them as blood-frenzy washed over her. At moments like this she could not deny her true faith. She fought in tribute to the Bloody-Handed God, making every cut as cruel and painful as she could, laughing mercilessly as the creatures tumbled away, gasping and choking, Khaine's symbol scored into their flesh.

There was an explosion of light, and the whole scene became a frozen tableau of silhouettes. Then the light vanished and Maleneth stumbled, blinded, as ghouls rushed at her.

Hot pain erupted across her back as claws raked over her skin.

She whirled around, lashing out blindly, cutting through muscle and cartilage as she jumped clear.

Once she had gained a safer vantage point she saw the source of the light. Trachos had taken some objects from his belt and clasped them together, forming a slender sceptre with an ornate mechanical cube at its head. The cube was trailing strands of smoke, and there was a charred heap where several ghouls had been standing.

'Steadfast and majestic!' boomed the Stormcast, still singing. 'Fiery hammer swinging!'

Maleneth grimaced and bounded up the shrine after Gotrek.

They reached the necromancer at the same moment, the howling Slayer barrelling through ghouls from one direction while Maleneth leapt gracefully from the other.

The necromancer whirled his scythe, and stone limbs stabbed towards the Slayer.

Gotrek was covered in blood and his grin was daemonic as he slammed his axe into the cages, shattering every corpse that tried to land a blow on him. He leapt through a storm of bone, blood and rock, grabbing the necromancer by the throat.

Maleneth arrived just in time to see the look of confusion on Gotrek's face as the hood fell back.

Rather than a wizened old man, there was a young woman staring back at the Slayer.

Gotrek froze, shocked into momentary silence.

The girl took her chance. As the Slayer hesitated, she sank her scythe into his chest.

There was another explosion, and this one was so powerful that it kicked Maleneth back from the pulpit, sending her crashing into the ghouls.

'Sound the starlit trumpets!' sang Trachos from somewhere nearby. 'Rouse the ardent host!'

'Trachos!' Maleneth howled, attacked on all sides and unable to rush after Gotrek.

The singing paused, and there were more flashes of light. Maleneth fought blind, weaving through the ghouls until she was back on the ground.

As her eyes adjusted to the glare, she saw Trachos swing his sceptre and hurl silver-blue flames. 'Never-ending glory!' he cried as the blast left a landslide of charred body parts at her feet. 'Foes vanquished and unbound!'

Maleneth ducked and rounded on another mordant, opening its throat with a backhanded slash before leaping clear.

When she turned to look back at the fight, it was over. Gotrek had hacked down half the ghouls, and she and Trachos had dealt with the rest. The shrine was empty, its stone branches lying in the dust.

'Where is he?' she gasped, glancing at Trachos.

He did not seem to hear. His head was thrown back and he was still gripping the sceptre in both hands, aetheric energy sizzling around his gauntlets. He was still singing, but only to himself now, the words muffled and faint inside his helmet. Then he shook his head and lowered the sceptre, turning to face Maleneth. The light faded from his eyes and he suddenly looked dazed from his exertions. He leant on the sceptre as a crutch.

'He fell when the necromancer stabbed him.'

They both looked around.

'We need to get out of here,' said Maleneth, looking past the Stormcast Eternal to the mist towers. There were hundreds more ghouls approaching from every direction. Even with the Slayer they could never face down so many. 'That sorcerer you put so much faith in has abandoned us.'

She leapt over the dead bodies, looking for Gotrek and the sorcerer, leaving Trachos to stagger after her.

They found the girl first. She had rolled down through the nest of spiny stones and landed in a heap at the bottom of the shrine. Her hood was thrown back, so they could see her flushed, furious face. Her teeth were bared, and she glowered at Maleneth like she wanted to tear her throat out.

She tried to rise, but Maleneth held a knife against her throat, smiling. 'Just give me a reason.'

The woman was shivering with rage. 'The Unburied will endure.' Her eyes were so bloodshot they looked wholly red. 'Morbium eternal!'

'Unburied?' Maleneth glanced at Trachos for an explanation, but the Stormcast shrugged.

The woman sneered, her words thick with hate. 'Kill me. Be done with it. I don't know how you uncovered the Iron Shroud, but this will not be the end of us. The ancestors will endure. As was will always be. The past remains in the now. The Unburied will still be here when the traitor-god is overturned and the–'

'Your walls are falling,' interrupted Maleneth, annoyed by the woman's pompous tone. 'Take a look.' She hauled her to her feet and showed her the line of shrines. All of them were collapsing under the weight of the ghouls' attacks, surrounded by storms of mist.

'Morbium will endure,' snapped the woman, her fingers trembling, her weapon lost.

'Your spiky shrub is the only one still standing, and that's only thanks to Gotrek,' said Maleneth. At the mention of his name, she remembered that the girl had wounded the Slayer. 'Where is he?' she muttered, looking across the still-twitching bodies.

Trachos barged past her, striding through veils of mist, his sceptre shimmering.

'Wait!' demanded Maleneth, still crouched over the woman with her blade at her throat. 'What are you?' she said, wondering if there was any reason for letting her live. '*Are* you a necromancer?'

The woman looked appalled. 'I'm the High Priestess of the Cerement.'

'Good for you,' said Maleneth, pressing on the blade.

Gotrek staggered through the mist, dazed but apparently unharmed.

He shoved Maleneth aside and dragged the white-robed woman to her feet. He held up the scythe she'd used on him and tapped it against the rune in his chest. 'Aim higher, lass, if you get another chance.'

'Prince Volant will have your head,' hissed the woman. 'When he hears you attacked the Iron Shroud, there'll be no sorcery in all of Shyish that can protect you.'

'The Iron Shroud?' asked Gotrek.

Maleneth leant close, speaking with mock discretion. 'I think she means this impregnable edifice.' She pointed at the ruined shrines that trailed away from them in both directions.

'Attacked?' Gotrek shook his head. 'What are you talking about?' He looked at the tides of ghouls racing towards them. 'You think these things are *mine*?' He waved at the bodies that surrounded them and laughed. 'Perhaps you didn't notice me trimming their necks.'

The woman shook her head. 'Then who are you?'

'Gotrek, son of Gurni, born in the Everpeak and–'

'Gotrek,' said Maleneth, drawing the Slayer's attention to the host thundering towards them.

He grunted, annoyed at the interruption, and looked back at the woman. 'How do I get to your master?'

'Prince Volant?'

'Prince who?' Gotrek shook his head. 'Is that the Morn-Prince? Prince Volant? Is he the one who can get me to Nagash?'

The woman stared at him. 'Nagash? You're insane.'

Maleneth laughed. 'She's a sound judge of character, at least.'

'They're almost on us,' said Trachos.

Maleneth glanced at Gotrek. 'Any suggestions?' There were so many ghouls charging through the mist that the ground was trembling.

The woman looked past Gotrek to the approaching horde and then back at the shrine.

Gotrek caught the glance. 'Is there something you can do? What have you got in that shrine?'

'Why do you seek Nagash?' asked the woman. 'To pledge allegiance?'

'Allegiance?' Gotrek laughed. 'I didn't come here to bend the bloody knee.'

'Trachos,' said Maleneth. The ghouls were only moments away. She could see their rolling, feverish eyes and the blood on their teeth. 'Your staff?'

He nodded, whispered a prayer and adjusted the cogs around the sceptre's head. Energy shimmered down the metal, splashing light over his faceplate. The air crackled as he strode away, launching into another tuneless hymn. 'Stooping from celestial spires, he rides the storm to conquer!'

Maleneth looked back at Gotrek. Even now he seemed oblivious to the host rushing towards them. He was holding the woman's gaze.

The woman stared at the dead ghouls Gotrek had scattered around the shrine. Her expression was tormented.

'If you can do something, it needs to be now,' said Maleneth, infuriated by the woman's indecision.

They all staggered as Trachos hammered his sceptre down onto the ground. An aether-wave splashed through the mist, hitting the front ranks of the ghouls, and Trachos' song rose in volume and fervour.

The ghouls ignited like kindling, howling as they fell, shrouded in embers.

The woman's eyes widened. She looked at the wreckage of the other shrines and then at Gotrek's axe and the rune in his chest, both of which were still glowing.

'The Iron Shroud is both wall and door,' she said. 'If it is the will of the Unburied, I may be able to return to Morbium and take you with me.' Her eyes were still burning with hate and outrage, but she kept glancing back to the shrine and she made no attempt to attack.

'Morbium?' Gotrek shook his head. 'That's it. That's the one. Get us there quick, lass, and I might forgive you for trying to gut me.'

They staggered again as Trachos unleashed another wave of light, toppling more ghouls as his song reached a triumphant crescendo.

The young woman gripped her head, drumming her fingers on her skull. 'Prince Volant was right to send me out here. The Shroud *has* been breached.' She shook her head, glancing at the shrine. 'I have to reach him.'

'If he knows the way to Nagash, I'll get you to him,' said Gotrek. 'Consider that an oath.'

She glared at Gotrek but seemed to be considering his offer. 'If the mordants have breached the Shroud, I may need protection.'

Gotrek tapped his bloody axe. 'If protection is what you need–'

'Slayer!' cried Trachos, rushing back and smashing his sceptre into the face of a ghoul. Its skull detonated, scattering flames and grey matter.

Maleneth dodged the gore then stopped the next one with a flurry of knife blows, and Gotrek dropped a third, crumpling its skull with his axe.

'Follow me to the pulpit!' cried the woman. She clambered quickly up the gnarled, twisted mass of stone, waving for them to follow.

They climbed backwards up the stones, still facing the ghouls, parrying their attacks.

Gotrek grinned as he fought, scattering heads and limbs as he hurried after the woman. Trachos used his sceptre like a hammer, swinging it with almost as much ferocity as Gotrek, and every blow triggered a flash of Azyrite sorcery that flashed over his armour, catching on the lightning bolts and stars that decorated the polished plate. His song had become a meaningless jumble of unconnected words. 'Swift! Blessed! Heart! Strife!'

When they reached the centre of the shrine, the woman waved them into the pulpit and indicated that they should sit beside her on the knotted shapes.

'Press your palms to the stone!' she cried.

Maleneth rushed to Gotrek's side. 'Is there anyone you *won't* put your trust in?'

The Slayer laughed and nodded to the chaotic scenes around them. The ghouls were in such a frenzy that they were turning on each other, tearing at their crooked limbs in their desperation to reach the last standing shrine. 'Stay here if you like.'

Gotrek slapped his meaty hand down next to the woman's, gripping a spur of stone that jutted up from the centre of the pulpit.

Trachos pointed his sceptre and lightning ripped from the metal, tearing a ghoul's chest open before lashing through another one's head. 'There's no option,' he said, using the sceptre to club a ghoul that leapt at him from another direction. He put his hand down next to Gotrek's, the metal of his gauntlet clanging against the stone.

Maleneth looked at the red-faced woman. She had gripped the stone in both hands and closed her eyes, whispering furiously. Indigo flames flickered between her fingers, and a breeze washed through the pulpit, causing Maleneth to shiver and curse. This was necromancy, whatever the woman claimed. She could smell death magic on the air.

The shrine began to judder, crumbling under the weight of the ghouls.

Maleneth muttered another curse and put her hand on the stone.

Cold rushed through her, and she gasped in pain. She tried to pull her hand free, but it was frozen in place.

'What is this?' she hissed at the woman, but the priestess was oblivious to anything other than her incantation. Her eyes were closed, her head was tilted back, and she was mouthing arcane, sibilant phrases.

'If you have betrayed–' began Maleneth, but her words were drowned out by a deafening grinding sound as the stone briar tightened its grip, clenching like an enormous fist, enveloping them all in a cage of bristles.

Maleneth cried out as thorns punched into her. She tried again to wrench her hand free, but it was no use.

Dozens of crumbling tusks sliced into her, and as the world grew dark, the talisman at her neck spoke up, its voice full of derision.

You can't even die elegantly.

CHAPTER SIX

MORBIUM

'Ditch maid!' roared Gotrek.

Maleneth was in darkness, but the Slayer's bludgeoning tones could only mean one thing – she was still alive. She had mixed emotions about this.

'It's Witchblade,' she muttered, struggling to sit up. She was tightly bound and her arms were numb from blood loss. She cursed herself for not killing the priestess.

'Aye,' replied Gotrek, sounding infuriatingly cheerful. 'Ditch maid. Get off your arse. Look at this.'

Someone moved towards her, and there was a grind of shifting stones. As her face was uncovered, she saw the heavens whirling overhead. The strange black stars had vanished, replaced by the usual glittering constellations, but they were hazy and faint, as though seen through a gauze.

Maleneth's neck was stiff with cold, but she managed to turn and see who had uncovered her. It was Trachos, starlight shimmering over his battered mask.

'The priestess was telling the truth,' he said.

'This is Morbium,' said the priestess. Maleneth could not see her, but she recognised her taut, furious voice, coming from somewhere up ahead in the darkness. 'Soul prominent. Last bastion of the Gravesward and the royal demesne of Prince Volant, nineteenth heir to the Sable Throne and Morn-Prince of the Lingering Keep.'

Trachos moved more stone off Maleneth, and she managed to stand, slapping her legs and arms, summoning blood back into her limbs. The stone was the remnants of the shrine. Its thorny limbs were in pieces and the corpse cages shattered, leaving the bodies to spill onto the ground, where they now lay motionless.

She looked around. They were on a ruined quay, but it was a quay that hung out over the strangest sea Maleneth had ever seen. Its towering waves were all motionless, as though they had been hammered from iron. She stared at the bizarre view for a moment, wondering if the water was frozen, but while the air was chilly, she was sure it was not cold enough to freeze an entire ocean. The waves just seemed to be paused in a moment, like a sea that had been made for a stage set.

Piers jutted out across the lifeless tides, constructed from the same fractured bones as everything else. The scale of the place was shocking. Maleneth had seen nothing so grand since leaving Hammerhal. Behind her, the quay joined an iron road, or a bridge of some kind, that led out across the sea, trailing off into the shadows.

'I haven't seen craftsmanship like this since the Hearth Halls of Karaz-a-Karak,' muttered Gotrek, staring out at the grand, crumbling piers. He almost sounded impressed. 'Who built this?' he asked, his breath coiling around him in the cold air.

The priestess was still picking her way from the ruined shrine and dusting her robes down, too dazed to realise she was being addressed. Maleneth noticed that she was mouthing words as she moved – numbers, by the look of it, as though she were counting something.

Gotrek repeated his question in even more bombastic tones, and the priestess looked up. 'The Morn-Prince,' she said. 'The *first* Morn-Prince, at the dawn of the Amethyst Princedoms.'

Gotrek stooped and picked up a piece of mangled metalwork. Even broken it was beautiful – intricately scored bone inlaid with strips of silver that depicted skulls and insect wings. 'Not bad for a bunch of ghost-botherers.'

'We do not "bother" our dead.' The priestess looked at her scythe, still tucked into Gotrek's belt, her eyes smouldering. Her face was flushed with anger, and Maleneth could see that she was struggling not to attack Gotrek. 'We watch over them just as they watch over us. We revere our ancestors.'

Maleneth nodded at the corpses slumped in the shrine's broken cages. 'Did you revere them?'

The woman sneered. 'They were mordants. I wiped their minds and turned them on their own kind. There are not worthy of anything more.'

'You're a witch?' Gotrek looked as though he had tasted something unpleasant.

'I am Lhosia, High Priestess of the Cerement. Spiritual adviser to the Morn-Prince.' She nodded towards the scythe at her belt. 'What power I have is tied to the ancestors.'

'Sounds like ghost-bothering to me,' grunted Gotrek, picking rubble from his mohawk.

Maleneth had climbed from the ruined shrine, and she stepped out towards Gotrek and Lhosia. 'This Morn-Prince you serve. We were told he could lead Gotrek to Nagash.'

The priestess frowned. 'Why would you *seek* the necromancer? Most people would do anything to avoid him.'

At the mention of Nagash, Gotrek's expression had soured. 'The gods owe me a doom. I don't care if it's the bone-head or the thunder-dunce – someone's going to give me what I was promised.' He waved his axe, causing its brazier to flicker. 'Either way, this thing will end up embedded in a god.'

Lhosia laughed in disbelief. 'You're at war with the gods?'

'We all are, lass. I'm just taking the fight to them.'

'The necromancer promised you something?' Lhosia glanced at Maleneth with a baffled expression.

Maleneth shrugged.

Gotrek's beard bristled. He stomped across the ruined metal, muttering in an archaic duardin tongue. 'I don't know who promised me what anymore,' he snapped, 'but I know I was robbed of my doom. Nagash knows what I'm owed. He'll remember me.'

There was a note of desperation in the Slayer's voice. Maleneth had the impression that Gotrek was propelled by fury more than facts. How much could he really remember? Was he seeking Nagash for revenge or because he didn't know what else to do? Did he just want to find someone who might know who he was? Since the moment she had met him, Maleneth had sensed that Gotrek was unsure why he was still alive. He was like a hound that had been kicked, bloodied and readied for the hunt, then thrown into a cage.

As Gotrek stormed around the ruins, swinging his axe and cursing, the rune in his chest started to glow.

'Can you get us to this prince of yours?' he demanded.

'I can,' said Lhosia. 'I *have* to reach him. He sent me to check that the borders of the princedom were sound, and they're in tatters. And if the mordants have breached the Iron Shroud, they could be anywhere.'

'What is this place?' asked Trachos. As usual, he seemed two steps removed from the conversation, consumed by whatever strange thoughts rattled around his helmet. He unclasped one of his devices from his armour and pointed its notched ellipses at the architecture. 'Why did you bring us here in particular?' He looked around at the empty streets and toppled buildings.

'It's my home,' Lhosia said. 'It was the easiest place for me to conjure from memory. Besides, before I do anything else I have to warn my family. The Iron Shroud is breached. Morbium has been revealed. I have to make sure our Unburied are safe.'

'It's a port,' said Gotrek.

She nodded. 'Some of your duardin kin used to pilot aethership here, before the fall of the princedoms. They called themselves Kharadron. They used to ship ore here. My ancestors fused it with bone to construct our temples.'

'There were dwarfs here?' Gotrek frowned, looking around the ruins with a suspicious expression.

Maleneth laughed. 'He's quite the celebrity amongst his own kind.' She lowered her voice to a mock whisper. 'They think *he's* a god. Oh, the irony...'

Lhosia stared at Gotrek's scarred, filthy muscles, looking even more baffled. 'A god? Why would they think that?'

Maleneth rolled her eyes. 'Because he crawled out of a hole and claimed it was the Realm of Chaos.'

'Slayers do not lie,' said Gotrek. 'The gods promised me a doom in the Realm of Chaos. Then the faithless bastards forgot about me. Now I'm here.' He peered into the ruins. 'Do dwarfs... I mean, do *duardin* still come here?'

Lhosia shook her head. 'No one comes here. When the other princedoms fell we built the Iron Shroud. Through the wisdom of the Unburied we hid ourselves from the necromancer and even from the Dark Gods. But without the Kharadron we lost contact with the other realms. We are alone.' She glanced at the corpses next to the shrine. 'Or, we were.'

'How can we reach your prince?' asked Maleneth.

Lhosia nodded to a building that looked more intact than the others. It resembled the bleached bowl of a skull, gleaming and chipped. 'My family is stationed here, guarding the ruins. They will have already seen that I'm here. It is only a small temple, but we have many Unburied loaning us their sight.' She waved for the others to follow as she began picking her way through the rubble towards the building.

'Unburied?' asked Maleneth. It was a strange word, and every time Lhosia spoke it there was reverence in her voice.

'The ancestors,' said Lhosia, glaring at her. 'The reason we are here. We exist to ensure their future. Our world is an antechamber to theirs – the world that is to come, where we shall join our forebears.'

Gotrek glanced up at that, seeming intrigued. He was about to speak when Lhosia faltered and came to a halt, squinting through the gloom at the building at the end of the pier.

Maleneth gripped her knives. 'What?'

'No light.' Lhosia's voice sounded odd. She nodded to the curved bone-white walls of the temple. The building was swathed in shadow and looked abandoned. She staggered on, looking dazed and troubled.

CHAPTER SEVEN

HARBINGERS

They rushed on, reaching the building together. It was a coiled teardrop of bone, edged with a silver tracery of symbols that Maleneth did not recognise. The bone looked ridged and grooved, as though made of irregular tiles. The silver glimmered in the starlight, but otherwise there was only darkness.

'Anyone there?' bellowed Gotrek, tapping the head of his axe against the walls.

There was an explosion of noise and movement.

Maleneth flipped gracefully back from the building, whipping her knives out of her leathers and landing in a crouch, only to find that Gotrek had disturbed nothing more dangerous than insects. What she had taken for tiles on the surface of the building were actually thousands of pale, diaphanous moths. They were now whirling around Gotrek and the others, fluttering against their faces and filling the air with a frenetic buzz.

Gotrek cursed and waved his axe around, nearly beheading Lhosia in the process. 'Damn things,' he grunted, trying to bat the insects away.

Maleneth laughed at the absurd sight of a Slayer doing battle with moths. 'You don't like them,' she snorted.

Gotrek glowered back at her. 'I like them a damn sight more than witch aelves.' He waded off through the fluttering cloud, muttering as he batted them away.

Maleneth was still laughing as she struggled after him, amazed by the ridiculousness of the Slayer. She had seen him kill beasts that could best armies and trade insults with a sylvaneth goddess. And here he was, cursing because a few insects were trapped in his beard.

'Stop!' cried Lhosia, grabbing Gotrek's axe and glaring at him in outrage. 'The harbingers! You'll offend them!'

Gotrek stared at her. 'The what?'

'She means the moths.' Maleneth laughed even harder. 'You're scared of them, and she's worried about offending them!'

'Where's the door?' cried Gotrek, scowling at Maleneth and then rounding on Lhosia. 'How do we get in?'

After a wary glance at Gotrek's axe, the priestess nodded and hurried past him, pointing her scythe at a bone archway that looked like the rib of a long-dead leviathan. Her eyes were wide with fear.

They all rushed after her, entering a circular courtyard with a hole at its centre and metal steps spiralling down into the darkness.

Lhosia hesitated at the top step, looking around the courtyard and shaking her head. She peered down into the darkness. 'Hello?' she called, taking a few steps down into the gloom. 'Mother? Father? It's Lhosia.'

A clattering echoed up the steps, followed by what sounded like a door slamming shut.

Lhosia glanced back at the others. Her pale, hard features twisted into a scowl.

Gotrek took the scythe from his belt and handed it to her.

She looked at the blade for a moment, then turned and dashed down the steps, vanishing from view.

Maleneth laughed again. 'By the Bloody-Handed, she's as eager to die as you are, Gotrek.'

'We need her alive if we're going to find this wretched prince,' he replied, and charged after Lhosia.

Maleneth turned to Trachos with a despairing look. The Stormcast took an instrument from his belt and fixed it to the head of his sceptre with a click. Cool blue light washed over Maleneth's shoulders, and she climbed down the steps after Gotrek and Lhosia, Trachos following closely behind.

She could make out the Slayer's squat, bulky form a few steps ahead as he halted in front of a doorway next to the priestess. The door was hanging from its hinges. As Trachos' light washed over an opening of curved, metal-edged bone, it revealed a glimpse of a large underground chamber beyond.

Lhosia swore under her breath and shook her head.

Gotrek grunted in annoyance and booted the door down, stomping into the room with his axe raised.

They rushed in after the Slayer, and Trachos' sceptre revealed a gruesome scene. Body parts were scattered across the floor, glistening in pools of blood and shrouded in fluttering moths.

Gotrek grimaced, but Lhosia fell to her knees as though she had been gut-punched, gasping, reaching out to the remains but not daring to touch them. Moths rose from the blood as her hands hovered over it.

Maleneth scoured the room for signs of the killer, but it was empty apart from the corpses, torn apart with such savagery that the whole chamber was splattered with gore. 'Impressive,' she muttered, nodding at the carnage.

Gotrek glanced at her and nodded to Lhosia.

Maleneth shrugged and gave him an apologetic smile.

The room was unfurnished apart from a few chairs arranged either side of a tall, curved door that led further into the temple. The door was ajar and there were trails of blood leading to it. A snuffling, grunting noise came from the next room, and then the sound of something heavy moving around.

'The Unburied,' whispered Lhosia, her words barely audible. She climbed slowly to her feet and staggered to the door.

Gotrek grabbed her arm and shook his head. 'Let me go first, lass,' he said, his voice softer than usual.

She wrenched her arm free and carried on, the others close behind.

Maleneth staggered to a halt on the other side, unable to understand what she was seeing. The room looked like a man-made orchard. The circular walls were punctuated by six trunk-like columns of bone that arched upwards and met in the centre of a domed ceiling. Each of the columns had a protruding limb about twelve feet in the air, and dangling from them was what looked like pale, rotten fruit, each one about the size of a man's head. No, realised Maleneth, they were more like cocoons – dusty, bone-white bundles, like elongated eggs made of paper strips. And they were not rotten – they had been attacked. The six cocoons had been slashed by claws or a knife, and dark, viscous liquid dripped from the shredded remains.

Lhosia howled at the sight of them, her expression more horrified than when she had seen the corpses in the previous room.

'What is this?' said Gotrek, reaching up to one of the torn cocoons.

'No!' cried Lhosia, her words rough with fury. 'They should not have been here! The prince swore that they would be moved!'

'What are they?' asked Maleneth, peering into one of the dangling sacks. She could see what looked like pieces of dried meat inside.

'The Unburied,' said Lhosia, her voice trembling.

'Your ancestors?' asked Maleneth.

'My grandmother!' gasped Lhosia. 'My great-grandfather! *His* great-grandmother! All of them. They were all–'

Gotrek silenced her by raising his hand and nodding to the next doorway. The light of Trachos' sceptre shone through into the next chamber, and there was something coming towards them.

Lhosia slumped against the wall, clutching her head. 'Prince Volant swore an oath.' She sounded furious. 'They should have been taken to the capital.'

One of the mechanisms fixed to Trachos' belt began to whirr and click. He looked like he was about to say something when the doorway exploded towards them.

Fragments of metal and bone filled the air as a huge shape smashed through, tearing half the wall down as it came.

'Grungni's Beard!' snarled Gotrek. 'That's more like it.'

The creature lumbered into the room, shrugging pieces of masonry from its shoulders. It was twice the height of Trachos. It was clearly a cousin of the ghouls they had fought on the borders of the princedom, with the same deranged eyes and slavering jaws, but it was massive, clad in thick, scarred muscle and bristling with mutant growth – every inch of its greasy flesh sported tusks of bone that jutted through its muscles like spines on a burr. Its face was smeared with the same dark liquid that dripped from the cocoons, and as it locked eyes on Gotrek, it let out a feral roar, dragging down more wall as it launched itself at the Slayer.

Gotrek answered with a roar of his own and leapt at the giant, swinging his axe as he flew through the air.

The blade flashed, thudding into the ghoul's chest with such force that the monster staggered back, carrying Gotrek with it. They smashed through the ruined doorway and landed in the room beyond.

Gotrek howled in annoyance as he stood atop the prone giant and tried to haul his axe free.

The blade refused to move. Rather than bleeding, the ghoul's chest had swallowed the axe head, puckering around it and holding it fast.

The ghoul rose to its feet and punched Gotrek with an enormous fist, sending him flying across the room. The Slayer smashed into a stone column and slammed to the floor.

'Gods,' he muttered as rubble pattered down on his scalp. 'You're a big lad.'

While Gotrek grabbed the broken column and tried to climb to his feet, Maleneth sprinted past him, knives drawn, and leapt at the monster's chest.

The ghoul lashed out with talons like swords, but Maleneth whirled out of reach, arching her back as she dodged the blow.

Before the monster knew what was happening, she dragged her blades across its throat and leapt away.

Maleneth landed with a curse. Her blades had remained embedded in the ghoul's neck. Just like Gotrek's axe, her weapons were being absorbed by the creature's flesh. Now that she saw it more clearly in Trachos' light, she realised that not only was the monster covered in spurs of bone, but also fragments of weapons – hilts and hafts jutted from between its ribs and shoulder blades, mementos from previous battles.

The ghoul locked its fist around Trachos' throat, lifted him into the air and slammed him into Gotrek like a club. They crashed to the floor just as Maleneth reached the monster, and the three of them ended up in a mangled heap.

They helped each other up and backed away, panting and limping.

Gotrek wiped blood and dust from his face. 'I didn't escape the Dark Gods to be pummelled by this oaf. Distract the bugger and I'll…' The Slayer's words trailed off as two more of the creatures stumbled into the room, just as massive and deformed as the first, their combined bulk almost filling the chamber. One was unarmed, but the second had wrenched a bone column free and was gripping it like a makeshift spear, its splintered point glistening with dark liquid.

'Three of them,' muttered Gotrek. 'And they swallow weapons…'

Maleneth was gripping her head, trying to quell the agony reverberating round her skull, and Trachos was leaning against the wall, sparks coiling around his neck brace as he took deep, ragged breaths.

Lhosia strode past Gotrek, gripping her scythe and glaring up at the three giants with no trace of fear. 'They murdered the Unburied.'

She sliced her scythe cleanly through one of the ghouls' legs, causing it to stagger, then whirled away into the shadows, swallowed by the darkness before the creatures could fight back.

Maleneth nodded, impressed by the girl's speed and bravery. She grabbed Trachos' sceptre from a shattered plinth and hurled it to him.

The Stormcast raised the light, dazzling the giants, as Gotrek bounded across the room and leapt for his axe again. 'Blazed pennants!' cried Trachos, launching into song as his sceptre shone brighter. 'And wondrous, gleaming pinions!'

The first ghoul staggered back into the other two, unbalanced by the impact of the Slayer slamming into it. As it fell, Gotrek roared in triumph, drowning out Trachos' song. Rune-light rippled across his knotted muscles, blazing in his beard.

With a final, ear-splitting roar, the Slayer ripped his axe from the monster's chest.

Gotrek cartwheeled backwards in an arc of blood, then rolled across the floor and charged back at the ghoul. This time, rather than sinking his axe into the monster's chest, he followed Lhosia's lead, swiping low and cutting through its ankle.

The monster fell heavily, smashing more columns and scattering cocoons.

As the ghoul landed, Maleneth dashed across the room, snatched a vial from her belt and hurled it into the monster's gaping mouth, dodging aside as it reached out to grab her.

Gotrek had already strode on to meet the other two giants. The first tried to land a punch, but the berserk Slayer was too fast and the blow only succeeded in smashing more bone from the walls.

Lhosia leapt from the shadows and hacked through the ankle of the next ghoul, sending it smashing to the floor before she vanished into the darkness again.

Maleneth was ready. The giant had hardly hit the ground before she hurled a vial down its throat and backed away.

Trachos marched past the downed ghouls and levelled his blazing sceptre at the one still standing, causing it to reel away from him, arms raised in front of its grotesque face.

Gotrek barrelled across the room and swung his axe with such force that it hacked straight through both of the ghoul's legs, dropping it in a shower of splintered bone. The creature slumped against the wall, and Maleneth hesitated, swaying from side to side as she tried to spot a route to its head. Then she had a better idea. She ran to the monster's butchered leg and punched her fist into the severed muscles, leaving a vial embedded deep beneath its pallid skin.

As Gotrek, Maleneth and Trachos backed away, Maleneth's poison took effect and the three giants began to smoulder. Smoke plumed from their mouths as they thrashed across the floor, clawing at their throats and eyes before erupting into flame.

The blaze was so ferocious that everyone was forced to back away to the doorway they had originally entered through.

Gotrek gave Maleneth and Trachos a grudging nod of respect. 'Not bad,' he yelled over the sound of the dying ghouls.

'The Unburied!' cried Lhosia, pointing her scythe at the door on the other side of the fire. The flames were spreading across the floor into the chamber the ghouls had emerged from. 'The others may still be alive! They'll be burned.'

Gotrek looked at the flames and laughed. 'Rather your paper eggs than us.'

Lhosia glared at him, still gripping the scythe. For a moment, Maleneth thought the priestess might try and attack the Slayer. Then she shook her head. 'Only the Unburied can guide me to Prince Volant. If you let them burn, you will never see the prince and you will never find Nagash. The prince could be anywhere in Morbium. And the princedom is vast – we could search for years and not find him. But the Unburied see all. They could tell me right now where Prince Volant is, and the best way to reach him without encountering more of the mordants.'

Gotrek stared at the fire. One side of his face was glossy with old scar tissue. He ran his finger over the burns. 'I've been through bigger fires.'

He turned to Trachos and Maleneth. 'Either of you know another way to find this prince?'

They shook their heads.

Gotrek gave his beard a thoughtful tug, looking at the priestess. Then he raced into the flames.

Maleneth cursed and headed after him, but the heat drove her back. 'Trachos!' she called. 'Your faith will protect you. Follow him!'

Trachos nodded and limped towards the fire.

'No, wait,' muttered Maleneth, putting her hand on his chest. 'I know what you'll do if he *has* immolated himself. You'll take the damned rune.' She glanced at Lhosia. 'Is there another way out of there?'

Lhosia nodded.

Trachos shoved Maleneth aside, heading for the flames again, raising his voice in skull-tightening song.

But before he reached the fire, Gotrek came charging back into the room, head down and cradling something, trailing sparks and smoke as he ran past Trachos and Maleneth and dropped to his knees, still laughing.

'Got it,' he said, standing up and grinning at Lhosia.

The priestess ran to him, ignoring the smoke and the heat as she prised his arms apart.

'Intact,' she whispered, gently lifting a cocoon from his grip. She closed her eyes and let her head fall gently against it.

'Now the others!' she said, staring back through the flames. 'There should be another cocoon, like this one.'

'It was empty.' Gotrek nodded at the mess scattered across the floor. 'Ruined like these.'

'You're lying!' Lhosia put the cocoon under one arm and drew her scythe, her lips quivering.

Gotrek raised an eyebrow, calmly ignoring the blade that was inches from his face.

Lhosia's eyes widened, and she drew the scythe back to strike.

Maleneth grabbed her arm. 'He doesn't lie. He really is that boring.'

The rage dimmed in Lhosia's eyes. 'All gone?' she muttered.

'Apart from that,' said Gotrek, nodding at the cocoon she carried.

Maleneth tried to get a better look at it, intrigued by the awe Lhosia obviously held it in. 'What is it?' she asked, struggling to see it clearly in the firelight. 'How is that your family?'

Lhosia sheathed her scythe and cradled the object like an infant. Then she nodded to the antechamber they had entered through. She walked towards it, indicating that they should follow. 'Let me show you.'

CHAPTER EIGHT

THE UNBURIED

Once they were gathered in the room, Gotrek shoved the door closed behind them, blocking out the heat and smoke.

Lhosia was still hugging the object and she gave them a wary look. 'You are not one of the Erebid. You do not understand the Unburied.'

Gotrek's expression darkened. 'I've just singed half my beard for this.'

'What is an Erebid?' asked Maleneth, amused by the woman's odd, nervous behaviour.

'I am.' Lhosia still sounded hollow and dazed, but she tried to explain. 'I mean, we are – the people of Morbium. It's what we call ourselves.' She waved them away. 'You must not stand so close. When I am communing with my ancestors I will be in a fragile state.'

Maleneth raised an eyebrow. 'Emotionally?'

'Physically. My form will change. You must not touch me until the rite is complete. If you touch me it won't only be me who is in danger. You will become part of the ritual. The Unburied will inhale your soul and your flesh will be transformed, made brittle.

You will be drawn into your past lives and the past lives of the Unburied.'

'I have no idea what you're talking about,' grunted Gotrek. He gave Maleneth a warning glance. 'But I'll make sure no one interferes with your spell.'

Maleneth gasped in mock offence. 'Always, you doubt me, Slayer.'

'Stay away from me until I am done,' Lhosia said. 'Or you risk more than just your flesh.'

She headed over to one of the columns that arched up the walls of the chamber and sat down against it. She muttered quietly under her breath. It seemed to be some kind of song.

'Oh…' Maleneth rolled her eyes. 'She's a *wise* woman. I imagine she reads palms.' She gripped the knives at her belt and smirked. She could show Lhosia how to perform a rite that actually achieved something. And it would not require any lullabies.

As Maleneth strolled around the chamber, waiting for the rite to finish, she considered her next move. She'd had no option but to follow the Slayer this far, but what if there really was some way he could reach the God of Death? Nagash was known for many things, but sharing was not one of them. If Gotrek reached Nagash, the Slayer would be destroyed, his soul would be enslaved and the rune would be taken. She had to find a way to get her hands on it before this ridiculous quest got out of hand.

Maybe if you paid attention to your surroundings, you might learn something to your advantage, said her mistress, causing the amulet to pulse warmth across her chest.

Unlikely, she thought. A berserk hog, a babbling necrophile and a Stormcast Eternal who's so confused he can barely speak. They're not likely to offer much in the way of insight.

Something caught in Maleneth's hair. She batted it away, realising it was one of the pallid moths. Another one fluttered across her face and then another, until the air was busy with the things.

She cursed and tried to wave them away. They were fluttering past her in a great cloud, heading towards Lhosia. They landed on the priestess like a pale robe, covering her and the cocoon in humming wings.

Lhosia's hands were sinking into the surface of the cocoon, vanishing from sight. Then a pale light started to shimmer inside it, like a candle in a paper lantern. The surface of the cocoon gradually became transparent and, as the light burned brighter, the cocoon's contents became unmistakable. At first there was a flurry of tiny shapes, circling like gnats, then one began to grow and take shape. Maleneth could not help but laugh. There was such a contrast between the reverence in Lhosia's gaze and the pathetic, grotesque thing hanging in front of her. It looked like a wizened foetus, no bigger than a human head, but with the grey, weathered features of a decrepit old man. It had long, thin, grey hair and patchy stubble on its jaw. Its limbs were atrophied and wasted and its eyes were milk white.

Gotrek grimaced. 'I risked my life for a pickled corpse? How could that thing have got any more dead?'

'The Unburied endure,' replied Lhosia, speaking in hushed tones, her eyes still closed.

She moved her palms beneath the surface of the cocoon as its contents began to move.

Trachos muttered and Maleneth smirked as the shrivelled thing kicked its legs, disturbing whatever fluid suspended it inside the cocoon. Slowly, it raised a withered hand and pressed it against Lhosia's palm.

Lhosia whispered a prayer of thanks and, when she opened her eyes, the pupils and irises had vanished, leaving featureless white orbs. Then she began to undergo a more profound transformation. As the moths fidgeted across her robes, the dusty, white texture of the cocoon washed over her, turning her whole body into luminous bone. The light of the Unburied pulsed through her and caught on the wings of the moths as they spiralled around her.

Then the shape in the cocoon began to speak. No sound emerged but its mouth was opening and closing and Lhosia nodded in reply.

'How did you create such a revolting thing?' asked Maleneth.

'*We* did not do this,' Lhosia's voice sounded odd – like an echo. 'No mortal can preserve souls. Not by natural means, at least.' Lhosia nodded to the moths spinning around her. 'This is the power of the noctuid.'

'Noctuid?' Maleneth frowned. 'The moths?'

Lhosia nodded, her voice hushed. 'Harbingers. Our link to the next life. They weave the shrouds and preserve the spirit. Every one of our ancestors has been preserved this way for countless generations. We built our faith on the wisdom of our bloodline. Nothing lost. Nothing forgotten.'

Maleneth looked back towards the room containing the ruined cocoons. 'Until now, you mean.'

Lhosia's expression hardened. 'They should not have been left here. Each one of those cocoons held hundreds of souls.' She placed her other palm on the cocoon and whispered more prayers. The light was burning so brightly it looked like she had caught an amethyst star. The glare flashed over her hard, opalescent face, making her look like a work of devotional art.

'How will this thing lead us to your prince?' said Gotrek.

Anger flickered in Lhosia's eyes at the word 'thing' but she nodded. 'We are in a Separation Chamber. I have separated my soul from my flesh so I can speak with my ancestor.' She gave them all a stern look. 'You must be silent. If my concentration is broken, my form may be altered.'

'Your what?' laughed Maleneth.

'I have sundered my soul from my flesh. I am holding an image of my physical self in my mind so I may return to find it unchanged.'

Maleneth frowned at Gotrek and shook her head.

There was a long silence as Lhosia held the cocoon with her eyes closed, her hands still pressed beneath its surface. The only noise was a vague rattling sound coming from somewhere above. After several minutes, the shrivelled corpse mouthed more words and Lhosia nodded. There was another pause, then the priestess opened her eyes. The moths scattered from her skin and her flesh lost its shell-like texture, becoming normal again.

She took a deep breath, then looked up at them. 'The prince is headed to see Lord Aurun at the Barren Points. Not far from here. Three day's walk if we make good speed.'

'Good,' said Gotrek, striding away from the light and heading for the door. 'Then we should leave now.'

Maleneth and Trachos followed but Lhosia remained where she was, whispering to the tiny corpse.

'What's that sound?' said Gotrek, pausing by the door and looking up, noticing the rattling noise for the first time.

They all listened. It sounded as though someone were hurling stones at the roof.

Maleneth looked at Lhosia.

The priestess dragged her gaze from the cocoon and listened. Then she frowned, disconnecting her hands from the cocoon, extinguishing its inner light and rushing past Maleneth to the bottom of the stairs.

Maleneth and the others followed her as she climbed back up to the quay. The noise grew as they climbed the steps, becoming a fierce, rattling din, like coins poured onto metal.

As they reached the entrance hall they were greeted by a spectacular sight. The sky was a veil of glittering shards.

'I've never seen this,' said Lhosia. She stepped towards the opening at the end of the hall, her hand outstretched.

Gotrek grabbed her and shook his head. 'Watch out, lass.'

Lhosia glared at him and pulled her arm free.

'He's right,' said Maleneth. 'We've seen this before. In Klemp they call it bone rain.'

Lhosia shook her head. 'Bone rain?'

Gotrek grunted and stepped back, avoiding the shards that bounced towards him. 'Weather from Nagash. It'll cut through you like knives.'

They stood in silence for a while, stunned by the spectacle of the scene. It looked like they were trapped behind a waterfall spilled from the stars, and the sound was deafening, like waves crashing against rocks.

Eventually, Lhosia looked at Gotrek. 'When will it stop?'

He shook his head. 'Could be days for all I know.' He scowled. Then he looked past her, back into the temple, a hopeful gleam in his eye. 'Do you people have anything to drink?'

CHAPTER NINE

THE HOUNDS OF DINANN

The war had been brutal but brief. King Galan had not expected the level of resistance, but he had expected the glorious devotion of his men. The Hounds of Dinann. What army, in all the realms, could hope to stand against such warriors? Never had he felt so alive. He was almost grateful for the uprising. To rise from his fur-strewn throne and take up his spear one last time. One final war. The Great Wolf had smiled on him.

The traitors had taken hold of an outlying keep, burning effigies and flying their colours from the walls in defiance of his rule, but King Galan could taste victory. He was days away from ending the rebellion and returning order to the entire kingdom. Loyal vassals from every corner of his empire had flocked to his banner when word of the rebellion spread. There were reports coming in from all the major engagements, describing victory after victory. By the time he reached the capital, there would barely be a rebel left to face him. He looked around as he rode towards the keep. Ranks of spearmen were arrayed around him, their golden torcs gleaming in the darkness, their breastplates flashing as they followed him to the gates. Behind them came serried legions of foot soldiers, their pennants flying and their voices raised in song as the sigil of the hound fluttered in the wind.

'Surrender your arms!' cried Galan as he stopped his horse near the shattered gates. 'I am no tyrant. Handle yourselves with dignity and you can live. The battle is over. The Hounds of Dinann are not savages. There need be no slaughter.'

There was no reply. He could see figures rushing through the darkness up on the walls of the keep, readying their weapons and war machines for a final, desperate defence. He had expected no more, but he had fought the whole campaign with dignity and pride. He was no fool. He was old. He had not expected this last chance for glory, but now that it had been given to him he would show his men how a king should lead.

'Very well,' he called. 'We have given them a chance to kneel and they have refused. They have turned their back on the Great Wolf.'

He raised his spear and pointed it at the keep. 'Hounds of Dinann! Advance!'

There was an oceanic roar. His army surged past him, howling war cries and rattling spears on shields as they rushed forwards.

His men moved with such speed that they seemed to swarm up the walls with barely any need for ladders or hooks, washing over the battlements and pouring into the reeling defenders.

Howls and screams filled the night as King Galan rode towards the gates of the keep. He did not have to wait long before the doors flew open, revealing the victorious faces of his men as they drove the traitors back, washing the courtyard with blood and setting fire to the buildings inside the walls.

He strode over to one of the fallen defenders. The man was still alive, and as Galan offered him a helping hand he started to scream desperately, trying to drag his broken body away.

'What are you?' howled the man.

Galan frowned. It was a strange thing to say, even for a dying man. And it was not the first time he had been asked this question. 'What am I?' He laughed. 'I am your king.'

The man would not stop screaming, and eventually, the sound started to infuriate Galan. This had happened several times during the campaign. Every time he offered his hand, giving the wounded a last chance to surrender, they panicked and shrieked at him. He stooped down and pressed his hand over the man's mouth, trying to stifle his cries.

'There's no need for this,' he said. 'Lay down your weapons. Rejoin the Hounds.'

The man thrashed beneath him, blood flying everywhere.

Too much blood, realised Galan. He had a broken leg, but there were no cuts on him. Why was he bleeding?

The more Galan tried to calm him, the more the air filled with blood.

'What are you?' cried the man again, but Galan found it hard to concentrate and the voice grew distant.

The air turned crimson and Galan backed away, shaking his head, confused. As he stumbled away from the man, he realised how hungry he was. In fact, his craving seemed to have confused him. He'd imagined he was still on the battlefield, but hunger and exhaustion were playing tricks on him, throwing him back into the past. He laughed, realising he was already at the victory feast. He leant back in his chair and grabbed some meat from a platter on the table. It was so rare it was almost raw. Blood rushed down his chin as he ate, delighting in his well-earned appetite.

CHAPTER TEN

REMEMBRANCE

Gotrek grimaced as he drank the wine Lhosia had found, but Maleneth noticed that he had managed to empty another skin. A few hours had passed since the storm had begun, and there was now quite a pile of them lying around him on the platform, all empty. It looked like he had been fighting overgrown bats and was now sprawled on their carcasses. He nodded to a row of shields that covered the walls. 'What do they say?'

They were sitting in a circle, just inside the archway, silhouetted by the flashing rain. The torrent of bones bathed the group in ripples of light, making it look like they were under water. The temperature had dropped so they had lit a fire, with Lhosia seated to one side of the Slayer and Maleneth to the other. Trachos was opposite Gotrek, his head bowed as he muttered to the flames, his face still hidden behind his helmet.

'The shield poems?' Lhosia's words were slurred. Despite her earlier protestations, she had eventually agreed to drink some of the wine. She claimed never to have drunk before, but grief had clearly given her a thirst. 'They record the deeds of the Unburied.

When an ancestor dies, we carve the story of their life into their shield and place it near the Separating Chamber. Then all who come seeking their wisdom will know how they lived and how they died.'

Gotrek bared his teeth in a grim smile. 'Death poems. We had such things where I come from.' He grabbed another wineskin, tore it open and drank, staring morosely at the fire.

'Where *do* you come from?' asked Lhosia. Maleneth had noticed that she kept steering the conversation away from herself and her loss, as though unwilling to share her grief with strangers.

Gotrek ignored her, hypnotised by the flames.

Lhosia looked at Maleneth.

'His world is gone,' she said. 'He says it was destroyed. Somewhere beyond the Mortal Realms. Although he won't say much else on the subject.' She sneered. 'He talks about his ancestors almost as much as you do.'

'You could never understand,' grunted Gotrek. 'You faithless aelves have no concept of history or tradition.' He waved at the shield poems. 'You have no regard for your elders, never mind your ancestors. All you care about is yourself.'

Maleneth shrugged. 'Someone has to.'

'My people respected the past and remembered their ancestors,' said Gotrek, giving Lhosia a sympathetic look. 'Much as you do. We recorded deeds on oath stones and...' His words trailed off and he shook his head, looking suddenly annoyed. 'What does it matter? They're all gone. All butchered. And, thanks to the treachery of the gods, I did nothing to help them.'

Lhosia was still holding the cocoon. There was no sign of the light or the figure inside. It looked like a rock, swaddled in dust and pale, fine-woven cloth. Maleneth noticed that she was counting again, mouthing the numbers in silence. Then she frowned and looked up at Gotrek. 'Why didn't you help your people?'

'Grimnir told me I was his heir. He tricked me into the Realm of Chaos, promising me that I would finally meet my doom. The mightiest doom ever achieved by a Slayer, he said. Lies, all of it.'

Gotrek lurched to his feet, staggering dangerously close to the archway. The bone shards were cutting into the ground just inches from where he stood, talking to the darkness. 'And while I languished in those wretched hells, forgotten, everything and everyone I knew was blown apart.' His voice grew hoarse. 'If I had remained to fight, I would have found a way to save them. But the gods tricked me. Everyone was killed and I was left alive. Sworn to die, and I outlived everyone! What could be crueller?'

It was the most Maleneth had heard Gotrek say about his journey to the Mortal Realms. The most she had heard him say on any subject, for that matter. Usually he just cursed, muttered or laughed. The wine had affected him differently to the ale he usually drank. He was still morose and bitter, but more willing to talk.

'What did you see in there?' she asked, trying to sound only half-interested, not wanting to spoil the moment by prying too eagerly.

Even Trachos ceased his muttering and looked up at Gotrek.

The Slayer stomped back over to the fire and sat down with a grunt, taking another swig of wine. 'Things with no names. Things beyond words. Citadels of sound. Songs of blood. Oceans of hate. You wouldn't understand even if I could show you. I couldn't understand them even as I saw them. For a long time I believed the lies. I believed that I *had* been given a great doom. To slaughter daemonic hosts for all eternity. Until I died or they did. But *nothing* dies in there. Not truly. I killed and was killed with no victory or defeat. The gods laughed at me.' His voice cracked with bitterness. 'Then forgot me.' He grabbed a burning stick from the fire and crushed it, the flames blinking in his eye, embers spiralling around his scarred face. 'They won't forget me again.'

He drank some more and fell quiet. His earlier high spirits had faded. Maleneth was about to ask Lhosia more about her own people when Trachos did something she had never seen him do before. He unclasped his neck brace and removed his helmet. The seals were dented and caked in filth, and they made a strange hissing sound as he prised them apart.

Even Gotrek looked up in surprise as the Stormcast Eternal's face was revealed. His hair was long, white and knotted into thick plaits. Released from his helmet, it tumbled down over the metal of his cuirass like ropes, giving him the appearance of an aged shaman. His skin was the colour of polished teak, and his face must once have been handsome in a fierce, leonine kind of way. It was not handsome now. Every inch was covered in scars. They were not the rippling burn marks that covered half of Gotrek's face, but deep, jagged cuts. One of them went right from his jaw to his forehead, wrenching his brow into a constant scowl. He looked warily at them, as though removing his helmet had made him feel exposed. 'How did you escape?' he said. Without his helmet on, Trachos' voice lost its thin, metallic quality and became a deep, rumbling tenor.

The combination of wine and surprise seemed to trick Gotrek out of his usual reticence. He stared at Trachos, then stared through him, as if picturing somewhere else.

'I began to see things,' he muttered. 'Things that had not happened yet, or maybe things that had happened long ago.' He shook his head. 'Losing my mind, I suppose. Fighting for so long. Furious at my betrayal. Struggling to remember my own name.'

He looked at Lhosia. 'I had a rememberer once too, like your shield poets. A manling. But not like most of that cowardly, cack-handed race. He was a skilled fighter. And brave with it. A good storysmith, too. He stood by me through everything. He would have come with me if I'd let him. Then, when the madness came over me, I thought I could see him, still alive, in some other world, preserved somehow through the long ages of my purgatory.' He laughed bitterly. 'I sometimes wonder if he's *here* somehow, in these damned worlds you call realms. But then I wonder if it was someone else I saw, leading me through the Realm of Chaos, bringing me through the flames.'

He seemed to notice everyone watching him and his face hardened. 'Whatever happened, my search spat me out into that ugly furnace you call Aqshy, surrounded by babbling idiots claiming to be Slayers. Descendants of Grimnir, they said. If they knew him like I do, they wouldn't be so keen to claim his kinship. Not one of them understands what a treacherous crook their god is.' He pounded the rune in his chest. 'They're as useless as him, though. So maybe they are his spawn. They made this bauble and then lacked the strength to use it.'

'What is it?' asked Lhosia, reaching out to touch it. She snatched her hand back as the rune singed her skin.

'Property of the Order of Azyr,' snapped Maleneth, giving her a warning glance.

Gotrek laughed, his mood lifting a little. 'Just you try and take it, aelf.' He moved his beard aside, trying to look at the rune. He grimaced as he revealed its design – the face of a duardin ancestor god. 'Look at him, sitting in my bloody chest. Taunting me every time I see his stupid face.'

'*That's* Grimnir?' asked Lhosia.

'Aye. His likeness, at least.'

'You wear a symbol of a god you despise?'

'Not by choice, lass. It didn't bloody look like this when I planted it in my chest. Besides, it has its uses. What do they call this stuff, again?' he asked, looking at Maleneth.

'Ur-gold.' She rolled her eyes. 'The fyreslayers say it's pieces of Grimnir, scattered across the realms.' She stared at the rune.

'Ridiculous, obviously, like all duardin legends, but ur-gold certainly has power. The fyreslayers hammer it into their bodies to fuel their battle rage, but none of them are equal to the one in Gotrek.' She let her gaze caress the metal. 'This is the *Master* Rune, forged by Krag Blackhammer himself. And when Gotrek destroys himself, I will take it to Sigmaron.'

Maleneth's pulse raced as she considered what that would mean for her. *She* would be the one who had secured a weapon powerful enough to win the war for the realms. Her slate would be wiped clean. No one would care what she had done in the past. None of her enemies in Azyrheim would be able to lay a finger on her. Sigmar would probably make her a saint.

'So,' said Lhosia, frowning at Gotrek, 'when you talk of your doom, you mean you wish to destroy yourself?' She shook her head. 'You say your culture reveres ancestral wisdom, but you're prepared to throw away everything you know? What greater crime could there be than suicide? It's a betrayal of your ancestors *and* your descendants. You should preserve your wisdom. You should fight to pass on what you know.'

'I'm a Slayer, lass,' said Gotrek. 'I have to atone for…' His words trailed off and he shrugged. 'I have things to atone for, though no one here can remember them.' He drained the last dregs of his wine and grimaced. 'Gods, this is drakk's piss.'

They sat in silence again, listening to the rain and the flames. Then Lhosia looked at Trachos. 'And are you the Slayer's servant?'

Maleneth laughed.

'I serve the God-King,' replied Trachos. His brutal features were exaggerated by the firelight, making his face almost as savage as Gotrek's. His eyes looked like stars, smouldering under his furious brow. 'And the Order of Azyr.' He glanced at Maleneth. 'We both do.'

Lhosia looked from Trachos to Maleneth. The enmity between

them was so obvious she asked her next question with a doubtful tone. 'You're working together?'

It was Gotrek's turn to laugh. 'The aelf wants the rune, and she doesn't care if that requires my death. Pretty boy here feels the same, but he's tying himself in knots trying to work out what the hammer-hurler would think is the right thing to do. He's desperate for the rune, but he doesn't want to behave badly. That's right, isn't it, smiler? You don't want to be a savage like me.'

Trachos' eyes flickered with emotion and his head kicked to one side, but he said nothing.

'You've been here before,' said Lhosia, leaning over to study Trachos' armour. 'You've been to the Amethyst Princedoms before.'

'What?' demanded Maleneth.

Lhosia pointed to the jumble of equipment that covered Trachos' belt. Tucked in amongst the measuring devices and weapons was a metal-framed hourglass filled with dust that shimmered as it moved. The piece was topped with an ornate, leering skull.

'Or did you buy that from someone else who has been to the Amethyst Princedoms?'

Trachos grunted and covered the hourglass up. He looked angrier than ever, and his head twitched again.

Gotrek snorted in amusement. 'Something to hide?'

Trachos grabbed one of the wineskins and drank. He ignored Gotrek and Maleneth's intrigued expressions and turned to Lhosia. 'I fought with a retinue of Stormcast Eternals along the southern reaches of the Amethyst Princedoms. They were Hammers of Sigmar. My own retinues had been…' He hesitated, then tapped his turquoise armour. 'I belong to a Stormhost known as the Celestial Vindicators, but I was the last of my retinue. I was headed back to Azyr when I was attached to the Hammers of Sigmar. We were strangers to each other, but we fought well. We took back the

Amalthea Keep then scoured the whole coast. No servant of Chaos now draws breath for nearly three hundred miles of those walls.'

Lhosia nodded. 'The Amalthea Keep. I know the name. The Radican Princes. In the ancient times they were our allies. There are still sacred texts written by Radican Princes held in the libraries of the Lingering Keep.' She shook her head. 'You have claimed back the keep? It is centuries, countless centuries since those lands were free of Chaos.'

Something flickered in Trachos' eyes, then vanished as quickly as it had come. 'We claimed the keep and the land around it. I was attached to the Hammers of Sigmar to perform a specific duty.' He tapped the devices clasped to his belt. 'My job was to send a signal to Azyr so that the rest of their Stormhost could find a route through the aether-void. While my comrades rounded up the locals and armed them, I helped the retinue responsible for repairing the keep.' He paused and took another deep swig of wine. 'Weeks passed. No word from Azyr.' He shook his head, frowning. 'Well, nothing I could recognise. Only howls and screams. Someone was trying to warn me. But it was like cries heard through a wall. "Necroquake" was the only word I could decipher, but I had no idea what that meant.

'We continued our work, scouring the plains for remnants of the Chaos dogs.' His gauntlet screeched as he crushed the wineskin tighter, as though imagining squeezing the life from someone. 'We had them on the run. We attacked. With ferocity. Such brutality. I showed the Hammers of Sigmar how Celestial Vindicators fight. Even the Bloodbound were not prepared. They had grown lax. They never expected anyone to try to reclaim the princedoms after so long. They thought these lands were theirs.'

His voice grew louder, as though he were addressing a crowd rather than three people sitting right next to him. 'But reclaim them we did! With barely a single loss. We tore down their idols and citadels. We ripped open their prisons. We freed wretched souls who hadn't seen light for decades. It was glorious. The hammer fell. The Bloodbound died.'

Maleneth took the wineskin gently from his hand, interrupting his memories. She took a sip and spoke quietly. 'And yet, when you approached me and the Slayer in Aqshy, you were alone. There were no Hammers of Sigmar with you when you found us on the Slain Peak.'

Trachos' head was shaking as he stared at her, rage bleeding from his eyes.

She slipped a hand discreetly to one of her knives, wondering if she had pushed him too far.

Trachos' anger subsided and he slumped back. 'We crushed Chaos. We did as we were forged to do. Those beasts could not break through the armour of our faith, but…' He hesitated. 'But Chaos is not the only threat in Shyish. The voices from Azyrheim grew fainter and more desperate, so we focused all our attention on fortifying the keep and arming the slaves we had freed. We knew it would not be long before word of our success reached the warlords in control of the rest of the princedom. We had taken the keep through speed and surprise, not through superior numbers. Without reinforcements we would be hard pressed. The slaves were terrified of us at first, but as the weeks wore on they saw a chance. A chance for revenge, if nothing else. Some still knew legends of the time before Chaos. Times when man lived free of tyranny. Under our care they grew stronger. Braver. We started moving out into the surrounding villages, fortifying them, spreading across the princedom. When the attacks came we were ready. And so were the mortals.

'But then we began to hear of other things.' His expression darkened. 'Cannibalism amongst the wretches we had armed and fed. We had shared Sigmar's word with them. We had told them that the Age of Chaos was over and that a new era had begun, but as soon as we left them to their own devices they fell back into savagery.' His voice trembled with rage. 'If people knew what we sacrificed to fight for these realms. If they knew what it meant. We are immortal but we–' He shook his head. 'After so long under the lash of Chaos, they had fallen back into the debased worship of the Blood God. Or, at least, that's what I thought. I rode out from the keep to see for myself what had happened.'

His voice fell quiet. 'It was not Chaos. They were not worshipping Khorne. I saw it as soon as I reached the nearest village. Worship of any kind was now beyond them. They were no longer human. They had crawled into the mass graves left by their oppressors and dug up the remains.' He grimaced. 'They were eating corpses, feeding on them like animals. After all we'd done for them, I could not understand it.' He pounded his fist against the ground, scattering embers. 'We freed them and they turned into animals. Couldn't they see that they were risking everything? They were leaving us open to attack. We saved them and they betrayed us! They did not even–' Trachos cut himself off again and shook his head.

'What did you do?' asked Maleneth, sensing that he was reluctant to finish the story.

Clearly the wine had had the same tongue-loosening effect on Trachos as it had on Gotrek. He looked torn, but he could not stop talking. Maleneth had seen humans like this before. Too ashamed to speak of their deeds but too tormented to stay silent.

'I was furious,' he muttered. 'Some of the Hammers of Sigmar were there and they tried to calm me, but I would not listen. I tore through the village. Those people were going to ruin everything, and I was determined not to… I butchered them. All of them. I showed them how the God-King deals with those who betray their saviours.'

Maleneth shrugged. 'Seems reasonable. You saved them and

they turned into ghouls. It's ill-mannered, if nothing else. I don't blame you for taking a hammer to them.'

Gotrek frowned. 'You said the other hammer-hurlers tried to hold you back. Why? You were doing the work of Sigmar. They were ghouls. Like the things we've fought here, in Morbium. Why shouldn't you slaughter them?'

Trachos would not meet their eyes, and his voice became flat. 'I was furious. It was a kind of madness. I could hear my comrades calling me, but their voices were like the screams of the aether-void. They made no sense. Like a pack of animals howling at me. My hammers rose and fell, smashed and crushed, filling my eyes with blood. Only exhaustion finally forced me to pause. And then I saw the bodies I had left.'

Maleneth nodded, finally guessing the truth. Finally understanding why Trachos' mind was as broken as his body. 'They weren't *all* ghouls, were they?'

Trachos did not answer.

'You were killing humans,' she continued. 'That's why the other Stormcast Eternals were trying to stop you.'

Trachos spoke quietly. 'I walked back the way I had come, but I could not make sense of it all – of the corpses. Some were *definitely* the things I saw gnawing at the graves. But others were…' He shook his head.

Gotrek grimaced, drinking more wine.

Lhosia looked at Trachos with new eyes, appalled.

'What did the Hammers of Sigmar do?' asked Maleneth.

Trachos' voice was a dull monotone. 'Tried to control me. Tried to… I fought them off.'

Maleneth laughed incredulously. 'You *fought* them? Your own kind?'

'No! Not that. I fought them off. I don't mean I attacked them. Not that, at least. Even now, changed as I am, I would not harm one of Sigmar's own. But I resisted them. I abandoned them. I left them to their fate. I could not rid myself of the faces I saw. I still can't.'

Gotrek was looking thoughtfully at him and spoke with softer tones than usual. 'The gods make fools of us. All of us. You were there because they ordered you to be there.'

'The God-King did not order me to kill unarmed families.'

Gotrek glowered at the rain. 'When the gods talk of Order or Chaos, they just mean glory – *their* glory. They have no interest in what happens to the people who win them that glory.'

'Changed as you are?' said Maleneth.

Trachos shook his head, confused.

'That's what you said,' she continued. 'You said, "Changed as I am, I would not harm one of Sigmar's own".'

Trachos stared at Maleneth, and for the first time since they had met, she felt something other than amusement when she looked at him. She did not feel that she was looking into the eyes of a man. It was not a human gaze. What were they, these Stormcast Eternals? She had never really considered it before, but now she felt a chill as she realised just how peculiar he was. In some ways, he seemed less human than the ghouls.

'I've lost myself,' he muttered, finally freeing her from his inhuman stare and looking back at the fire. 'I died for the first time at the battle of Visurgis. It was glorious. Agony, yes, but glorious. When I felt my soul, still intact, blazing in Sigmar's halls, hammered on the Anvil of Apotheosis, I knew I had been reborn. Reforged so that I could fight again. Then I died again, fighting greenskins at the Orrotha Pass. The pain was greater that time, but still, the glory was unimaginable. A chance to live again, to fight for the God-King, to fight against all that is wrong in the Mortal Realms.'

He looked up at the stars. 'The third time I died, the pain seemed like it would never end. Perhaps something was wrong? Perhaps I was too broken to be saved? I could not be sure. But the torture seemed endless. And that was not the worst of it. Once it was over, and I rejoined the host, I could not quite remember what it meant. Why were we fighting? Everything that had previously seemed so important felt like stage directions in a play, or the words of a song. Nothing seemed real.'

He turned to Gotrek, shaking his head. 'I could not remember my family. Not even the name of my father. Or the place of my birth.'

'And then you were sent to Shyish,' said Maleneth, guessing what came next.

He nodded, without meeting her eye. 'All I could remember was the songs. The hymns we learned in Azyr. Those glorious tunes. I sang them as I fought, praying that the words would hold me in check – that they would guide me when my mind could not. But the truth is that I do not know what I am. I have killed so many in Sigmar's name, thinking I was doing his work. But was I? Always?' He frowned and fell quiet again.

No one spoke for a while. Even Gotrek looked troubled by Trachos' speech.

Something occurred to Maleneth. 'What will happen to you when you return to Azyr? Word of your flight from Shyish might have reached them. Unless the Hammers of Sigmar all died. What will your commanders say when you return empty-handed and without your men?'

'I will not return empty-handed. I will submit to whatever judgement is deemed appropriate, but I will not return with only failure to report.' He gazed at the rune in Gotrek's chest. 'I will return with a prize.'

Gotrek's laughter boomed around the hall. 'Of course! You want me dead too, just like Ditch Maid. So you can cut this thing out of me and–'

'No.' Trachos tightened his fists. 'I am *not* a murderer. Whatever I did in the past. I will keep you alive. I will let no harm come to you until I can convince you to come with me to the Celestial City.'

Gotrek staggered to his feet, unsteady with drink, and grabbed his axe. 'Murder?' The calm, sympathetic tone had vanished from his voice, replaced by a savage roar. His face was contorted by rage and amusement. 'There need be no murder, manling. Face me in honest combat. *Earn* the bloody rune!'

Trachos remained seated. 'I will not. You are not a creature of Chaos or an agent of the Ruinous Powers. Nor are you a revenant summoned by the Great Necromancer.' He shook his head. 'In truth, none of us know what you are. I doubt you know yourself. I will not fight you.' He opened his hands and stared at the scarred, riveted palms of his gauntlets.

Gotrek stood for a moment longer, then dropped heavily back down beside the fire, grabbing another wineskin. His belligerence had lacked its usual fervour, almost as though he were going through the motions because it was expected of him. 'Pity,' he muttered.

Maleneth considered what she had just learned. A Stormcast Eternal whose faith had been shaken was far less of a threat than the hard-line zealot she had thought she was travelling with. There was no hope of convincing Gotrek to stroll up to Azyr and hand himself over to the Order to offer himself in service to the God-King. And if Trachos was too battle-weary to kill the Slayer and take the rune, that meant she was the only one with a chance of getting it back to Azyrheim. She leant back, sipping more wine, and grabbed some of the food Lhosia had fished out of the temple storerooms, feeling happier than she had for a while.

'And what about you?' asked Lhosia, turning to face her. 'Are you here to protect the Slayer too?'

Maleneth stifled a grin and Gotrek snorted.

'She'll protect me unless my death offers a better chance to get the rune,' he said.

Maleneth splayed her hand against her chest in mock offence.

'And what about the soul you carry?' asked Lhosia.

Maleneth laughed. 'You don't want to know what's in my soul, priestess.'

'No,' replied Lhosia. 'I don't mean *your* soul. I mean the one you carry around your neck.'

Trachos and Gotrek both glanced up, surprised.

Maleneth clasped her hand around the amulet.

She knows what you did! Her mistress laughed wildly, delighted by the turn of events. ***How will you explain this one?***

'What do you mean?' Maleneth said, pitching her voice a little too loud. 'It's just a memento of a kill.'

Lhosia frowned, looking suspicious. 'Surely you know it's more than that? If not, I can help explain. I'm the High Priestess of the Cerement. Even the most shrouded spirit is visible to me. I see every soul in Morbium.'

Maleneth cursed inwardly. She needed to silence the idiot woman before she ruined everything.

'It's stopped,' said Trachos.

'What?' snapped Maleneth.

'The rain.'

'Finally!' cried Gotrek, leaping to his feet.

They watched as the last few shards rattled across the platform and ceased, then looked at Lhosia, but she was still staring at Maleneth's amulet.

Gotrek stomped out onto the platform, holding his palm up to the stars. 'Looks like marching weather!'

CHAPTER ELEVEN

SOMETHING MORE
THAN BLOOD

While Trachos headed back into the temple to fetch supplies for the journey, Gotrek and the other two wandered around the platform, examining the damage, running their fingers over the scars that now covered every inch of the bone-work. There were still storm clouds overhead, glinting oddly as they rolled and swelled, but they were heading south, away from the quay.

When Trachos returned, he nodded to the far end of the platform, where wide, sweeping steps led up to the beginning of another huge structure. 'That way?'

'Yes,' said Lhosia. 'And we had better move fast. The whole princedom might be infested with those flesh-eaters. They could come back at any time.'

They climbed the steps and, despite Lhosia's request for urgency, had to pause at the top to admire the strangeness of the view. They stood at the entrance to a great road built of the same combination of bone and iron as the temple below. It swept out over the sea, curving as it vanished into the gloom. Far away, sections of it were illuminated by what looked like pale, low-hanging moons.

'The prominents,' explained Lhosia, nodding to the lights. 'Home to the living and the Unburied.' She looked pained. 'There should be far more of them. The whole sky should be lit up.' She turned and looked south, where there were almost no lights at all. One half of the sky was only punctuated by the faint spectral stars.

'They've been destroyed?' asked Maleneth.

'Perhaps. But even if they are still intact, they must have been defiled. They were built to preserve the souls of the Unburied. And the light of the Unburied should be visible from here. I had hoped that Prince Volant would have done as he planned and evacuated the occupants – keeping the Unburied and their guardians in the capital where we can keep them safe. But something must have gone wrong. My own temple had not been emptied. My family were still there when…' Lhosia shook her head.

Gotrek studied her for a moment, then peered down the road. 'Is *that* a fortress? Is that one of your "prominents"?'

Lhosia and the others came to stand next to him. There was a light flickering lower than the others, on the surface of the road. It was hard to gauge distances in such a strange landscape, but Maleneth guessed it was only four or five miles away. Rather than the blue lights of the others, this was a golden glow, the colour of flames.

'That would be the gatehouse,' said Lhosia. 'Each branch of the wynd is guarded at various points along its length by gatehouses.'

Gotrek waved his axe at the surface of the road. There were bloody footprints leading away into the distance. 'It looks like the gatehouse received the same visitors as this temple.'

Lhosia nodded. 'We should move. The sooner we reach the prince, the better.'

As the group rushed down the road, Maleneth heard a familiar voice in her head. *Did you hear what that girl said?*

She slowed down until the others were a few paces ahead of her. 'What?' she whispered, glancing down at the amulet hung from her neck.

Before she joined herself to the little dead thing – didn't you hear her? When she was talking about Separating Chambers. She said something interesting. Surprising, I know, from someone so ugly and boring, but she did.

Maleneth frowned. 'She said the Unburied could lead us to the prince and that the prince can help Gotrek find Nagash.'

Not that, simpleton. What did she say when she shooed you away?

'She said she had to concentrate. She said that if she lost her thread, there was a risk she might not return intact.' Maleneth stumbled to a halt, realising that her old mistress had a point. 'What did she mean by that?'

You always were such a poor student. So dim.

Maleneth smiled as she started walking again. 'And how does that reflect on you, mistress? Even someone this dim-witted was able to out-think you.'

You never out-thought me, you–

'I killed you.' Maleneth smiled. 'Surely that is the very definition of out-witting you?'

And what now, you ridiculous creature? What will become of you when you finally return home to Azyr?

'I will return with the rune. Nothing else will matter.'

That Slayer won't die. Can't you see that? He's not like the others. Even if you could get some poison through his thick hide he wouldn't notice. Something has changed him. Look at him! He talks about god-killing, but he's half god himself.

Maleneth nodded. 'The rune changed him. He's not like any other duardin I've met. He has so much power.'

It's not just the rune. Think what he was like when you first met him in the fyreslayers' cells. That was before he took their Master Rune, but he was already unstoppable. Something more than blood burns in his veins.

'What do you want to tell me about the Separating Chamber?' snapped Maleneth, irritated by her mistress' games.

The amulet fell silent, and Maleneth whispered a curse.

She picked up her pace and caught up with the others as the road curved and gave them their first clear view of the gatehouse. It looked like a larger version of the cocoon Lhosia was carrying, like a pale, curved tear, built around a pair of large, leaf-shaped gates. It must have once been an impressive structure, but there were now flames washing across it, filling the darkness with embers and smoke. The walls had cracked in several places, dropping huge slabs of bone onto the road.

'No sign of mordants,' said Lhosia, hurrying on.

'Not that way,' laughed Gotrek, nodding back the way they had come. There were dark shapes pouring from the temple they had just left. Even from here, it was clear that there were hundreds of them.

Lhosia spat a curse and drew her scythe.

'We'll never outrun them,' said Maleneth. 'Look how fast they're closing the gap.'

'Move!' yelled Gotrek, waving them on to the gatehouse.

As they neared the building, they began to see bodies scattered across the road. At first it was only ghouls – identical to the wiry, semi-naked wretches they had fought on their way into the principedom. But then, a while later, they saw the corpse of a man who looked far less savage. It was a tall, powerfully built knight, dressed in black armour and a white, feathered cloak. His throat had been ripped out and he was clearly dead, but there were dozens of butchered ghouls lying all around him. Even in death, he was still gripping a bloody, two-handed scythe.

Lhosia shook her head. 'Gravesward. There's not much hope if even they can't hold these things back.'

'Hope's overrated,' said Gotrek. 'Sheer bloody-mindedness, that's the thing.'

As they reached the gatehouse they had to shield their eyes from the glare. The fire was ferocious.

'Not much good as a gate anymore,' laughed Gotrek. The front curve of the building had completely collapsed, consumed by the flames. It was possible to see the road on the far side, littered with more corpses. Again, they were mostly ghouls, but Maleneth spotted a few more of the black-armoured knights.

Gotrek crouched down on the road, looking at the metalwork at the base of the building. 'Is that an axle?' He glanced back at Lhosia. 'How do these gatehouses work? Do they just bar the way? Are they *just* gates? Or something more complicated?'

Lhosia shook her head and then nodded, her eyes narrowed. 'Yes, I see what you mean – they *are* more than just gates. It's possible to raise a section of the road, like a drawbridge. I'd have no idea how to operate it though.'

'Here's your chance, manling!' Gotrek grinned, pointing Trachos to the mechanism beneath the walls. 'You're an engineer, aren't you?' He stepped back and gazed up at the burning building. 'Looks like the whole structure works as a counterweight. We saw a bridge that worked this way when we were back in Nuln. Do you remember? The one that crossed the Reik.'

Trachos shook his head. 'Nuln?'

Gotrek rolled his eye. 'No matter. The point is that we should be able to lift a section of the road up.' He examined the mass of arcane equipment at Trachos' belt. 'Does a fancy title like Lord Ordinator mean you know how to use a spanner?'

Trachos stared at Gotrek, clearly surprised. He shook his head. 'I have never seen this kind of design before.'

Gotrek jabbed him in the chest with a blocky finger. 'What are you scared of? Trying and failing? If you do nothing we die anyway.'

Trachos hesitated, then turned to the building, examining the layout. 'Perhaps.' He paced back and forth for a moment, then edged around the flames and dropped out of sight, climbing down into the mechanisms underneath the gatehouse. A few seconds later, clanging sounds rose up from the shadows.

Maleneth looked back down the road at the fast-approaching crowd of ghouls. 'I guess ten minutes. Maybe less.'

'We can do better than that,' said Gotrek, hefting his axe in both hands. 'Help the manling. He's more capable than he thinks. Call me when he's done.' He started pounding back down the road towards the ghouls. 'But don't be too quick. This looks like fun.' He howled a war cry, dropped his head and charged.

'They'll tear him apart,' muttered Lhosia.

Maleneth watched Gotrek go with exasperation. 'You really would think so, wouldn't you?'

She turned back to the fire and tried to spot Trachos. At first she could see no sign of the Stormcast, but then the sound of tuneless singing led her to him. He was wailing strident verses to himself as he worked. She held up her arm to shield her face as she approached the walls, feeling her hair shrivel in the heat.

Trachos was crouched on a framework of curved metal, grappling with a series of ash-covered cogs. He was holding what looked like a pair of riveted, golden callipers, and he was trying to fix them to the struts beneath the road.

There was a furious bellowing from behind as Gotrek reached the first ranks of ghouls. They were close enough that Maleneth could see their faces as the Slayer axed them down, scattering bones and blood.

She wondered whether to go and help Gotrek or stay with Trachos. 'Can you work it?' she called down to him.

Trachos' callipers were now clamped around one of the struts, and the tool was alive with aether-light. Trachos leant his weight against it, singing too loudly to hear Maleneth's question.

'Will it work?' she yelled.

He twisted around, shaking his head. 'No. The gates are warded by sorcery. I can see a lock, but we don't have the key.'

'The gatekeeper would have it!' cried Lhosia, peering through the ruined gate at the bodies on the other side. 'If you could get me into the building, I would be able to spot his corpse from the others. He might still be wearing the key.'

Maleneth stared at the wall of flames. 'We'd cook. We'll have to wait for it to die down.'

'No time,' said Trachos as he hauled himself back up onto the road, fastening the callipers back to his armour. He took his helmet from his belt and fixed it back in place, then took out both his hammers and marched towards the gates. He showed no sign of feeling the heat as he reached the inferno. He paused for a moment in front of the tall, bone-wrought doors. He leant forwards to peer at the hinges and nodded. As Gotrek careered through the crowds of ghouls, Trachos began to attack the gate, smashing the hinges repeatedly with his hammers, surrounding himself in clouds of sparks and smoke. The doors, already weakened by the flames, began to judder, and Trachos hit them with even more fury, swinging the hammers with such force that they began to spark and crackle. Finally, with a monstrous groan, the gates started to lean backwards.

Trachos retreated, lowering his hammers as they slammed down onto the road.

A wall of flames and smoke rolled towards Maleneth, forcing her back. Then the fire ebbed away to reveal the doors lying flat on the ground, still sparking and smoking but with nowhere near the same ferocity.

Trachos glanced at her. 'How fast can you run, Witchblade?'

She nodded and darted past him, sprinting over the toppled doors and dodging the flames until she reached the road on the far side.

Through the fire she saw Trachos march over to Lhosia. They exchanged words – Lhosia seemed hesitant. Then she nodded, and Trachos picked her up, throwing her over his shoulder like she was a bundle of clothes.

The rest of the gatehouse was still engulfed in flames, but as Trachos jogged through the fallen gates with Lhosia in his arms, he was able to protect her from the few still licking around the opening.

Even from this side of the building, Maleneth could see the absurd odds Gotrek faced. The Slayer looked like he was trying to hold back a tidal wave.

'The rune,' she muttered. She turned to Trachos. 'If they kill him...'

Trachos nodded. 'The key,' he said, looking at Lhosia. 'Which one of these bodies is the gatekeeper?'

Lhosia rushed back and forth. Apart from the dead knights, all the bodies were ghouls. She shook her head. 'None of them. He's not here!'

Maleneth moved further on down the road. 'Then he must have fled.'

'No.' Lhosia stared at the ruined building. 'The Gravesward would never have let him abandon his post. It would be treason.' She rushed from body to body, turning them over and shaking her head.

Gotrek cried out in frustration, and they all turned towards him.

The ghouls were driving him back. They could not manage to land a blow on him, so they were using sheer weight of numbers to overwhelm him, hurling themselves on the bodies of the fallen and creating a landslide of fists and claws.

'We need that key,' said Trachos, surveying the gruesome mess that surrounded them. 'Are you sure none of these are him?'

'Sure,' muttered Lhosia, 'but that makes no sense.'

There was another roar of defiance as the crowds pushed Gotrek back towards them.

So you die, said the voice from the blood vial, whispering smugly in Maleneth's head. *Slaughtered like cattle, miles from anywhere, in an abandoned gatehouse. A worthy end for someone like you.*

Maleneth hissed a curse. She cast her gaze over the ruined walls and the empty buildings on either side of the fallen gates. There were several doors, some smashed, some intact, all of them splattered with blood. 'I wonder,' she muttered.

'What?' said Trachos.

'Can you give me a few more minutes?' She nodded towards Gotrek. 'Can you help the hog hold them back for a little longer?'

He looked at her in silence for a moment, clearly suspicious. Then he shrugged and stumbled back through the flames, launching into another hymn. Maleneth guessed his logic – better to be near the rune than stuck with the murderous aelf. It didn't matter. As long as he could buy her a few more minutes.

As the road lit up with flashes of Azyrite sorcery, Maleneth rushed to the nearest ghoul corpse and dropped to her knees, whipping out her knives.

'It's already dead,' said Lhosia, staring at her in confusion.

Maleneth ignored her, slamming the blades down into the corpse's chest. There was a dull cracking sound as she wrenched them apart, ripping open the ribcage and revealing the glistening mess beneath.

Lhosia cursed in disgust and backed away.

You can't do this, said the voice of her dead mistress. *What are you thinking? You really are a fool. Do you think that just because you watched me at work, you can perform a blood sacrament?*

Maleneth thrust her hand into the wound and grabbed the still-warm heart, then stood up, ripping it from its cage in a spray of crimson. *I did more than watch you, mistress,* she thought. *You thought me a blunt-minded tool, but I was always preparing, always planning for the day I would take your place.*

With the blood still pumping, she began cutting the heart, gouging intricate sigils into the muscle, all of them centred on the symbol of her beloved, blood-thirsty lord, Khaine. When she had covered every inch of the heart, she cried out an invocation and the organ began to smoulder, spilling smoke between her fingers.

For a moment, nothing else happened. Maleneth cursed. Perhaps she *was* a fool, trying to pray to Khaine in such a rushed, slipshod way.

You absurd creature. If you'd really been learning from me you would know that–

Maleneth cried out and leant back, arching her back as Khaine's fervour jolted through her. She laughed in ecstasy. The blood rite had worked. The might of the Murder God shook her with such violence that she cried out to Lhosia. 'Help me! Hold the heart!'

Visions flooded her mind and, for a moment, they were utterly confusing. She was riding with proud warriors, clutching spears and pennants, charging into battle on glorious steeds. Their colours were unfamiliar, and the language was an ancient tongue that bore no relation to anything she had heard anywhere else in Shyish.

The riders were nothing like the black-armoured knights Lhosia had referred to as the Gravesward, but the landscape *was* familiar. The riders were charging down the same road she had just travelled – a highway of bone hung across the Eventide. The horsemen cried out as they saw the gatehouse up ahead. The building was still intact and there was no sign of a fire. Figures were racing back to the gates, but they were too late, caught unawares by the attack as the riders hurled spears and drew longswords, killing them before they could reach the mechanisms that raised the road.

The horsemen tore on into the gatehouse itself and began battling the defenders waiting inside – a ragtag mob of savage, sallow-faced barbarians clutching clubs and knives. Maleneth felt a wash of fury at the sight of these craven savages. Who were they to steal land from the Hounds of Dinann?

The savages fought desperately, but they were massively outnumbered and it was the work of moments to knock them from the walls and slice them apart.

There was another man in the gatehouse, though, unarmed but clearly a kinsman of the rest of the barbarians. He dashed away as the fighting began, bolting to a door at the bottom of a tower and slamming it shut behind him. Maleneth rushed towards him, outraged, but before she could reach the door, blood filled her vision and she fell heavily to the ground.

'What happened?' cried Lhosia, staring at Maleneth. The priestess was helping her grip the bleeding heart, her face a disgusted grimace as the gore flowed down her arms. 'What are you doing?'

Maleneth squeezed her eyes shut, confused, the words 'Hounds of Dinann' still echoing round her head. What did that mean? The gatehouse was in ruins again, flames rippling across the walls. There was no sign of the proud riders on their horses or the savages they had been fighting. She had no idea who any of the warriors might have been, but Khaine's vision had still told her what she needed to know. The door she saw slamming in the vision was still there, unchanged, with the same bloodstains across its handle and the same corpses piled in front of it.

'He's in there!' she gasped, dropping the heart and hurrying over to the door. The blood rite had left her exhausted and dazed, but also exhilarated. She had joined her soul to Khaine's! She could still feel his power hammering in her pulse. It was dizzying and wonderful. She grinned, waving for Lhosia to follow. 'Your gatekeeper is a coward. He's hiding.'

There was an explosion of shouts and splintering bone as Gotrek and Trachos staggered back through the broken gateway, hacking and lunging wildly at an enormous mound of grey bodies. The ghouls were as frenzied as Gotrek, oblivious to even the most horrific wounds as they tried to claw over the dead.

'Here!' cried Maleneth. 'Open this door!'

Gotrek barely broke his stride. He hacked the head from a ghoul, sidestepped a raking claw, slammed his face into the door, ripping it from its hinges, then lunged back into the scrum, blood sizzling on his chest rune.

The second the door fell, a figure tried to run at Maleneth, but she moved with fast, easy grace, dodging around him and then grabbing him by the collar, jolting him to a halt.

It was the man she had seen in her vision. He howled as he struggled to escape, staring at the legions of ghouls attacking Gotrek and Trachos.

Maleneth could not entirely blame the man for his fear. The creatures did make a horrific sight. She did not feel inclined to be sympathetic, though.

'Keys – quick!' she hissed in his ear, pulling him close and pressing one of her blades to his throat.

He scrambled at his belt and unclasped a bundle of keys, holding them up for her to see, his hand shaking violently.

Maleneth snatched them and let him go. As he sprinted past Lhosia and raced off down the road, Maleneth considered putting a knife in his back. She decided it would be a waste of a good weapon and turned away.

'Trachos!' she cried, hurling the keys.

He paused, mid-strike, and caught them.

Maleneth shook her head in disbelief as she rushed to join the fight. It looked like a mass burial falling on top of her.

Trachos sprinted away, leaving her alone with the Slayer. Gotrek was now using his head as a club, his face entirely crimson and covered in bits of skull and teeth. When he looked her way, there was no sign of recognition. He was like an animal in a feeding frenzy, tearing and clawing through the throng.

Maleneth had only been fighting for a few seconds when she realised that it was hopeless. There were too many. Cuts opened across her legs and face as the ghouls lashed out blindly, smothered by their own numbers.

'Pull back!' she gasped, though she knew the Slayer was too far gone to hear.

She was about to stagger free when the ground shook and she lurched backwards, struggling to keep her footing as the road heaved into motion.

'Trachos!' she cried. 'He did it!'

She backed away, knives raised, as the road began to rise, throwing ghouls dead and living towards her. She had to duck and weave as the bodies flew, crashing off the walls and bouncing down the slope. The brainless horrors could not seem to register what was happening, still trying to drag Gotrek down to the floor as it fell away from them. While dozens of ghouls hurtled towards Maleneth, many more fell back the way they had come, sliding from sight.

'Gotrek!' roared Trachos, reappearing on the road and battling his way towards the Slayer.

Gotrek was too busy smashing brains to hear.

'Gotrek!' repeated Trachos, slamming a hand down on the Slayer's shoulder.

Gotrek whirled round, snarling like a maddened dog and drawing back his axe to hack Trachos down. At the last moment he hesitated, finally noticing that the ground was rising beneath him.

'Manling!' he gasped, grinning through the blood.

More ghouls smashed into them both, and they staggered towards Maleneth, smashing the creatures away and reaching for handholds as they found themselves suddenly standing on a steep slope.

'Back here!' cried Maleneth, running down the slope to where the road was level again.

Lhosia was already there, staring up at the incredible scene in amazement.

As the gatehouse rocked back and gears whirred, the road lurched up into the air.

Gotrek and Trachos fell rather than ran the last few feet, and landed gasping and coughing beside Maleneth.

As she helped them up, ghouls began thudding down all around them, crashing onto the road with weird, wheezing groans.

Maleneth dealt with the first two, her knives slashing back and forth, then Gotrek and Trachos handled the others.

As the road juddered higher, it began to change. Iron and bone struts slid apart, splaying like the fingers of a hand, forming into a fan. After a few seconds, Maleneth laughed, realising what shape it was forming. The section of road that had risen up in the air, nearly fifty feet high, had created a piece of intricate sculpture – a pair of ancient, riveted wings, complete with the same spiralled markings that Maleneth had noticed in the temple.

'A moth?' she said, looking around for Lhosia.

Lhosia was gazing in wonder. For the first time since she had found her family's remains, it seemed as though her grief had been eclipsed by something. She nodded. 'A harbinger. Waiting here since the elder days. Ready to serve.'

Maleneth broke away to cut down some more of the ghouls that had fallen on their side of the wings. 'Very pretty. But I don't think we should spend too long admiring it.'

Gotrek nodded. He was panting heavily and drenched in ghoul blood. Usually, after such a brutal fight, he would seem pleased with himself, but he was staring at the rune in his chest with a furious expression on his face.

'Gotrek?' Maleneth said, trying to rouse him from his reverie.

It took a moment for his eye to focus on her, and when it did he was clearly thinking about something else. 'He's trying to…' He shook his head, looking increasingly annoyed.

'Who's trying to what?' she asked. The Slayer was moody at the best of times, but now he seemed confused.

'Bloody Grimnir,' muttered Gotrek, staring at the rune again and slapping one of his meaty hands over it, hiding the face of the Slayer god. 'When I was fighting, lost in the glory of it, the rune lent me its strength.'

She nodded. 'It's ur-gold. Fyreslayers don't hammer that stuff into themselves just for fun. You know that. That rune has been making you stronger ever since you took it from the Unbak Lodge.' She raised an eyebrow at the heaps of bodies. 'You've never minded before.'

'But Grimnir's still trying to get into my head!' Gotrek gripped the rune tighter, as though he wanted to tear it from his ribs. He was talking to himself as much as Maleneth. 'He's still trying to change me.'

Gotrek removed his hand from his chest and scowled furiously at the rune. 'He's trying to change me into *him*. Every time I use this bloody rune it gets worse.' Gotrek punched his own chest. 'Think again, Grimnir! I'm Gotrek! Son of Gurni! And I mean to stay that way.' He ran his fingers over the golden streaks threaded through his beard. 'None of these were here before I had the rune, were they?'

She shook her head.

'No more!' he growled. 'I've slain daemons and dragons without any help from you, Grimnir.' Gotrek stomped off down the road, still hurling abuse at the rune as he headed away from the gatehouse, trailing bits of hair and bloody flesh.

Lhosia followed him, cradling the tiny cocooned corpse of her ancestor and whispering to it.

Trachos limped after her, his head twitching and lightning flickering from the joints in his armour. He mumbled a hymn as he walked, celebrating their victory in a grating monotone.

Maleneth watched the strange trio go, shaking her head in disbelief. 'Am I the only one who's sane?' she asked the vial of blood at her neck.

CHAPTER TWELVE

THE MORN-PRINCE

Lord Aurun watched as a sleeping girl was lifted up into a cart. The driver took her carefully and placed her with the other sleeping children. She was around six or seven, younger than any of the others nestling in the sacks and blankets, and she looked tiny. As the cart rattled away from him, the girl looked like an infant, frail and defenceless. He tapped his scythe against the ground, feeling his pulse quicken. *I will not fail them*, he thought. *I have the strength to do this, and I will not fail.*

'No one would judge you if you left,' said a voice behind him.

'*Everyone* would judge me.' Aurun's voice was stern. 'Above all, the Unburied. And they would be right.'

He turned to face the man standing with him at the East Gate, a frail septuagenarian with sharp, brittle-looking features – a priest dressed in white robes. Corsos was hunched by age, and he was leaning on a femur as tall as he was. The enormous bone had been bleached and carved with sigils, and an iron padlock hung from one end. Corsos was the most senior priest in the Barren Points, and the intricately engraved lock was a symbol of his authority.

Aurun had also seen him use it to club sense into some of the younger acolytes.

'We have lived through blessed times,' Aurun continued, gazing at the buildings behind Corsos. The prominent was almost empty. Most of the windows were dark. The only light came from the souls embedded in its heart. 'All these generations, hidden from everyone. Nothing required of us other than to watch and wait. Who in all the Mortal Realms has lived as we have? Who else has known this peace? And now, at the crucial moment, we have a chance to show our worth.'

Corsos nodded. 'The Morn-Prince will soon come. I have seen it. The Unburied have seen it. We need only hold the walls for another day or so. Prince Volant left the capital with a host unlike anything he has ever mustered before. It does not matter how all these mordants found their way into Morbium. None of them will leave.'

Aurun smiled. 'Bold words from a man armed with a bone. If you could have dragged yourself away from those holy texts, you would have made a good general.'

Corsos laughed and raised his arms, revealing his scrawny frame. 'I *do* have the physique of a hero.'

They both looked back at the train of disparate vehicles rolling away from the fortress, dwarfed by the vast, rigid breakers of the Eventide. 'Well,' said Aurun. 'Whether the prince arrives soon or not, the Barren Points will stand.'

They walked back through the gates towards the centre of the fortress. Soldiers in the black of the Gravesward were dashing from building to building, readying defences and fetching weapons before moving out to the city walls.

Aurun saluted them as he passed, filled with pride. These men had sworn their oaths as children. None of them knew what the words really meant. To serve in life and death. To preserve the

Unburied, whatever the price. What does a child know of such things? But when he gave the orders for evacuation and allowed them the chance to leave with the civilians, not one of them had even considered going. The sky around them was almost entirely dark. The prominents had all died, dragged beneath the dead tides, their lights extinguished. But his men were like beacons, their lacquered armour flashing in the light of the Unburied. It was a glorious sight. Aurun had waited his whole life for this chance to prove himself, living in the shadow of the ancestors, with their tales of heroism and glory. And now he would have his chance to earn a place in their ranks, not as a subordinate but as an equal.

'Have you met the prince before?' asked Aurun.

Corsos shook his head. 'I have read all the histories of the Morn-Princes, though. I know they are more than men.'

Aurun nodded. 'Volant is larger than a normal man. And stronger. But I would not say he is more than us, Corsos. Merely different.'

'Do you like him?'

Aurun shook his head, surprised by the question. 'Like? "Like" would be a strange word to use in relation to Prince Volant. I respect him and I trust him, much as I think he trusts me.' He shrugged. 'He is hard to explain. But you should soon be able to judge him for yourself.'

Aurun spent another hour inspecting the defences and talking to his men. He had expected to find them anxious and afraid, but if anything, they seemed excited. He could understand it. They had spent their whole lives being told that they were born for one purpose, to protect their ancestors, and now they were going to have a chance to finally show that they were worthy of all that trust. The more time he spent talking to the men on the walls, the more proud he felt. Their excitement was infectious.

They would easily hold the walls until Prince Volant arrived, and then he would explain to him why they need not leave. And then the people of the Barren Points would be free to return home.

As they climbed the walls and headed towards Aurun's chambers, excited voices rang out.

'The prince!' cried the men on the ramparts. 'All hail the Morn-Prince!'

All along the walls, the sound of horns rang out, bright and bold, seeming to drive back the shadows.

Aurun grabbed Corsos by the shoulder, and the two old friends grinned at each other.

Two worlds were visible to Prince Volant – the first was illusory, full of pain and doubt, and the second was true, full of life yet to be lived, where understanding would be attained. He alone in the princedom could see so clearly and so far, and his royal attire was designed to symbolise the duality of his vision. Like his subordinates in the Gravesward, he wore lacquered black armour and a white, feathered cloak, but his helmet was of a unique, ceremonial design. It was intricately worked so that one side resembled a snarling face, obsidian black and shockingly ferocious, and the other side was palest ivory, its expression serene. The Morn-Prince had a habit, perhaps a subconscious one, of turning his head as he talked, depending on which side of his mask best represented his mood. As he looked down from his saddle at Lord Aurun, only the black side of his mask was visible.

His steed was a skeleton drake, its gleaming bones clad in the same black as its rider. As the prince leant out from its back, the drake settled its enormous wings with a sound like rattling spears. Behind Volant were knights of the royal Gravesward, scythes gleaming and pennants trailing. Their steeds were smaller kin of the beast the prince was riding. It was an impressive sight. Aurun had never received such a visit before. In fact, he had never heard of *anyone* receiving such a visit.

Behind the pennants was a less cheerful reminder of the prince's power. Dozens of cylindrical cages were raised up on poles, swaying above the knights' heads, and each held a pitiful, emaciated wretch, stripped of their clothes and painted with runes. These were the Barred. They were men the prince had deemed unworthy – men who had failed to protect the Unburied. Some were already dead, dangling from their cages, but others would last for days, their cries growing weaker until they finally died from their wounds or lack of water.

'Did you receive my order?' said the prince. He spoke softly, but the words chimed through his helmet like a temple bell.

'Your highness, I did,' replied Aurun, determined not to be cowed before his men. 'But the messenger was wounded and confused. He did not make sense. And I'm afraid he did not survive more than a few days. Even if he had lived, I could not have complied with the order.'

The prince stared down at Aurun for a moment. They were outside the fortress, near where the wynd rose to meet its gaping North Gate. The Barren Points was one of the largest fortresses in the princedom, second only to the prince's own palace, the Lingering Keep. The light of the Unburied was pouring through the walls and flashing across the knights' scythes, making it hard for Aurun to see the prince. He had to hold up a hand to shield his eyes. The desperate cries of the Barred rang out from their cages, pitiful and deranged as they called for mercy. Aurun knew they were wasting their breath. Prince Volant was known for many things. Mercy was not one of them.

'We have ridden a long way to reach you, Lord Aurun,' prompted one of the prince's captains.

Aurun started, shocked to be addressed so casually by a subordinate.

He bit back an angry reply, conscious that the prince was still staring at him, and stepped back, waving the royal knights through the temple gates. He called for grooms and servants as the deathless steeds clanked past.

'Give me a few minutes,' said the prince as his attendants helped him from the drake. Aurun was not lacking in height, but the prince towered over him, eight or nine feet tall and bristling with lacquered ebon plate. His voice sounded like an echo in a crypt. 'Then join me in my chambers. We have only a few hours to prepare.'

Aurun hesitated, confused. He had been waiting for this moment for years, but now that it had come, it was not playing out how he had expected. He bowed, and was about to reply when he realised the prince had already strode off across the courtyard, preceded by a scurry of servants and courtiers.

Corsos looked as shocked as Aurun. 'A few hours to prepare for what?'

Aurun shook his head. The column of knights was still riding into the square, and as they passed, Aurun noticed that many of them were wounded, their armour gouged and battered, as though they had been grappling with animals. Their faces were speckled with blood, the crimson stark and shocking against their bone-white skin, and several looked little better than the prisoners suspended above their heads. More shocking than that were the numbers.

'Is that all of them?' whispered Corsos, his eyes wide as he leant on his bone staff, peering out through the gates.

They both stared in shock as they realised that there were no more knights coming down the wynd.

'That's barely two dozen men,' said Aurun, shaking his head. 'I thought this was meant to be the greatest host ever to ride out of the Lingering Keep. Did the Unburied give you no word of this? Did they make no mention of the prince's situation?'

Corsos looked uncomfortable. 'Nothing. But you know what I have already told you. They're troubled and strange. They do not speak with voices I am accustomed to. The last time I prayed to them, they–'

Lord Aurun silenced him with a wave of his hand, already aware of his friend's concerns. 'It matters not. We are prepared.' In fact, thought Aurun, if the prince's numbers were reduced, it would give him all the better chance to show what the men of the Barren Points were capable of. 'Do not let this interrupt the usual observances. Make sure everyone gathers for pallsong as usual. Fetch the shield poems from the reliquary and choose something appropriate. I will speak with the prince. When he learns how we have prepared for this day, he will want to come and sing with us.'

Corsos bowed. He turned to leave, but hesitated. 'My lord,' he said, nodding at the wounded knights. 'This must be to do with whatever made the other temples vanish. The prince must have come here because we are–'

'What happened at the other temples will not happen here.' Aurun raised his chin. 'We are different.' The haughty tones of Prince Volant had given him a new surge of determination. 'These are the Barren Points. We will not be sent into disarray by the negligence of others. We will not abandon our wards because others cannot tend to theirs.'

Corsos nodded, but seemed unable to drag his gaze from the darkness.

'Corsos!' called Aurun, heading back into the temple. 'Ready the shields. Gather the choir.'

'They're *gone?*' Aurun found a chair and sat, staring at the floor, his breath quickening.

The servants had put the prince in a room on the south face of the fortress with a balcony that overlooked the wynd. From up here, the huge iron bridge looked like a gossamer thread, glittering with hoarfrost, floating over a gelid storm. Volant's advisers were waiting outside in the hall, and the two knights were alone.

'Gone,' repeated the prince. 'Nearly half of our keeps. Thirty-two prominents.' His voice was rigid. He had removed his ceremonial helmet and his face was striking – pale and harsh, with brutal, angular features. 'There are many souls we will never recover.'

Aurun shook his head, dazed by the scale of the defeat. His chest felt tight. 'There must be a way. You are the Morn-Prince. Surely you are able to–'

'They are gone. You know why these temples were built, Lord Aurun. If our ancestors are not anchored to prominents, they go the way of every other soul.' The prince was squeezed awkwardly into the chair opposite Aurun, his voice dangerously soft. 'They go to the Nadir, Aurun. To the necromancer. They go to Nagash.'

Aurun gripped the arms of the chair. It was rare for anyone to use the name of the soul-thief so openly. 'But how? The Iron Shroud kept us hidden all this time. Even when the other princedoms fell. Why are we in danger now?'

'The Great Necromancer's power has grown. The Unburied tried to warn me, but Nagash's power has muffled their voices and muddied my vision. I knew there was a problem, but I thought I still had time. I thought I would still be able to complete my work. The necromancer has performed an act of great sorcery, Aurun. The Unburied showed me a black pyramid turned on its head, ripping souls from the sky. After all these centuries, the necromancer has played his final hand.' There was a fire snapping in the hearth beside them, and Volant stared into the flames. 'This is a new death magic. Whatever he has done is too powerful even for the Iron Shroud. Nothing is safe anymore, not even Morbium.'

Aurun thought of the little girl in the cart, out on the wynds, with only half a dozen Gravesward to watch over her.

Prince Volant leant closer. 'My messenger should have explained all of this. Why are you still here?' The two men had met before, as children, in the Lingering Keep, but Volant gave no sign of recognising Aurun. 'Why haven't you acted?' he demanded.

'Your messenger did talk of mordants destroying temples, but that is not a thing we need be concerned with here. We have heard the same vague warnings as you, my prince, and we have been preparing for months.' He tapped his armour. It was a new design, cunningly crafted by Aurun's artisans, beautifully engraved and studded with white gemstones. 'We have refined and strengthened our defences, your highness. Every aspect of the Barren Points has been tempered and readied. You have not seen us in action before, but now I will show you what this prominent is capable of. No mordants could hope to breach these walls, whatever Nagash has done.'

The prince studied him in silence, but Aurun noticed that he was gripping the arms of his chair so tightly that the wood was starting to creak.

'Where have they come from?' asked Aurun. 'I have heard of an occasional outbreak of flesh-eaters, but never whole armies entering the princedom.'

The prince stared at him for a moment longer, then replied in the same soft voice. 'The Iron Shroud has been damaged. Morbium has been revealed to the other princedoms – lands desecrated by the necromancer before you or I were born. The mordants can now see us. They can cross our borders as though we are just another territory. They have travelled down the wynds, murdering the gatekeepers. They're a plague, sweeping through the princedom, devouring everything. Our ancestors mean nothing to them. They are insane.'

Aurun felt the darkness pressing in, suffocating him. Then he recalled the legions of men he had trained and armed. 'We can stop them, your highness. This invasion will halt at the Barren Points. And the victory will be all the sweeter with you at our side. You have skill to match the necromancer. You are the Morn-Prince. The wisdom of the Unburied is in your blood. Their power is in your hands.'

'I am not a god. And I am no match for a god. What power I have is bound to the Lingering Keep. Outside my palace I can do little.' Volant's voice was still neutral, and Aurun could not gain any idea of what the prince was feeling. Was he furious or relieved?

'I intended to gather every soul in the princedom and return them to the capital.' Some of the rigidity had slipped from his voice, and for a moment, he just sounded like an exhausted man. 'I have lost hundreds of my own royal Gravesward.'

'Is he here, then? Is Nagash in Morbium?'

'No. The mordants are animals. They are revolting, inhuman things. But they bleed and they die. They are not born of necromancy. Perhaps they pay some kind of allegiance to Nagash, but they are too feral to be his true allies. They serve nothing but their own vile hunger. If the Great Necromancer's gaze had fallen on us, we would be facing spirit hosts rather than these mindless flesh-eaters. His sorcery has toppled our gates, but it was not specifically directed at us. He has summoned a great power and cast it over *all* the underworlds. All of Shyish. I do not think he has even noticed our existence yet. The mordants are savages. They have no idea what they've found.' Volant shrugged and poured himself a cup of wine. 'But they will destroy us just the same.'

'Destroy us? How could you say such a thing?'

The prince hesitated, then shook his head, the cold, flat tone returning to his voice. 'I can do little out here on the wynds, but it's a different matter in the capital. With the help of High Priestess Lhosia, I have been working on a new defence, a new Iron Shroud. We may not be able to safeguard the whole of Morbium anymore, but I have found a way to hide the Unburied in the capital, even against this new power the necromancer is wielding. I provided her with a powerful relic called the Cerement Stone. She is currently inspecting our defences, but I have been assembling the Unburied in the Lingering Keep so that when she returns, I can harness their souls through the stone and Lhosia's rites and preserve them.' He finished his wine and poured another cup. 'I have sent word to all the temples. Everyone who still can is heading to the capital. All the prominents have been destroyed or abandoned.' He paused. 'Apart from yours.'

'So that's why the lights have died?' Aurun looked out into the darkness. 'The Gravesward have taken the Unburied back to the capital?'

'You are not listening. Half the fortresses have been *destroyed*. They have sunk into the Eventide. The souls are gone. Caught in the nets of the necromancer. And without the souls of ancestors to keep them afloat, the prominents have fallen beneath the dead waters.' The prince shook his head. 'And I cannot guarantee that everyone who fled will make it to the Lingering Keep. The mordants are too numerous. They have taken many of the wynds. Even the Gravesward will have a hard fight crossing those bridges, especially when burdened with their ancestors' caskets.'

Aurun shook his head. Only the thought of the caged corpses outside stopped him laughing in disbelief. 'This *cannot* be, your highness. You would have me believe that in a matter of weeks Morbium has gone from impregnable to defeated. This princedom has defied the necromancer for centuries. How can it have so easily collapsed?'

Prince Volant sipped his wine, studying Aurun over the rim of his cup. 'The mordants are headed here next,' he said, ignoring the question. 'We heard word of them everywhere we went. Yours is the last light in the sky. They are coming for you.'

'Which is what you meant when you said we only had a few hours to prepare our defence. Why are we sitting here? I will muster the Gravesward and prepare the ballistae. The archers are already assembled. I will ready the defences.'

'You are not listening to me. There *is* no defence. Not out here on the wynds. You will return to the Lingering Keep. All of you, living and Unburied. You have a few hours to prepare for the journey and perform the necessary rites.' The prince looked around the room. 'The Barren Points is one of the largest citadels in the princedom. You have hundreds of Unburied here, contained within those twelve cocoons. Thousands, maybe. I will not risk losing them.'

Aurun sat up in his chair, trying to shrug off the grim atmosphere Volant had created. 'It's impossible,' he said, raising his voice. 'We cannot move the Unburied.'

Volant's eyes flickered and the arms of his chair creaked. 'In a matter of hours you will be besieged. Mordants will butcher you, and then they will destroy the Separating Chambers. Every soul in this fortress will be lost.'

Aurun was horrified by the prince's bleak manner. How could someone so unambitious, so lacking in faith, rule Morbium? He wondered if this despair and defeatism were the cause of the entire problem. 'You do not understand, your highness. It's not *possible* to move the Unburied. And even if it were, there would be no need.'

Prince Volant stood, his expression rigid as he loomed over Aurun, his massive frame all the more impressive in the tiny confines of the room. 'Every noble in Morbium has done as I ordered. Everyone has headed for the Lingering Keep. Only you have failed to obey. Only you have remained out here on the wynds, far from my reach, endangering the souls I have entrusted to you. Why is that, Aurun? And why have we had no word from you during all this time? Is there something you wish to hide?'

Aurun stood to face him. 'Are you accusing me of treason, your majesty?'

'Why are you still here?'

Aurun shook his head, biting back his rage. Then he waved to the door. 'Let me show you.'

The innermost coils of the fortress were like the chambers of a shell, spiralling and shimmering as they plunged deeper beneath the surface of the Eventide. The prominents had not been built by tools and hands but by the sorcery of an earlier age, when the gods still fought together against the Ruinous Powers and their supplicants could harness even the most violent aether currents. They were bone constructs, pale, translucent vessels woven from the air and suspended in a lifeless sea.

As the prince's attendants rushed through the streets, their torches quickly became superfluous. The ivory light radiating from the walls grew stronger as they approached the heart of the Barren Points. The chill grew the further they descended, and the damp air tasted of salt. Aurun led the way with Prince Volant at his side. Ahead of them went the elderly priest, Corsos, with a phalanx of Gravesward, their armour shimmering in the bone-light.

At each intersection they were met by a pair of priests clad in the white robes of their order, but Corsos waved them away with his bone staff, muttering prayers as the guards admitted them into the fortress' innermost districts. Finally, they reached a building even grander than the previous ones, constructed of the same intricately carved bone but blazing so brightly that Corsos squinted as he pushed the doors open.

They entered a vast circular hall with curving, spine-like columns that stretched up the walls and disappeared into a blazing inferno of amethyst light. The glare was so great that it was only just possible to make out the shapes of twelve cocoons hanging overhead. They were enmeshed in a labyrinth of pipes, chains and cables, all of which were shimmering.

Prince Volant strode into the middle of the hall, his iron-shod boots clanging across the bone floor as he looked up into the light.

'The Barren Points are unlike any other prominent,' said Lord Aurun, waving up at the machines. 'The Unburied are bound into the walls. The twelve caskets are part of the foundations. These engines were designed by the Kharadron at the dawn of the princedom.'

Volant shook his head. 'Do you think I don't know my own princedom, Aurun? Did you think I knew nothing of how the Barren Points were designed? Remove the Unburied from these machines.'

'But, Prince–' began Aurun.

Volant spoke over him. 'There is no other way. Get everyone you can out of the city, then remove the Unburied from their cradles. There will be time to flee the fortress before it sinks.'

Aurun was too furious to respond, so Corsos spoke up on his behalf.

'Prince Volant, forgive me, but there *is* no way to remove the Unburied from the machines. The devices are alien and ancient. Their workings are a mystery even to the Unburied themselves. Only the duardin who built this hall could remove them. If we abandon the Barren Points, we will be abandoning the Unburied.'

Volant stared at him, then turned towards one of his own priests.

The man looked panicked. 'Dontidae Corsos is learned in matters concerning the Unburied. If he says it is so, then it must be so.'

Prince Volant was silent for several moments, gazing up at the machines and the cocoons embedded in them. 'How many are there?' he said eventually, his voice much quieter than before.

'Unburied?' said Lord Aurun. 'In all twelve cocoons? There must be over a thousand.'

Volant closed his eyes.

Aurun tried to hide his triumph. 'Your highness. We are prepared for this. We have sent everyone away who is not needed. This fortress is ready for war. We are ready for whatever the mordants can throw at us.'

Volant's voice sounded hollow. 'Show me.'

They marched from the Separating Chambers, and ten minutes later they were clambering up onto the ribs of the fortress, causing a noisy commotion as white-robed priests and black-armoured Gravesward dropped to their knees, whispering prayers as the prince passed by.

Once they had reached the battlements, Prince Volant inspected the defences, striding up and down the lines of men. He towered over them like a demigod, reordering the troops and repositioning the war engines.

'It is a fine sight,' said Corsos, speaking quietly in Aurun's ear as they surveyed the ranks of knights. Reinforcements from other prominents had been arriving all day, and it was the largest muster either of them had ever seen. As well as the knights, there were lines of archers dressed in a lightweight version of the black Gravesward armour, with white plumes on their caps in place of the feathered robes worn by the knights.

Aurun nodded, but his eye kept coming back to Prince Volant's knights. Volant had positioned them directly above the main gates into the fortress, and as they formed into ranks, Aurun was near enough to see how savagely they had been attacked. Gravesward armour was made of thick, lacquered leather, treated so cunningly that it formed into plates as hard as steel. But it had not been strong enough to protect the prince's men. Their wing-shaped shields were dented and their armour was torn, exposing deep, bloody wounds.

'How can mordants do that?' he asked as the prince returned to stand at his side.

'What?'

Aurun nodded to the wounded knights. 'What weapons do they use that can tear through our armour?'

Volant shook his head. 'No weapons. Only naked fury. They are deranged. It gives them unnatural strength.'

Volant looked around, frowning. 'Where are the rest of your men?'

Aurun nodded, trying to hide his pride. 'This is barely a third of our reserves, Morn-Prince. I have deployed the bulk of our army out on the wynd.' He nodded to the gatehouse barring the road, about half a mile out from the city gates. 'The approach to the fortress is only a hundred or so feet wide. There will be a bottleneck. My men will be able to hold the mordants back for as long as we need in such tight confines.' He smiled. 'Meanwhile, my archers will butcher them. They will never even reach the fortress.'

Prince Volant stared at Aurun. 'You have to call them back.'

A bell clanged, up on one of the towers.

'Too late,' muttered Volant, sounding dazed.

'What do you mean?' asked Aurun. 'Too late? Too late for what?'

The prince ignored him, stomping over to the walls and leaning out into the night.

A hush fell over the lines of knights as they all peered out into the darkness, straining to see what had triggered the alarm.

The bell clanged again, followed by another further down the wall, then dozens more followed suit, until the whole fortress rang to the sound of the alarm.

'The sea is moving,' muttered Corsos, confused. The black waves had started to ripple and surge for miles in every direction. 'How? The Eventide is solid. How can it move like a normal sea?'

'It's not the sea,' replied Volant.

'What do you...?' Aurun's words trailed off as he understood. The entire ocean, every mile of the Eventide, was swarming with crowds. Thousands of mordants were surging through the darkness.

'They're not using the wynds,' breathed Corsos, gripping his bone staff as though he were about to collapse. 'They're crossing the sea.'

'How?' cried Aurun as the dark legions poured past the gatehouses like an oil slick. 'It is impossible to walk on the Eventide!'

'Why?' said Prince Volant, sounding calm again despite the horror of the scene below.

'Because it means madness. No one can touch the Eventide without losing their mind.'

'How do you break a mind that has already been shattered?'

Aurun stared, trying to make sense of the numbers, but the prince climbed up a few steps, making himself look even more like a giant, and raised his scythe high into the air. 'The ancestors are with us!' he cried, his voice magnified somehow, so that every soldier and knight on the walls turned to face him. 'They're in our hearts! In our blades! Every generation of Erebid is on these walls. Those godless creatures have no idea what they're about to face. I came here because this is where the war will be won!'

The prince's voice boomed with such conviction that Aurun almost found himself believing him, even though he knew the prince had only come to order a retreat.

'Here is where we make our stand!' roared the prince. 'Today we end this sacrilege. Today we drive the mordants out!'

The soldiers on the walls raised their scythes and howled, full of righteous fury, their fear forgotten.

Aurun remained silent. As the knights revelled in the glory of fighting with their prince, Aurun watched the gatehouse half a mile away vanishing under a tsunami of grey, feral bodies.

'Look at them,' he whispered, staring at the tides of ghouls rushing towards them.

'Look at *him*,' said Corsos, nodding at the prince.

Volant had returned to his skeleton steed and climbed up into the saddle. He looked like a figure from legend, head thrown back and scythe raised as his mount reared beneath him.

'Gravesward, to war!' he roared as the skeleton pounded its fleshless wings and launched him into the sky.

All along the wall, Volant's honour guard drove their steeds from the fortress, gliding out into the darkness, pennants snapping.

The skeleton mounts looped in formation, like a single, mountainous serpent, then dived, plunging towards the wynd and the battle at the gatehouse.

Aurun shook his head, awed by the sight. Then he stood up straight, dusted down his armour and began marching through the lines of knights. His initial shock was fading. Nothing had changed. They were prepared for this. 'Ready the ballistae!' he cried, waving his scythe at the towers that punctuated the walls. War machines rumbled into view – huge iron bolt-throwers decorated with wings of bone, designed to resemble the moths that circled constantly overhead.

'Load the barrels!' he called, and huge, smoking vats of oil were ratcheted up into place on the walls.

'Archers take aim!' Hundreds of bowmen rushed past the knights and readied their weapons, targeting the crowds surging towards the walls.

Aurun was ashamed of how he had hesitated at the sight of the mordants. The Morn-Prince had taken to the air with bravery and determination, despite the fact that he had never intended to make his stand here. None of this was as Volant had intended, but he had rallied the men with as much confidence as if this had been planned months ago. Aurun resolved to do the same. As he strode back and forth, howling his orders, his determination grew. The Unburied could not be moved, but neither would they be abandoned.

Corsos stumbled after him, gripping his bone staff. He had just opened his mouth to say something when he halted and peered out into the darkness.

The battle at the gatehouse was raging, a clamour echoing across the Eventide, but Corsos frowned and put a hand to his ear. 'What is that?' he cried.

Aurun paused to listen. 'What?' All he could hear was the din of battle and the sound of the bells ringing behind him.

Corsos held up a finger to silence him, still listening intently.

Then Aurun heard it – a thin, ululating shriek.

'What is that?' he muttered.

A captain rushed over to him, asking for clarity on his orders. Aurun answered his question, and by the time the captain had gone, the shriek was much clearer. It was quickly getting louder, and something about it caused Aurun's blood to cool. It was like dozens of tormented voices screaming in concert.

He shrugged and tried to ignore the sound as he saw that the mordants not attacking the gatehouse had now reached the foot of the fortress walls and were starting to climb up its twisting, claw-like buttresses.

'On my order!' he cried to the archers.

The mordants moved with unbelievable speed, scrambling up the walls like spiders bursting from an egg, swarming towards them with no need of ropes or hooks. The sight of them filled Aurun with revulsion. They were beings without souls. Men without minds. Vessels for a grotesque hunger and nothing else. He held his hatred in check, keeping his hand raised until he was sure they would be easy targets. Then he swept his hand down and launched hell.

A storm of arrows sliced into the mordants, tearing through their sagging flesh and ripping them away from the walls. Dozens tumbled back through the air, trailing arcs of blood and crashing into the mob below.

As the archers loosed wave after wave of arrows, the screaming sound grew so loud that some of them started to miss their marks, wincing and cursing as they shot.

'There!' said Corsos, pointing into the distance.

A shape was rushing through the clouds towards the fortress, a grotesque parody of the prince's skeleton steed. Rather than an elegant serpent of gleaming bones, it was an ugly, snub-faced thing, with ragged, fleshy wings and scraps of intestine trailing from its butchered chest. It looked like the carcass of an enormous bat, and its mouth was open, revealing long, cruel incisors and filling the air with that hideous shriek.

As the sound grew in volume, Aurun's head started to pound and he became gripped by an overwhelming sense of dread. His heart hammered in his chest, and his hands began to shake.

'A terrorgheist,' gasped Corsos.

Aurun shook his head, trying to escape the sound. 'A what?'

'It will send us mad!' cried Corsos, covering his ears. 'The sound will send us mad!'

Aurun looked across the wall and saw that some of the archers had staggered away from the battlements, shaking their heads and dropping their longbows. Even the lines of Gravesward standing behind them were lowering their scythes, gripping their heads and cursing.

'Block your ears!' shouted Aurun. He grabbed some dust from the ground, spat in it and jammed it in his ears, waving for his men to do the same. 'Block out the noise!'

All along the wall, knights and soldiers dropped to their knees, seizing fistfuls of dirt and trying to cram it into their ears.

The dust lessened the sound for a moment, but as the terrorgheist hurtled towards the walls, the noise became unbearable.

'Fire the ballistae!' cried Aurun, and the men in the towers struggled to comply, triggering their war machines as best they could while reeling from the sound.

The bolts went wide, whistling off into the clouds as the terrorgheist crashed into the battlements, hurling bone and masonry in every direction as it waded onto the top of the wall, screaming furiously at the soldiers scrambling for cover.

The monster was huge – thirty or forty feet long, with enormous leathery wings that thrashed violently as it tried to find a steady perch on the wall.

With the archers scattering, the Gravesward rushed towards the creature, raising their scythes to attack.

The monster hit them with a scream like a body blow, causing them to stumble and stagger. Most of them failed to land a blow, and those that did only hacked through flaps of dead, ragged skin.

The terrorgheist's head lunged forwards and ripped through the knights.

Aurun stumbled through the carnage, dodging around staggering knights in his attempt to reach the monster.

This close, the scream was horrific. It felt like his head was being split open, and he struggled to see clearly, his eyes were so full of tears. There was also a nauseating smell pouring from the monster's heaving carcass. Several of the knights near Aurun were doubled over, gagging on the foetid stink.

He reached the creature and landed a blow, slamming his scythe into its chest. The blade cut easily through the exposed ribs, but the wound had no effect. The terrorgheist did not even seem to notice him as it dropped a fresh corpse from its mouth and waded into the crush of archers and knights, locking its jaws around another man and ripping him in two.

Aurun tried to attack again, but before he could, the monster reared back and let out its loudest screech yet.

Aurun fell to his knees, deafened and in so much pain that he could not see.

Other knights collapsed all around him, helpless to defend

themselves as the monster lurched forwards, ripping and tearing, filling the air with blood and howls.

The scream grew until Aurun curled into a foetal position, his muscles locked with cramp and his breath caught in his chest. His lungs burned and his oxygen-starved brain began to withdraw into itself. The cries of his men and the scream of the terrorgheist faded, becoming distant and vague, as though he were remembering his death rather than experiencing it.

Light burned into Aurun's mind, and he mouthed a prayer, preparing to meet his ancestors. Then he realised that as the light grew, the terrorgheist's scream was faltering. His vision was also returning. He saw that the light was not in his mind, but burning through the walls of the fortress. It was the amethyst fire of the Unburied.

His muscles loosened enough for him to breathe, and he managed to sit up and look around. All across the wall, men were struggling to rise as the scream dropped away, but rather than attacking, they were staring up in shock.

The Morn-Prince was circling overhead.

He still had his scythe raised, and he had been transformed by the Unburied. Their fire had leapt from the walls of the fortress and ignited his armour. He was burning with the power of the ancestors.

Prince Volant lashed out with his scythe, and purple light ripped through the air, slamming into the terrorgheist's face.

The monster fell backwards, pounding its wings, trying to right itself as amethyst fire drummed into its flesh, engulfing it in sparks and smoke.

The terrorgheist launched itself from the wall and locked its jaws on the neck of Volant's steed. The winged goliaths looped and dived, screaming and roaring as they tore at each other.

'The walls!' cried Aurun as dozens of figures poured over the battlements. He cursed when he realised that whatever happened to the terrorgheist now, it had done its job. While it kept his men occupied, the mordants had scaled the walls and were now pouring into the fortress.

He rallied the knights nearest to him and led a charge, howling as he cut down the first mordant to reach him.

It was frenzied and desperate. The mordants clawed at the knights like animals, and there were so many of them, flooding onto the walls with a roar of snarls and grunts.

Aurun staggered backwards, swiping, hacking and slipping on blood. The knights around him fought with the same furious, silent determination and managed to hold their ground until a massive shape crashed down beside them, sending a violent tremor through the walls and causing everyone to stagger.

Aurun dragged himself clear of the scrum, up onto the battlements, and saw that the two winged monsters had crashed to the ground.

Volant slammed onto the wall and rolled away as his steed collapsed and fell in the other direction.

The terrorgheist leant back and opened its bloody jaws, preparing to scream again, but Volant's armour was still ablaze with the power of his ancestors, and he hurled it from his scythe.

The terrorgheist's head jolted back, and as it tried to shake away the flames, Prince Volant dived across the wall and sank the full length of his curved blade into the monster's skull.

The creature jolted upwards, trying to fling the prince away, but he gripped the haft of his scythe and yanked it down, splitting its head in two.

Archers and Gravesward cheered as the terrorgheist crashed to the ground, juddered, then lay still.

The Morn-Prince turned to face his men, light still shining from his black armour. He held his scythe aloft, trailing strands of blood from the blade, and his men howled even louder.

'The Unburied are with us!' cried Prince Volant. 'Now and forever. And when this battle is—'

His words became a pained cough and he stumbled forwards.

Then he dropped to his knees, revealing the figure standing behind him. It was a mordant, and it was gripping a bloodstained shard of iron as long as its arm. It stood over the prince, panting hungrily, about to pounce on him, but dozens of arrows kicked it backwards through the air, sending it hurtling from the battlements.

'To the prince!' howled Aurun, running through the battle and climbing up the terrorgheist's corpse.

Gravesward formed a circle around Volant, holding back waves of mordants.

As the flesh-eaters continued tumbling onto the wall in great crowds, swamping the fortress' defenders, Lord Aurun dropped to Prince Volant's side and grabbed his bloody armour.

At first he thought the prince was dead, but then Volant coughed, spraying blood through the mouth grille of his helmet.

He managed to sit up and grab Aurun's arm. 'We've lost the gatehouse. Can you hold the wall?'

Aurun nodded, then glanced around. 'No,' he admitted. He was determined to show the same fortitude as the prince, but he could not deny what he was seeing. Thanks to the terrorgheist, the mordants were flowing freely over the battlements. As well as the ones climbing over the embrasures, there were some with wings, like smaller versions of the terrorgheist's mighty pinions. There was no way to use the oil or war machines. 'The walls are lost.'

He thought the prince would be outraged, but he simply nodded, pulling Aurun closer. 'Get your men to the Unburied. I need time to think.' He coughed and stiffened in pain, then grabbed Aurun again, his voice growing more steady. 'Fight every inch of the way.'

CHAPTER THIRTEEN

THE VICTORY FEAST

'What happened to us?' asked Queen Nia. She was seated at King Galan's side, at the head of the feast. Lords Miach and Melvas looked up at her words, but Galan knew she was talking to him. The war had ignited something in her soul. Her tiredness was gone, her bitterness forgotten. She looked wonderful – twenty years younger and flushed with pride. The firelight flashed in her glistening eyes, and he realised he could not remember the last time she had looked at him with such passion and focus.

He reached out and took her hand. 'What do you mean?'

She nodded at the Great Hall. They were surrounded by victorious warriors, vassals and kinsmen, their faces ruddy from wine and the heat of the fire, their eyes burning with pride as they leant back in their chairs or danced through the smoke. 'How did we forget this?' she said. 'How did we forget how to live?'

Galan laughed and drank more of his wine. 'It is not our place to choose the why and the when. The Great Wolf chose this moment to rouse his pack. We must just be grateful that he remembered us. He is behind everything. This rebellion would not have come as a surprise to him. I believe he sent us these traitors as a test – a final chance to prove our strength and loyalty.'

She smiled, squeezing his hand so hard it hurt. 'I love you.'

Galan raised her hand to his lips and kissed her fingers. 'I saw you at the gates, my love. So brave. So beautiful. You looked like a goddess – like Netona reborn.'

She blushed and looked away, then raised her chin and looked proudly down the table, the very image of a noble regent. For years she had hidden in her chambers, nursing a hurt he could not ease, the agony of not giving him an heir, but now she looked as though she had rid herself of a terrible weight, no longer hunched, no longer bowed. The lines on her face no longer looked like the cruel wounds of time, but badges of honour.

Galan turned to the warrior seated at his other side, Lord Melvas. 'What news from Lord Curac?'

Melvas was drowsy with exhaustion and drink, and his gaze was fixed on the dancers and musicians at the far end of the table. He sat up and rubbed his face, struggling to focus on his king.

Galan laughed. 'No one celebrates as well as you, my old friend.'

Melvas gave him a rueful grin. 'I have waited until tonight, King Galan. We will be on the road for two days or more after this. I will have plenty of time to recover before we reach the capital.'

'Then Curac has won?'

Melvas grinned. 'Very nearly. It took less than a day to reach the northernmost castle. He's attacking it as we speak. If the traitors refuse to surrender, Curac will take their heads just as easily as those of all the others.'

'Then he has no need of our aid?'

'No, your majesty.' Melvas emptied his goblet and poured himself another glass of wine. 'We are free to enjoy the fruits of our labours. And then, in the morning, we can set off for the capital.'

King Galan closed his eyes, picturing the scene. Once the Hounds of Dinann had captured the capital, the whole kingdom would be his once more. The sign of the Wolf would fly from every castle in the land, and the bards would sing of the day King Galan and Queen Nia crushed the rebels who had turned their backs on a thousand years of tradition and fealty.

He sensed Melvas watching him.

'I can't eat with you staring at my ear,' laughed the king. 'Speak your mind. What are you worried about now?'

'Curac could join us within a few days, your majesty.'

Galan shook his head. 'Not this again.' On another night, his general's doubt might have annoyed him, but he was in such good spirits that he smiled. 'Speed is everything, Melvas. I have told you this from the day we left Ruad. The rebels are a disorganised rabble, but if we give them time to join together against us, this war could become a tedious slog. I will not end my days locked in some drawn-out tussle over a backwater I had forgotten the name of until a few weeks ago. We move fast. We take their heads before they have time to get them together and form an alliance. We don't *need* the extra numbers from Curac.' He nodded at the meat heaped on Melvas' plate. 'You're just getting too comfortable here. You want to spend a few more days stuffing your gut.'

Melvas was about to protest, but Galan held up a hand to silence him. 'I'm joking! You're a good man, Melvas. Would I let you lead the Hounds if you weren't?' He shook his head. 'But I won't wait here for Curac. I needed him to take the north so that we wouldn't have an enemy at our backs, but you tell me he's dealing with that, so we will set off for the capital tomorrow. If Curac is as good as you claim, he will join us quickly enough to see me plant the false king's head on the battlements.'

Melvas seemed about to argue again when Queen Nia laughed at him. 'Know when you're beaten, Melvas. We'll leave in the morning.'

The warrior held up his hands and smiled. 'I'm not fool enough to argue with both of you.' He rose slowly to his feet, holding the back of his chair to steady himself. 'So I will dance.' He bowed, almost falling in the process, then stumbled down the length of the table towards the dance at the far end. As he went, warriors reached out, grabbing his hand and patting him on the back, roaring his name.

Galan was still smiling as he turned to Nia. 'Are we going to let that rogue have all the fun?'

She looked shocked. 'You haven't asked me to dance since...' She frowned. 'Have you *ever* asked me to dance?'

He shook his head in mock outrage, then stood and bowed to her. 'Queen Nia, heroine of Sarum Keep, will you consent to dance with me?'

She raised an eyebrow. 'Will your back hold out?'

He laughed as he took her hand and crossed the hall. People backed away, forming an impromptu processional, bowing, smiling and raising their drinks.

As their regents approached, the musicians struck up a new tune, playing faster and louder, and Nia laughed as Galan whirled her into the dance.

Faces blurred as the king turned at pace, lifting his queen off her feet and crushing her to his chest.

Colour and sound blazed in his mind, ignited by the wine and his quickening heart. Some of the dancers were swinging red ribbons, and as he spun, King Galan found himself surrounded by a spiral of crimson strands.

CHAPTER FOURTEEN

THE BARREN POINTS

The road headed south for a mile before it started to bend west and climb towards the stars. Gotrek walked just a few paces from the edge, staring out into the void and shaking his head. 'What do you call these roads again?' he asked, looking back at Lhosia.

'These are the wynds,' she replied. 'This is the Great South Wynd, one of the largest highways in the princedom. From here we will pass the Sceptred Wynd and the Wynd of Foreknowing. Beyond that we will reach the Barren Points, home of Lord Aurun, Warden of the Northern Climbs. There we shall find Prince Volant.'

Gotrek nodded and looked back out from the road. 'How are these things suspended? Sorcery?'

'The wynds are the veins of the princedom. They are hung from the prominents.'

'The prominents are your fortresses?' asked Maleneth, studying the few lights that still shone on the horizon.

Lhosia nodded. 'And our temples and homes. The greatest of them are vast. There are thousands of people in a fortress like the Barren Points or the Lingering Keep. There are many kinds of–' She cut off mid-sentence and stared up at the empty tracts of ocean.

'The Lingering Keep?' asked Maleneth.

'Morbium's capital,' said Lhosia, her voice flat. 'Home of Prince Volant, and home to the Amethyst Princes since the dawn of time.'

Gotrek was still gazing out at the lonely lights of the temples. 'So the roads are hung from your cities, but what keeps the cities afloat?'

'The Unburied,' said Lhosia, touching the cocoon she carried. 'We preserve our ancestors, and they, in turn, loan us their immortal power, feeding life into the prominents. Or at least, that's how it has always been until now.'

They trudged on in silence for a while, the only sound coming from Trachos' twisted boot as he dragged it along behind him. After walking for a few hours, his limp had become even more pronounced. Maleneth imagined he would like to rest but was too proud to ask. The thought of his stoical, grimacing silence made the journey slightly more entertaining.

Every dozen yards or so, they passed another corpse – either a dismembered ghoul, one of the knights in a flamboyant, feathered cloak or one of Morbium's civilians – pale, emaciated wretches like Lhosia, dressed in white or dark purple robes. Every one of the corpses was surrounded by a mobile shroud of tiny moths that scattered when Maleneth and the others approached, filling the darkness with movement and noise. It took a few minutes for Maleneth to realise that one of the bodies up ahead was still moving, trying to fend off the moths.

'Gotrek,' she said, nodding towards the struggling shape.

He nodded and veered back into the centre of the road, slinging his axe from his back as he reached the man.

When the Slayer hauled the terrified wretch to his feet, Maleneth recognised his face. 'The gatekeeper,' she laughed. 'You didn't get far.'

'Traitor!' cried Lhosia, barging past Maleneth to confront him. 'How dare you abandon your post? If you had done your duty, the mordants could have been halted. How could you hide yourself away while the Gravesward fought for their lives?'

The man tried to pull away from her, shaking his head, but he was trapped firmly in Gotrek's iron grip. 'High priestess... forgive me.' His voice was shrill. 'What could I do?'

'What you were trained to do!' Lhosia exclaimed. 'What you were sworn to do!' Her voice was taut with rage. Maleneth sensed that she was venting all the grief and rage that had been tormenting her since she had left the port. She drew her scythe and brandished it at the quaking man. 'Your cowardice will have risked countless souls! I should execute you for your–'

'They came so fast,' said the gatekeeper, shaking his head. 'There was no time to lock the gates or raise the wynd. Even the Gravesward could not hold them back.' His eyes flicked towards Lhosia. 'I've never seen so many mordants. Where are they coming from? Why are the prominents growing dark?'

'The Iron Shroud has been breached,' said Lhosia, not looking at the man. 'Something has broken through the power of the Unburied. We have been revealed to the rest of the princedoms.'

The gatekeeper looked like he might be sick. He shook his head and muttered something to himself. 'You're headed somewhere,' he said. 'Where?'

'Prince Volant is at the Barren Points. And I have promised to take this duardin to him.'

The man stepped away from Gotrek, staring at him in confusion, taking in the chest rune and the streaks of gold in his beard and mohawk. Then he turned towards Maleneth.

Her leathers were drenched in gore and her hair was clotted

with blood, sticking up from her head at a deranged angle. She gave him a friendly wink.

'Take me with you, priestess,' he gasped, looking back at Lhosia. 'Don't leave me with these…'

Maleneth wondered whether he was more afraid of her or the ghouls.

Lhosia did not meet his eye, but nodded.

'Only if you can keep up,' said Gotrek, and marched off down the road.

As the road climbed higher, they saw other highways passing beneath them, criss-crossing the sea, made of the same amalgamation of bone and iron. After a few hours, lights began to wash over the metal, coming from up ahead.

'Is this it?' asked Maleneth, peering at the distant shape. 'Is this the fortress where we will find your prince?'

Lhosia nodded.

Maleneth looked again at the shape in the distance, frowning as they walked towards it. 'Did you say the lights come from the…' She hesitated, gesturing at the cocoon Lhosia carried. 'From those things?'

Again Lhosia nodded. 'The Unburied.'

'And did you say that your prince took all the Unburied back to your capital, so that they would be safe from the flesh-eaters?'

Lhosia hesitated, staring at the lights.

'It would appear he's overlooked some,' said Maleneth.

The priestess strode on, gripping her scythe and picking up her pace.

'Finally!' grunted Gotrek, jogging after her. 'Someone with a sense of urgency.'

The Barren Points were nothing like the fortress they had seen at the port. Rather than a shell-like spiral curve, it resembled an overgrown version of the shrine where they had first met Lhosia – a gnarled, briar-like tangle of bone towers, each knotted around the others to make an impenetrable tangle. The whole tormented mass reached up like flames, as large as a city and as strange as everything else they had seen in the princedom. Somewhere deep inside the knotted walls was the source of the purple light, which spilled through the gaps between the towers, landing on the sea in a jumble of rippling shafts.

'Looks as buggered as the last place,' said Gotrek.

The far side of the fortress had collapsed, and hundreds of fires littered the ruined walls. There were figures battling through the fumes, silhouetted by the flames. Even from half a mile away, it was clear that most of the figures were ghouls. They were breaching the walls in a way that no sane warrior would attempt, swarming over the defences like rats, scrabbling over each other in a frenzy to reach the defenders that had gathered to face them. War engines hurled comet-like missiles, huge spheres of purple flame that exploded on impact, drenching the ghouls in liquid heat and adding to the fires that were spreading quickly through their ranks, but the shots were wild and sporadic.

Lhosia stared at the carnage. 'If the Barren Points fall, there is nothing to stop them taking the Northern Wards.'

'Are they more of your sacred moths?' asked Maleneth, peering at the clouds of tiny shapes that tumbled around the fighting.

Lhosia frowned in puzzlement, shaking her head.

'We would not see moths from this distance,' said Trachos. He took a carved ivory box from his belt and flicked a clasp on its side. A dozen linked boxes rattled out of it, each one smaller than the previous one, creating a long, square-sided tube. He snapped the clasp back, locking the boxes in place, then held the tube up to his helmet, looking through a lens at the narrow end. He muttered something and handed the spyglass to Maleneth.

She grimaced as the scene over the walls swam into focus. The flying shapes were ghouls with vast leathery wings, and as the knights reeled away from them, the creatures swooped down and tore them apart. 'No one is leading the defence,' she said. 'Look. It's mayhem. Where is this prince you've been telling us so much about? Is he the kind of prince that directs his troops from the local hostelry?'

They each took a turn with Trachos' spyglass, but when it came to Gotrek, he held it for a long time, muttering under his breath. 'There are thousands of ghouls at the front gates. They're everywhere. I presume the gates on this side will be locked, and I don't fancy our chances of climbing the walls. Any ideas how we get in?'

Lhosia was still staring at the battle on the walls. 'Where is the prince? Or Lord Aurun?'

'Priestess,' said Maleneth, causing her to turn round in surprise. 'Can you get us in? I can't imagine it will be long before the ghouls take a look at this side of the fortress.'

'Of course. I have my own routes into all of the prominents.' She waved at the approach to the gates, where several smaller paths snaked away from the main one, then started to hurry on along the road. 'Quickly.'

As they neared the fortress walls, they heard the sound of winged ghouls whirling overhead in the darkness. Some of them were making a thin, scraping, gasping sound. It was like a knife being dragged across porcelain. Maleneth would have found the noise easier to cope with if Trachos hadn't tried to drown it out with another grating hymn. He tried to look proud and triumphant as he marched on, but his wounds made him more tragic than fearsome.

Think how easy it would be to lace one of your knives and jam it through those splits in his armour, whispered her mistress.

'I serve the God-King,' she muttered. 'I serve something bigger than myself. You wouldn't understand what that's like.'

You were meant to serve me! You serve yourself before any god. And you need Gotrek dead if you're going to claim the rune for yourself. How else can you guarantee that he won't end up marching back into Azyr with it?

'Look at him. He's half dead already. I just need to bide my time and he'll do the job for me. That way I'll get the rune without breaking the oaths I swore in Azyrheim. The Order of Azyr won't last long if we murder each other every time there's a chance of glory.'

You're getting soft in your old age. You care about him.

Maleneth laughed. 'I haven't changed *that* much.'

'This way,' said Lhosia, leading them down a side road that followed the curve of the fortress walls, heading down as it went.

Maleneth glanced up. This close, the fortress looked even stranger, like a forest of heat-warped bones.

'Look out!' cried the gatekeeper as a ghoul dived at them from its perch on the wall.

Maleneth cursed. The thing was huge, like the ghouls they had faced at the port.

Gotrek ran at the wall of the fortress with such speed that he managed to take a few steps up its sheer side and hurl himself into the air.

The ghoul screamed in confusion as the full weight of the Slayer hit its back. It struggled furiously, forcing everyone to back away, blinded by clouds of dust, but Gotrek was still laughing as he struggled to keep his footing on the monster. He reached down, grabbed its chin and snapped its neck.

Maleneth ducked as another ghoul attacked, but she was too slow and a fist slammed into the side of her head. She stumbled like a drunk, swerving across the road. Then her breath exploded from her lungs as she tripped over rubble and thudded to the ground.

She was vaguely aware of a figure standing over her, fending off the ghouls, but she did not realise who it was until she heard Trachos' voice, booming out, 'Mallus-born and fiery-eyed! Godly lightning in my hand! Turning back the darksome tide! From Sigmar's golden starlit land!'

As the dust cleared, she saw him battling for her life, chin high and voice raised in triumph. He whirled his hammers back and forth, ignoring his wounds and his pain, smashing down every ghoul that scrambled towards her, punching sigmarite into their deranged faces. There was something horribly desperate in his words. It did not stem from fear of the ghouls, she realised, but fear of his own state of mind.

With a few of the ghouls down, the screams were more bearable and Maleneth managed to stand, staring at Trachos as he staggered away from her, dragging his ruined leg and looking for another target.

'You're such a dunce,' she said. 'Why were you protecting me? Without me around you'd have a chance of getting that rune.'

'I will protect you with whatever strength Sigmar spares me, Maleneth Witchblade, servant of the God-King.'

She rolled her eyes. '*So* brave.'

'This way!' cried Lhosia, dashing under an archway and continuing on down the road.

Maleneth ran after her and Trachos followed as quickly as he could, but Gotrek stayed in the centre of the road, roaring at the horrors above. Some were clambering over the walls and others were pounding torn, rotten wings as they circled overhead. Deranged as they were, the ghouls appeared reluctant to go anywhere near a raging Slayer. 'Get down here!' he cried. 'Or on my oath, I'll sprout wings and come up there after you!'

'Gotrek!' shouted Maleneth, waving her knives at the archway. 'The prince! He's in the fortress, remember?'

Gotrek grunted, gave the ghouls one last glare, then stamped through the carnage towards the arch, shrugging gore from his massive shoulders.

The road followed the curve of the wall, and after a few minutes, the clamour of battle began to fade.

They passed through a low arch. Lhosia unlocked a small hidden door, and they entered the fortress, emerging onto a wide paved area surrounded by windows and doors, all of which had been shuttered and barred. They could hear battle all around them, but there was no sign of soldiers or ghouls. The place seemed to have been overlooked as the fighting raged all around it.

The glow they had seen outside the fortress was brighter here, and the buildings looked like shards of alabaster held before a fire, pale and shimmering with amethyst light. Lhosia looked furious as she studied the lights. 'The Unburied should be safely in the capital by now. I explained to the prince. We didn't need to lose a single soul, as long as he took them to the Lingering Keep.' She waved her scythe at the lights. 'And here they are, still at risk, surrounded by mordants.'

'Where is he, lass?' said Gotrek, wiping blood from his face as he trudged into the square.

She shook her head and gestured them on, across the square. She led them to a narrow lane that looped up behind one of the buildings, lined with dozens of market stalls.

As they neared the top of the steep road, the sounds of fighting grew louder.

They readied their weapons as they crested the hill and saw another square spread out below them.

A brutal clash was in full swing. Gravesward, black-armoured archers and white-robed priests were all backing slowly into the square as mordants tumbled from every wall and roof. The ghouls were in such a frenzy that they were killing themselves to reach the defenders, leaping from rooftops and smashing themselves across the flagstones or else being crushed by the weight of bodies.

The scene was dominated by an enormous fossilised serpent that towered over the soldiers, its bleached-bone wings rattling as it lashed at the ghouls, flinging them through the air.

The Erebid numbered no more than a couple of hundred, but every building was carpeted with frenzied ghouls and more were looping overhead, pounding their wings as they looked for a place to attack. Maleneth guessed that in the streets around the square alone, there must have been thousands of the creatures, all thrashing wildly as they tried to reach the scythe-wielding knights. The Erebid had formed a tight circle around one of their fallen comrades. Maleneth struggled to see the wounded warrior they were so desperate to protect, but he looked to be unconscious, slumped in the arms of another knight. It was a desperate scene. The Erebid were massively outnumbered, and most of them were bleeding from multiple wounds. As they backed into the square, mordants rushed towards them from every direction, spilling out of streets and windows in a flood of grey, mottled flesh.

'This is not a fight we can win,' said Maleneth, searching around for a place to take cover. 'We need to think carefully about how we–'

'Who's the prince?' bellowed Gotrek, swinging his axe cheerfully as he strode out into the square.

CHAPTER FIFTEEN

THE HIDDEN CITY

Most of the Gravesward were too busy fighting to register Gotrek's question, but some looked round in surprise at the sight of a Slayer storming towards them.

Maleneth cursed and ran after Gotrek, with Trachos and Lhosia following close behind. The gatekeeper took his chance to flee, sprinting off up a side street.

Ghouls dashed at Gotrek as he broke from the shadows, but he hacked them down without breaking his stride.

'Halt!' cried one of the knights, breaking from the fight to level a scythe at Gotrek. 'Who are you?'

The skeletal drake reared up behind him, a furious edifice of bone, locking its empty eye sockets on the Slayer.

'I could ask the same of you,' replied Gotrek, glaring at the knight, clearly unimpressed by the massive beast looming over him.

Maleneth muttered another curse.

'You're clearly not the defenders of this fort,' continued the Slayer, 'or you'd be up on the walls instead of hiding down here.'

Maleneth had to step aside as a ghoul broke from the scrum and leapt at her, its face rigid with bloodlust. She opened its throat and booted it into another of the creatures, then bounded over the first one and hammered a knife into both their faces. She flipped clear and landed at Gotrek's side. Her pulse was hammering, willing her to abandon herself to the slaughter, but she held her bloodlust at bay.

A knight pushed through the crush, trying to reach Gotrek. It was the warrior carrying the fallen knight.

'Who are you?' he called, struggling under the weight of his burden.

'Where's your prince?' shouted Gotrek, punching a ghoul to the ground and slamming his axe through its neck. 'Well? Anyone got a tongue in their head?'

'Take their weapons,' said the knight. His armour was more ornate than the others', engraved and filigreed and studded with white gemstones.

The Slayer rumbled with laughter, gripping his axe in boulder-sized fists and dropping into a battle stance. 'Just you bloody try.'

The knights hesitated, thrown by Gotrek's psychotic grin.

The Slayer shrugged, swapping the axe from hand to hand. 'Not much of a weapon, to be fair.' He tapped it against his chest rune with a clang. 'I got it from the same mewling runts who made this. But it'll do for the likes of you.'

The knights staggered backwards as ghouls continued to pour from the surrounding streets. Trachos limped past them, pummelling ghouls and singing.

'Wait!' cried the knight in the ornate armour. 'Lhosia?' He pushed towards her, still dragging the fallen warrior, but then hesitated when he got within arm's reach of Gotrek.

'Lord Aurun,' said Lhosia, rushing past Gotrek and embracing the knight.

He smiled, clearly shocked.

'Prince Volant!' said Aurun, looking down at the man in his arms. 'It's the high priestess!'

'*You're* the Morn-Prince?' cried Gotrek, striding towards the prone knight.

There was a loud clatter as the Gravesward locked ranks, raising shields and readying scythes.

'Wait!' Lhosia raised a hand. 'The duardin is not an enemy. I would not have reached you without his help. He killed countless mordants to get me here.'

The prince managed to raise himself up and look at Gotrek.

It was only then that Maleneth realised how big he was – almost twice as tall as her, larger than Trachos, even. His armour was filthy and damaged, but he was unmistakably the leader. His face was hidden inside a tall black-and-white helmet that displayed a snarling face on one side and a serene smile on the other.

'Your majesty,' said Lhosia, backing away.

'Who are you, duardin?' gasped the huge knight, ignoring Lhosia. His voice was rough with pain, and there was blood pooling beneath him. 'Why do you fight for Morbium?'

The ghouls surged forwards again, and there was a flurry of blows as the knights struggled to hold them back.

'I'm Gotrek Gurnisson,' bellowed the Slayer over the din, 'and I fight exclusively for Gotrek Gurnisson.' He hacked down a pair of ghouls with one savage swipe. 'I'm here because I've been told you can get me to Nagash.'

'Nagash?' Prince Volant turned to Lhosia, shaking his head. He had to pause as more ghouls broke through the lines of knights. There was a furious flurry of scythes, and then, when there was another gap in the fighting, Volant stared at Gotrek. 'No *sane* person wants to reach the Great Necromancer.'

Gotrek laughed. 'Sane?' He waved his bloody axe at Lhosia, still holding the cocooned corpse she had taken from the docks. 'You live in bones and worship moths.'

Prince Volant looked past Gotrek towards Maleneth. But before he could say anything, the ground juddered and the sounds of distant battle swelled in volume. A low, booming explosion echoed down the streets.

'Grungni,' muttered Gotrek as a shadow loomed over the city. It looked like a column of smoke pluming from a volcano.

'What *is* that?' said Maleneth as the shape moved into the light.

'A mordant,' said Prince Volant, his tone bleak.

The ghoul looked similar to the others apart from its size – it was a colossus, hundreds of feet tall and teeming with legions of smaller ghouls. It smashed an enormous fist down into the battlements, destroying the rows of explosive charges lined up for the ballistae. Flames blossomed through the walls, lighting up the giant's grotesque face. It was just as hunched and sinewy as its smaller kin, but there was a gleam of cruel intelligence in its eyes, quite different from all the others. It dragged its fist sideways through the battlements, hurling men and war machines through the air and creating another drum roll of explosions.

'To the Separating Chambers,' snapped Volant, turning towards Lord Aurun. 'Protect the Unburied.'

Aurun nodded and ordered his men back across the square. They were completely surrounded and it was slow going, but the knights fought with impressive discipline, carving a path through the frantic crowds.

The fury of the fighting made more conversation impossible, so Gotrek, Maleneth and Trachos fought alongside the knights in silence as they made for a building on the far side of the square.

It was a huge, undulating structure built in an architectural style unlike anything Maleneth had seen before. It looked like a marquee of white silk, frozen at the moment its peaks were caught in a breeze, all ripples and bulges, but it was made of the same hard, bone-like material as the rest of the fortress.

'Into the Hidden City,' shouted Aurun, waving for everyone to follow him as he dragged the prince up the steps with the help of some of his men.

As most of the knights formed a semicircle at the bottom of the steps, raising their shields, Aurun unlocked the door, flinging it open and spilling purple light over the battle.

They hurried inside, hurling ghouls back down the steps as they backed into the hall. There was a fierce scrum at the threshold before the knights managed to shut the doors with a resounding slam.

'Bar them!' cried Lord Aurun, leaving the prince on the floor and rushing back to the doors. They were vast, imposing things wrought of iron-threaded bone, with thick crossbars mounted on either side. As Aurun waved his men back and forth they slammed the bars down. When each bar landed, it triggered a mechanism that whirred like an enormous timepiece, turning and interlocking and creating a lattice of bolts.

The sound of the mechanisms seemed to draw Trachos out of his habitual daydream, and he wandered over to them, fingering the locks with interest.

'What is this place?' asked Maleneth, looking up at the distant vaulted ceiling. There were twelve cocoons, identical to the one Lhosia was carrying.

'Who are you?' demanded Prince Volant, still sprawled on the floor and clutching his wounds. His skeleton steed was circling him protectively, its hollow gaze locked on Gotrek and Maleneth.

'I serve the Order of Azyr.' Maleneth nodded at Trachos, who was still studying the locks. 'We're escorting the Slayer through the princedoms.'

'You serve Sigmar?' The prince waved at Gotrek, who was stomping around the hall, staring up at the ceiling. '*He* doesn't. Why are you helping him?'

Maleneth spoke up quickly before Trachos could tell the entire crowd about the rune. 'He's unusually powerful. And he's an enemy of the Chaos Gods.'

'*Any* gods,' clarified Gotrek. He walked over to the prince. 'Get me to Nagash and I'll demonstrate.'

The prince removed his helmet and studied Gotrek. Like the rest of the Erebid, Volant's head was pale and hairless, but unlike the others, his face was inked with a complex spiral of tattoos – slender black lines that coiled down from his eyes, mimicking the markings of a moth's wings. His long, angular face was unmistakably regal, but it was twisted by pain. He gasped as he climbed to his feet, towering over everyone present. He stooped and tapped Gotrek's rune with a long, tapered finger. 'And this?'

Maleneth struggled to hold back a curse, wondering if there was anyone in the Mortal Realms who *wouldn't* immediately pick up on the rune's importance.

Gotrek laughed bitterly. 'The reason for my sudden popularity.'

Prince Volant waited patiently for him to elaborate.

The Slayer shrugged. 'Just a rune. And a bloody ugly one at that. Can you get me to Nagash?'

'Why would I help you?'

Gotrek made a low growling sound, but before he could respond, Lhosia strode across the room and addressed the prince, her face rigid with anger.

'We've come from the Anceps Docks. The Unburied were left to the mordants.' Her voice trembled as she waved at the cocoons hanging overhead. 'As they have been here. You swore that you would get the ancestors back to the capital, Prince Volant.'

'You swore the Iron Shroud would hold long enough for me to do so.' The prince's nonchalant mask slipped and his eyes flashed.

'Do you think you're the only one who cares for the safety of the ancestors?' He pointed at Aurun. 'I sent an order for the Unburied to be moved months ago, and when I arrived, only hours ahead of destruction, I find Lord Aurun doing nothing.'

'Nothing?' Lord Aurun looked outraged. 'We can't move the Unburied, high priestess,' he said, addressing Lhosia. 'I have explained all this to the Morn-Prince. We stayed here to defend them because it's either that or abandon them. They're bound into the workings of the fortress. They're part of the old duardin engines. It would take months to separate them from the architecture. Years, maybe.'

Lhosia shook her head, looking up at the cogs and wheels fixed into the ceiling. 'The Unburied are *trapped?*'

Aurun nodded. 'The forefathers completed their work here.' He tapped the haft of his scythe on the cobbles. 'This was the final prominent to be completed. They sealed it with the souls of the Unburied and then sailed back to the Lingering Keep. The Unburied are bound by mechanisms too complex to understand. And even if we could understand them, we don't know how the Kharadron powered these machines. And there's no way I could have broken the ancestors out before the mordants arrived.'

Maleneth shook her head. 'Did you say sailed? How could anyone sail in this place? Your sea isn't liquid. It looks like it's made of lead.'

'It's impossible to cross the Eventide now,' said Aurun. 'Even touching it means madness and death. But our forefathers crossed it regularly. They had to – there were no wynds until they built them. They borrowed engineering skills from the Kharadron. They brought the Unburied here in great engines that were able to cross the Eventide.'

Gotrek's eye glazed over. Maleneth had seen this happen before. It tended to precede either sleep, an idea or an explosion of extreme violence. It was worryingly hard to predict which.

'Right,' said the Slayer, looking up at the Morn-Prince. 'I have business with a god.' He waved his axe at the moth-shrouded shapes hanging overhead. 'How about this – I get your corpse eggs back to your capital, and you tell me how to reach Nagash?'

Lord Aurun laughed incredulously, and the prince simply stared.

'Well?' demanded Gotrek as something heavy boomed against the doors. 'My guess is that you have five minutes before the morons break in and start chewing your skulls. Do you want my help or not?'

'You're insane,' replied the prince.

'Agreed. If I get these twelve cocoons to safety, will you get me to Nagash?'

There was another blow at the door, and it gave a low groan as the frame started to give.

'Brace it!' cried Lord Aurun, waving more of his men towards it. 'Jam your scythes against the metal!'

Gotrek was still standing in front of the prince, waiting for an answer.

Volant winced and staggered. Knights rushed to help him, but he shrugged them off. He frowned at Gotrek, as though struggling to make him out in the dazzling light. 'You are peculiar. Quite unlike anyone I have ever met.'

Gotrek shrugged.

The door shook again, and the soldiers cried out as they tried to hold back the weight.

'How could you get the Unburied to the capital?' asked the prince. 'Lord Aurun says it would take weeks to break those machines.'

Gotrek turned to Lord Aurun. 'Are these doors the only way out?'

'There's another exit, but it only leads to the Eventide. The chambers at the rear of the hall join with the city walls, and then there's nothing there but dead sea and the *Spindrift*.'

'The *Spindrift*?'

'An aether-ship. The transportation used by the forefathers when they built the prominents – before they made the wynds.'

'An airship?' Gotrek shook his head. 'Why in the blazes aren't you using it?'

'It's a useless relic,' replied Aurun. 'Powered the same way as those.' He waved his scythe at the machines overhead.

Gotrek looked over at Trachos. The Stormcast Eternal was helping Aurun's men as they struggled to hold the door.

'Right,' he said, turning back to the prince. 'If I rescue your corpse sacks, you'll help me reach Nagash, agreed?'

Prince Volant sneered and seemed about to dismiss Gotrek again, but the Slayer's tone was so confident that he hesitated.

'He has a habit of surprising people,' said Maleneth. 'And he's *tediously* honest. If he says he can do it, he probably can.'

'How?' asked the prince, his expression a mixture of outrage and intrigue.

'Tell them, manling,' Gotrek called over to the Stormcast Eternal.

Trachos was not following the conversation. He was staring at the mechanical doors, muttering to himself.

'Trachos!' shouted Maleneth.

He looked over. As usual, his face was hidden behind his helmet's gleaming deathmask, and it was hard to know what he was thinking.

Gotrek waved him over. 'The moth people want their corpses back. They need them out of those machines.' He gestured with his axe at the ceiling. 'Duardin engineering. Shouldn't be hard to untangle.'

Trachos stared at the Slayer in silence, as though he had forgotten who Gotrek was.

Maleneth felt like jamming knives into his helmet.

The prince waved a dismissive hand. 'These people are ridiculous.' He turned away. 'Aurun! Get some of your archers up on those balconies. Fast!'

A low rumbling started in Gotrek's chest, and he stood up to his full – if not very impressive – height. He gripped his greataxe, and Maleneth saw quite clearly what was coming next. The prince was about to find out what happened to pompous nobles who refused to take Gotrek seriously.

'They're like the engines in Azyr,' said Trachos, talking to the ceiling. 'In the Sigmarabulum. In the alchemical forges. Those machines were designed almost entirely by duardin engineering guilds. These look similar.'

Maleneth looked from Trachos to Gotrek and back again, realisation dawning. 'You've studied duardin engineering?'

Trachos was still talking to the ceiling. 'Of course. Most of Azyr is built on the principles of duardin engineering. I have studied several methods of containing aetheric matter – Baraz Cylinders, Gromthi Coils. They're no different to any other...' He shook his head and began mumbling to himself.

Gotrek nodded. 'Between the two of us, we could untether these cocoons.'

Trachos lowered his gaze from the ceiling and stared at Gotrek. 'What?'

Gotrek's grin froze on his face, and he gripped his axe tighter. 'I said we could *release* them, you tin-headed lump.'

'Oh. Yes, perhaps. It would require an influx of aetheric energy.' Trachos tapped some of the arcane devices jangling at his belt. 'I should be able to trigger the correct currents.'

Gotrek had just opened his mouth to say more when the doors gave way.

CHAPTER SIXTEEN

THE MASTER RUNE OF KRAG BLACKHAMMER

Maleneth ducked as bone and iron whistled through the air.

Tree-sized fingers clawed at the doors, ripping away the frame, causing the walls to crumble.

Then, as the giant ghoul backed away, hundreds of its smaller kin poured into the hall, howling and snorting, their eyes rolling with kill-frenzy.

'Shield wall!' cried Lord Aurun, and the Gravesward locked together, forming a row of tightly packed shields just before the ghouls crashed into them.

The knights staggered under the impact but held their position. As one, they swiped their scythes beneath their shields, cutting the legs from the creatures. Ghouls slapped to the floor, thrashing in their own blood.

'Trachos!' bellowed Gotrek, waving at the stairs that lined the walls. 'Get those bodies down!' He was running as he shouted, rushing to join the battle. He vaulted a toppled column and leapt over the shield wall with a joyous howl, crashing into the heart of the ghouls.

Prince Volant waved Lord Aurun and Maleneth over. 'Help me up!' he called, pointing at his steed.

The skeleton drake had already lowered its head in readiness, but Aurun shook his head. 'Morn-Prince! Your wounds!'

'It's an order, Lord Aurun.'

Maleneth scoured the hall for the other exit, cursing as she realised she might have to abandon her plans, after all she had endured. They were cornered like rats. It was going to be a massacre.

The other doors lead to the sea. There's no point trying them. Her mistress' voice was not as sneering as usual. It sounded alarmed. *You heard them. Walk on those dead waters and you'll lose your mind. There's nowhere to go.*

Maleneth hissed in annoyance. Her mistress was right. Her only chance was that Gotrek's lunatic plan might somehow work. Trachos was still only halfway up the wall, struggling to climb because of his wounds. 'Your prince will last longer on that thing than on the floor,' she muttered, glancing at Aurun. 'Get him on there.'

Aurun looked appalled that she was addressing him in such a commanding tone, but he gave a grudging nod and, between them, they hauled Volant up onto his mount.

The prince seemed reinvigorated to be looming over the fighting, and he raised his scythe. 'Morbium eternal!' His steed reared beneath him and the Gravesward roared in reply, their shield wall unbroken as they cut down row after row of ghouls.

Volant's drake jerked its head forwards, jaws gaping, spewing a column of dust across the hall. It hit the ghouls with such force that it carved a path through the centre of the scrum, toppling dozens of the creatures. But as Maleneth climbed some rubble for a better view, she saw that the blast was doing more than simply knocking them over. As they tried to rise, their movements grew stiff and awkward and their flesh hardened. Within a few seconds, every ghoul that had been hit was lying cracked and lifeless on the ground.

Maleneth nodded, impressed, then remembered Gotrek. 'The Slayer is out there!' she cried.

'Aye!' shouted Gotrek, climbing onto the toppled door, the head of a ghoul in one hand and his axe in the other. He raised the weapon and grinned.

'Watch out for Gotrek!' she called to Prince Volant, pointing at the Slayer.

He nodded and cried out the same command, and his steed vomited more dust in the opposite direction.

Trachos was still struggling to reach the ceiling, so Maleneth bounded up the steps. As she approached him, she shook her head in disbelief. The idiot was singing to himself, as though he were enjoying a moment of quiet reflection.

She grabbed his arm and hauled him up the last few steps. They reached a balcony suspended just below the ceiling, and were now within arm's reach of the machines. Trachos' song faltered.

'Incredible workmanship,' he said, removing his helmet and fastening it to his belt so that he could study the devices in more detail.

'We're about to *die*,' said Maleneth.

Trachos fixed her with a flat, blank stare. 'I will not die.'

'Oh, well that's all fine then.'

He continued staring at her.

'The machines, Trachos,' she prompted. 'Can you make them work?'

He looked back at the engines and the rows of pale ovoid shapes they cradled.

From up here Maleneth could see the twelve cocoons clearly.

They were just like the one Lhosia carried – like oversized eggs wrapped in dusty gauze. Now that she knew what they contained, she found the sight of them revolting.

'Think of all those withered little corpses,' she muttered.

Trachos shrugged. 'Gotrek won't leave without the prince, and the prince won't leave without the corpses.'

There was an explosion of howls from below as the ghouls broke through the shield wall. Knights scrambled to block the gap, but it was like trying to stem a ruptured dam. Ghouls rushed in every direction, leaping and clawing and tearing soldiers to the ground.

'Quickly!' cried Maleneth. 'Get those things out!'

Trachos turned back to the machines. He singled out a particular piece of the workings and rotated cogs with his fingers, clicking them into a new position, aligning the duardin runes engraved into the ancient metal.

Maleneth laughed with relief as light shimmered through the metalwork, edging its wheels and levers.

The fighting became a desperate rout. Gravesward staggered in every direction, trying to fend off claws and teeth as their shields were ripped from their grip.

Gotrek whirled through the carnage, hacking, laughing and lunging.

'His rune,' whispered Maleneth.

Trachos was too engrossed in his work to hear. He had taken a spherical golden cage from his belt and fixed it to the cogs. The instrument was pulsing with the same light as the rest of the ceiling and making a bright ticking sound.

Maleneth stared at Gotrek. He was lost in the moment, fighting so ferociously that Grimnir's face was blazing in his chest. His blocky, savage features looked like they were rising from a brazier, underlit by a hellish glow. 'It will change him,' she muttered.

Trachos paused. 'What?'

'The rune.' She pointed one of her knives at Gotrek. 'It's consuming him.'

Trachos stared blankly at Gotrek's frenzied attacks, then went back to turning the cogs.

The lights flashed brighter over the ceiling and he nodded, taking another instrument from his belt and attaching it to the first.

'To me!' cried Prince Volant, still clinging weakly to the back of his steed as he waved his scythe. 'Form a circle!'

His soldiers tried to cross the room towards him, but so many ghouls had crushed into the hall that many of the knights were surrounded. Lord Aurun led a group of soldiers to the prince, and they formed an island of black armour in the heaving mass of grey.

'If we don't go now it's over,' said Maleneth, leaning over Trachos, trying to understand what he was doing.

Every part of the machinery was flickering, and there was a low humming emanating from the cradles holding the Unburied, but Trachos shook his head and backed away, leaving his implements hanging from the cogs.

'Not enough power.'

'What?' Trachos was nearly twice as tall as Maleneth and clad in hulking sigmarite, but she reached up, grabbed his arm and hauled him round to face her. 'You're giving up?' She shook her head in disbelief, waving at the battle that was ending below them. The Gravesward around Prince Volant were falling fast, vanishing beneath mounds of frantic ghouls. 'If we don't get these things out, we're all going to be butchered.' She pulled him close. 'You might not die, Trachos, but what will your next Reforging be like? And what will be left when you come out the other side?'

He loomed over her, his voice taut. 'I *know* what this means for me, Witchblade, but I still don't have the power to trigger those engines. They've been inert too long. It would take massive amounts of aether-fire to reignite them.'

Down below, the prince's steed let out an unearthly scream as ghouls tore into it, snapping bones in its legs even as it lashed out with foot-long claws. The prince howled a command and the drake spat more lethal dust, but it was like punching a mountain. Ghouls continued tumbling towards the prince.

'Try again!' Maleneth shouted, infuriated by Trachos' fatalistic tone. 'Even if I have to drag you–'

He barged past her, whipping his hammers from his belt.

Her fighter's instinct told her to duck, and she heard a crack of breaking bone.

She whirled around, knives drawn, to see ghouls lurching and scrambling up the steps.

'Get to the knights!' she gasped.

Trachos nodded, and they began fighting their way back down the steps.

Maleneth tried to kill as she had been trained, to honour the Murder God with every cut, but she was too mired in grasping limbs. The best she could do was use her momentum to bound over the heads and shoulders of the ghouls.

Trachos resorted to similar tactics, using his weighty, armour-clad bulk to smash through the crush.

By the time they reached the bottom steps, Maleneth could barely see, her face was so drenched in blood, but she managed to stagger into the circle of knights around Prince Volant.

Trachos punched his way after her and began hammering anyone who broke through the lines. He was unusually quiet, fighting in grim silence and glancing up at the machines still glowing overhead.

Gotrek was a few feet away, fighting outside the circle, his face locked in a scowl.

'What happened?' he cried, snatching a glance at Trachos.

'It can't be done!' yelled Trachos.

Gotrek attacked the ghouls with renewed fury, his axe a golden blur. 'Can't be done?' His words were contorted by rage.

The Slayer battled towards the base of a toppled column and climbed up onto it, wiping his face and staring out at the deranged figures crashing around him. He looked like the captain of a listing ship, standing at the prow as waves swelled around him.

'So *this* is my doom?' The rune in his chest was blazing constantly now, fuelled by kill-fever. 'These wretched things? In this wretched place?' He was talking to himself more than Trachos. 'I'm glad you never lived to see it, manling. It would not have been worthy of a poem.' He pounded the dazzling rune. 'Redeem yourself, Grimnir! Give me something better!'

At the far end of the hall, the door shook, hurling masonry through the air as the giant tried to shoulder its way into the chamber. Its grotesque face was so vast that only half of it was visible through the tumbling walls.

Gotrek laughed. 'Aye, I suppose *he'll* do.'

The Slayer glanced back at the group battling around the prince. 'Get out!' he shouted. 'I can't save your dead, but I can save you. I'll hold the morons back. Go. While you can.'

Lord Aurun called out to his men, waving them forwards. 'To the Slayer!'

'Don't be a fool!' yelled Gotrek. 'Go!'

As the Gravesward charged, Aurun cried out. Despite the carnage, he sounded clear and determined. 'What are we without the wisdom of our forebears? What use living if we lose the past?'

Gotrek's eyes flashed, and for once it was with something other than rage. 'Well said!' He bared his teeth in a grin, looking back at Lord Aurun. 'Well bloody said, manling!'

He raised his axe, letting the fury of the rune blast from his chest and up into the blade. He looked like a fallen comet, burning as the world collapsed around it. 'Then we meet our dooms together!' He locked his single, burning eye on the colossus at the far side of the hall. 'And that one's mine!'

Maleneth struggled to keep her footing as the knights shoved their way deeper into the ghouls. 'No!' she spat. 'I refuse to die *here*.'

Knight after knight fell, shields torn from their grip and necks ripped open. It was grotesque. And brutal. Whatever Gotrek thought, Maleneth saw nothing noble in the sacrifice. These men were dying for no reason, which might be fine for them, but not for a Bride of Khaine.

She fought furiously, buying time to think, but it was all going to be over in minutes.

There was no way to reach the exit at the back of the hall on her own – there were too many ghouls in the way. She looked to where Gotrek was charging head down through the creatures, making for the giant. He was consumed by his determination to reach the grotesque monster, burning so brightly now that it was hard to look at him.

'God of Murder,' gasped Maleneth. 'Why didn't I think of it? Trachos!' she howled, opening a ghoul's belly and standing on its back as it doubled over, raising herself over the crush.

Trachos was only a few feet away. His turquoise armour had been painted crimson by blood, but he was still swinging his hammers, towering over the battle. He looked her way.

'Power!' she cried, dodging a blow and trying to point at Gotrek.

Trachos shook his head, confused.

'The rune!' she shouted, enraged by his stupidity. 'The Rune of Blackhammer! Power!'

Trachos hesitated, only for a moment, but it was enough for a wave of ghouls to attack him. He fell, vanishing beneath the crowd of bodies.

'*Damn* you!' howled Maleneth, shaking her head violently as she fended off another blow.

Don't be a fool, said her mistress. *What do you know of engineering?*

'He hesitated!' she snapped, too far gone to care if anyone heard her addressing a ghost. 'Trachos hesitated. Because I'm right!'

She shrugged off the despair that had been threatening to overwhelm her and leapt from the back of the ghoul, landing on the shoulders of another one. Determination and hope thrilled through her veins, giving her a furious surge of energy. She bounded from one wretch to the next, moving so fast that they barely registered her footfall before she had leapt clear.

In a few seconds Maleneth left the Gravesward behind and crossed the hall, arriving next to Gotrek with a final, acrobatic leap.

The Slayer turned on his heel, axe raised, ready to behead her, his face contorted.

'Gotrek!' she said, holding out her knife in warning, squinting into the inferno that had engulfed him. 'It's me!'

Recognition flickered across his eye. He axed down a pair of ghouls without looking away from Maleneth.

'Aelf?' His voice was hoarse from shouting. He looked barely recognisable. Golden light was slicing through the pores of his skin and rippling across his mohawk. He looked like a weapon plucked from a forge.

They were a few feet from the wall, and Maleneth pointed at the pipes stretching to the ceiling. They were still shimmering with the power Trachos had triggered.

'The machines...' she said, but her words faltered as Gotrek stepped closer. The sweating, porcine oaf had vanished, and she found herself facing something quite different. He looked like an avatar of war, gilded with bloodlust and burning with power.

Gotrek dealt out a storm of brutal blows, cutting a path around

Maleneth. Then he shook his head. 'It's my time, aelf.' Even his voice sounded different – deep and calm rather than harsh and boorish.

He turned to go.

'No!' cried Maleneth, leaping in front of him.

Fury burned in Gotrek's eye. 'Step aside!'

Maleneth saw one last chance. One hope of survival. She shook her head, crouching before him. It was suicide, but she gripped her knives and dropped into a battle stance.

Gotrek glowered, outraged, and swung his axe at her head.

She ducked, rolling clear, and Gotrek was thrown forwards by the force of his blow.

His greataxe smashed into the shimmering pipes.

Power rushed through him, pouring from the rune down the haft of his axe and into the machines.

Maleneth was hurled backwards, engulfed in white heat.

CHAPTER SEVENTEEN

THE LAIR OF THE GREAT WOLF

'For Dinann!' howled King Galan, standing in his stirrups and lifting his spear.

'For Dinann!' His soldiers filled the night with noise, their horses rearing and screaming, pounding their armoured hooves on the dusty road.

Nia was at his side, triumphant on her white destrier, grinning as she raised her spear. She was bold and beautiful, her auburn hair plaited down her back and her voice as ferocious as any of the men's.

The Hounds of Dinann kicked their horses into a canter, and the highway rang to the sound of metal-shod hooves.

The capital was still half a mile away, but Galan could already see soldiers rushing to man the battlements.

'These are our lands,' said Nia, her voice hoarse with anger. 'The birthright of the Dinann. The lair of the Great Wolf. How could they fail us so badly? What could have driven them to betray us?'

Galan waved his spear at their glorious host. 'Who cares? It will soon be over. This battle might be larger than the others, but it will be just as decisive. And when we are done, the kingdom will be restored and we can end our days in peace. We can be proud of our reign, Nia.'

She held his gaze, and an unspoken thought passed between them.

He leant closer. 'We might not have produced heirs, but we have rebuilt the kingdom and given our people hope. That is worth far more. We *can* be proud, Nia.'

'Your majesty,' said Lord Melvas, steering his horse towards Galan.

Nia smiled at Galan and rode away, chin raised and eyes flashing.

Melvas looked troubled, and Galan slowed his horse to speak with him. The warrior seemed unable to talk, grimacing and struggling to meet Galan's eye.

'What is it, man?' Usually, Galan would have found his general's awkwardness amusing, but not on the cusp of battle. 'Speak up.'

Melvas shook his head. 'I'm not sure…' He still looked pained. 'Now that I come to say it, it sounds absurd.'

'Pull yourself together, Melvas. I can't have you pulling faces and cowering when we're about to attack. What *is* it?'

Melvas frowned. 'This morning, when I was inspecting the rearguard, I saw the strangest thing. For a moment, I thought I saw the men eating something…'

'What are you talking about, Melvas?' snapped the king. 'Eating what?'

He grimaced. 'It looked like they were eating the men they had just killed.'

'Eating the bodies? What are you talking about? You're saying they were cannibals?'

Melvas stared at him a little longer, then laughed and shook his head. 'I know. It's absurd. Forgive me, your highness. I think I really *did* drink too much at the feast.'

Galan leant closer. 'We've been fighting too long and sleeping too little, all of us.' He slapped Melvas on the back. 'Soon you'll be back at home with your feet up, boasting about how you did all the real work.' He laughed. 'Cannibals!'

Melvas tried to smile, but his eyes remained fixed and dull.

'Galan?' called Nia from the other side of the road. 'Is there a problem?'

'Only Melvas' inability to hold his drink! I warned him this would happen!'

She laughed and rode on.

Galan pulled Melvas so close their faces were almost touching. 'We are about to end this uprising. The men will be looking to you for guidance. Understand?'

Melvas nodded and sat up in his saddle. 'Of course.'

Galan loosed his arm, and the general's horse carried him back into the flow of riders. Melvas barked orders as he went, but his commands lacked their usual vigour.

Galan shook his head and rode on, frowning until he saw Nia, just ahead of him, laughing with one of the men, radiant and glorious.

'For Dinann!' he howled, grinning.

The host echoed his call.

CHAPTER EIGHTEEN

THE SPINDRIFT

Maleneth's breath exploded from her lungs as she landed, hard, on the floor. As she lay there, dazed and breathless, blinded by dazzling light, a great roaring came from somewhere and the ground started to shudder.

'Gotrek!' she gasped, her throat full of ash.

You've killed him! Finally!

Maleneth's skull was pounding where it had hit the floor, and nausea rushed through her as she stood, swaying, surrounded by coruscating light.

'Nice work, aelf,' boomed Gotrek, staggering through the glare. 'If in doubt, blow it up. Always a good plan.'

She tried to speak, to explain herself, but her breath was still trapped painfully in her lungs.

Gotrek's bludgeoning tone told her that he was himself once more. Whatever transformation had been threatening to overcome him had ceased. He was the hog again. He laughed. 'Did you *attack* me?'

'The cocoons,' she said, taking a deep, juddering breath. 'The power of the Master Rune. You sent it into the machines.'

He shook his head, looking at her as though she were insane. Then he laughed. 'By Grungni. Only an aelf could be so devious. If that's worked, I'll buy you a barrel of Bugman's.'

He hauled her across the hall, carving a path through the dazed ghouls until the light dimmed and they saw the effects of the blast.

The explosion had given the Gravesward a chance to regroup around their prince. There were more of them left than Maleneth had guessed, and they had locked their shields back together, forming a circular wall that bristled with scythes. Trachos was there too. His armour was even more damaged than the last time she had seen him, but he was still standing, staring up at the ceiling.

Maleneth followed his gaze and laughed. 'It worked!'

The pulleys and chains that held the Unburied were jolting and unfolding like spider legs, snapping and clicking as they lowered the cocoons.

'Gravesward, advance!' cried Lord Aurun, leading the knights forwards. 'Keep the mordants from the Unburied.'

As Maleneth's eyes adjusted to the light, she saw that the blast had torn through the ghouls. Her own body was unharmed, as were the Gravesward, but the aether-fire had devastated the mordants, burning flesh from their limbs and leaving most of them lying broken and smouldering.

'The aether-fire,' she muttered. 'It burned through them.'

The Gravesward crashed into the wounded revenants, avenging the brothers they had lost on the walls. The slaughter that followed was quiet but brutal. The hall rang to the sound of scythes cutting through meat and bone.

The far side of the building had almost entirely collapsed, its facade scattered across the square outside, and the giant ghoul was towering over the rubble, shielding its eyes from the blaze.

'Get the corpse eggs,' shouted Gotrek, running across the hall. 'I'll deal with Tiny.'

Maleneth whirled around and sprinted back towards Trachos. His neck armour was damaged and something was happening to the burnished sigmarite – it was pulsing with inner light, as though there were flames moving beneath its surface.

Lhosia was beside him, staring up at the unfurling machines with a rapt expression on her face. 'It's a miracle,' she whispered, looking from the ceiling to Trachos.

'It's engineering.' There was no pain in his voice. If anything, Maleneth thought, his tone seemed lighter than usual. He sounded almost pleased.

Prince Volant rode over to them, his enormous steed moving in a swaying, drunken gait similar to the wretches that had wounded it. The prince stared over the heads of his men, to the doors at the far side of the hall, where Gotrek was running towards the giant.

'What is he?' It was hard to tell if Volant was impressed or disgusted.

'Demented,' snapped Maleneth. 'Anyway, *I* was the one who had the idea to–'

'Look!' cried Lhosia.

The columns had reached the floor of the chamber, and at the base of each was a cocoon, lying safely on the debris-strewn floor.

'Quickly!' Prince Volant waved his honour guard towards them. 'Gather up the Unburied. That was only a fraction of the mordants. More could arrive at any moment.'

Rune-light was still shimmering through the columns, and the knights became silhouettes as they lifted the cocoons from their cradles.

Another shudder rocked through the hall, causing them all to stagger.

Maleneth wondered if the whole place was coming down, then realised that the noise had come from outside. The giant ghoul had fallen backwards across the square and toppled into the buildings opposite, smashing walls and sending up clouds of dust. The Slayer was just visible, like a dazzling ember on its chest, roaring as he hacked repeatedly with his axe.

Prince Volant shook his head as his men brought the cocoons towards him. 'Leave the hall. Make for the East Gate. We'll see if that wynd is still clear.'

'No!' said Lhosia. 'They'll be on us before we get half a mile.' She waved at the cocoons. 'Think how slow we'll be carrying those.'

'What do you suggest?' snapped Volant. 'Waiting in here for the next attack? We will be–'

He had to pause as, outside in the square, the giant fell through another building, rune-light flashing across its skull as Gotrek attacked its face.

'Use that,' said Trachos, nodding to the back of the hall, towards a looming, shell-like curve that reached almost as high as the ceiling.

Maleneth shook her head. 'What?'

'The aether-ship,' replied Trachos.

'The *Spindrift*?' said Lhosia. 'Do you think you could revive it the same way as the other machines?'

Trachos shrugged. 'Why not? Duardin engineering is built to last. It's probably just inert.'

Prince Volant shook his head. 'The forefathers used obscure techniques – the rune-science of the Kharadron.'

Trachos nodded. 'They used aether-gold.' He peered at the vessel. 'Is it likely to have been plundered?'

Lhosia looked appalled by the suggestion, and Volant shook his head. 'We revere the past. Our relics are sacred to us.'

Trachos nodded and limped off to the back of the hall.

Maleneth rushed after him. He had taken out his sceptre and clicked a new device to its head. It looked like a square goblet, formed of wire mesh and studded with gems.

The aether-ship was in the one part of the hall not illuminated by the light of the Unburied – a gloomy, barrel-vaulted recess like the undercroft of a cathedral. The half-visible leviathan loomed from the shadows like a promontory on a stretch of coast.

The mesh at the end of Trachos' sceptre blazed into life, spilling fingers of cool blue light.

'Khaine,' whispered Maleneth as the light washed over the prow. The figurehead was in the shape of a fierce, howling face, with a long, stylised beard and a thunderous brow. The face was as large as a house, and as Trachos' light glinted across the tarnished metal, it seemed to glower and snarl.

'It looks like him,' said Maleneth.

Trachos glanced back at her. 'Who?'

'The hog. Gotrek.'

Trachos nodded. 'Whatever he is now, he was a duardin once. The shipwrights who made this were too.'

He strode over to the hull and climbed onto an iron ladder that led up between the gun ports. A thunderclap of moths exploded from the darkness, thousands of them, alighting from every corner of the ship.

Maleneth shielded her face, and Trachos had to pause until the tumult ceased, then continued climbing. Maleneth wondered at the size of the vessel. She guessed it was fifty feet tall from rudder to gunwale, and she could just make out an armour-plated dome rising from the deck. It looked more like an impregnable fortress than a ship.

The moths had disturbed centuries of dust, and as she stepped onto the deck, Maleneth felt as though she had walked into a sandstorm. She coughed and cursed as she looked around. The vessel was unlike any ship she had ever seen. The deck was built in the shape of an enormous cross. It was actually four decks, arranged like the spokes of a wheel and linked by a circular walkway. The whole thing was like an enormous cog.

With the dust still whirling around her, she stumbled after the hazy silhouette of the Stormcast Eternal. He reached the dome at the intersection of the four decks, the hub of the 'wheel', and dropped to one knee, taking another device from his belt. There was a whirr and a click, and just as Maleneth reached him, a circular hatch opened in the deck. It slid aside with a mechanised rattle, and pulses of light shimmered under Trachos, flickering over the ruined plates of his armour.

Without a word, he turned around and climbed down into the darkness. Maleneth hurried after him.

Trachos' light flashed over a tangled forest of pipes and cogs. The belly of the ship was crammed with machinery, and as it flickered into view, Maleneth was surprised to see how well preserved it was.

'No rust,' she said, touching a row of pistons, tracing her finger over the carefully worked metal. Every inch was engraved with runes.

Trachos' faceplate looked almost as fierce as the ship's figurehead. The usual impassive gaze of his Stormcast Eternal helmet was rent beyond recognition, and with the light of his sceptre washing over the buckled metal he seemed to leer at her. He turned back to the machines and began working at them.

The light grew brighter, shimmering across cables and turbines, just as it had on the machines outside, then flickered and died.

Trachos took out the pair of callipers he had used at the gatehouse, measuring and twisting the mechanisms. He worked calmly at first, but after a few minutes he grew agitated, muttering curses under his breath.

He clanged the callipers against the pipes and strode across the engine room, examining cables and wiring and tapping gauges.

'It should be working!' He wrenched a circular hatch open and prodded the workings inside the case. 'The aether-gold *is* still here. There's no reason for the engines not to fire.'

He halted, spotting something in the forest of pipes and levers.

'Of course!' He grabbed it. 'The conduits have split. There's no pressure.'

Maleneth stepped closer and saw the two lengths of cable he was holding. Unlike everything else, they had perished and crumbled.

'Aether-gold is corrosive.' Trachos dropped the pipes and wiped his gauntlets on his armour. 'The Kharadron probably replace these conduits regularly to keep them working.'

'So we can't fire up the engines?'

'We'd need some way to channel the aether-gold.' Trachos stared up at the hatch. 'It's not so different from the machines that were holding the Unburied.'

'So we could use Gotrek's rune again?'

'Perhaps. If he's happy to come down here and let the aether-power blast through him. If he doesn't mind being used as an engine part.'

Maleneth raised an eyebrow. 'Ah…'

They stood in silence for a moment, then heard footfalls up on the deck and clambered back up the ladder, weapons readied.

It was Gotrek. He was trembling with battle fury and staring wildly. Rune-light rippled over his skin and his beard, spilling through the gloom. The knights of the Gravesward were behind him, carrying the cocoons onto the deck under the watchful eye of Prince Volant. Lhosia was there too, standing with the prince, and the pair were locked in a whispered debate.

'Did you kill it?' asked Maleneth as she rushed towards Gotrek.

'What?'

'The giant ghoul.'

He shrugged. 'He won't be breaking any more doors, let's put it that way. Unless someone puts his ugly head on a battering ram.'

'What do you intend to do?' asked Prince Volant, looming over Gotrek. 'You swore to preserve the Unburied, and we are running out of time.'

Gotrek looked at Trachos.

'The engines are intact,' said Trachos. 'And there's plenty of aether-gold on board. We just need a conduit – a way to channel the power. A powerful piece of ur-gold would do it.'

Gotrek nodded, then realisation dawned in his eye. 'Me? You want to use me as an engine part?'

'Your rune is powerful enough to channel the aether-gold.' Trachos' voice remained dull and flat. 'Nothing else could handle it.'

Gotrek tapped the rune. 'And what would be left of me when the journey was over? How much would be Gotrek and how much would be Grimnir?'

His beard bristled, and he looked so furious that Maleneth backed away, readying herself to dodge his axe.

'Grungni's teeth,' he snarled, scowling at the rune. It was still rippling with energy. The aether-light was spreading from the rune into Gotrek's veins, pulsing across his chest and revealing the arteries beneath his scarred skin. It looked like rivulets of molten gold passing under his ribs.

'I refuse to keep doing this,' said Gotrek, not looking at Maleneth. 'I did not come all this way to give my soul to the one god who betrayed me more than any other.'

Trachos grabbed one of his massive biceps. 'There *is* another way.'

Gotrek glanced up at the Stormcast Eternal in shock. Then he glowered. 'What way is that? Trot meekly into one of Sigmar's sparkly towers and prostrate myself before his greatness? Oh, Hammer Lord, let me comb your mighty beard! That sort of thing?'

'There's no need to worship him. Your soul is your own. Your faith is your own. The Order of Azyr only needs the power you wield.'

'And how exactly would you get it out of me? Last time I checked, my ribs weren't hinged.'

Trachos seemed oblivious to Gotrek's rage. 'The power isn't just in you. It's *part* of you. If you harnessed it in Sigmar's name we could–'

'In Sigmar's name?' Gotrek's face flushed with anger and the rune pulsed brighter. He slammed against Trachos, about to yell something else, when they were interrupted by the sound of fighting back in the hall.

'Mordants!' cried several Gravesward as they ran towards the ship, struggling under the weight of the last few cocoons. 'Hundreds of them.'

Volant cursed. He knelt down so that he was facing the Slayer. His tone was an awkward mix of outrage and desperation. 'I *could* send you to Nagash, Gotrek, son of Gurni, but only if you get my ancestors to the Lingering Keep. And only if we leave *right* now.'

A growl rumbled up from Gotrek's chest and he gripped his mohawk, wrenching his hair back and forth as though trying to rip it out. He stared at the shapes rushing through the shadows towards the ship, muttering angrily under his breath. Then he nodded, spat on the deck and climbed down the hatch, waving for Trachos to follow him.

Maleneth shook her head. 'I never dreamed he'd do it.' She looked at the cocoons. 'I suggest you tie those things down.'

CHAPTER NINETEEN

THE EVENTIDE

I refuse to be sick, thought Maleneth as the world turned around her. Even over the roar of the engines, she could hear people groaning and vomiting across the deck. She had lashed herself to the railings, but the ship was shaking so violently that she was covered in bruises.

'God of Murder,' she groaned. 'How long will this take?'

'Hours at most!' cried Lord Aurun from a few feet away. He looked exhilarated. 'Look how fast the *Spindrift* is!'

She shook her head and looked out at the sea. The waves were shimmering, illuminated by the ship's blue-green light. It gave them the illusion of movement, and seen in such snatched glimpses, it could almost have been a natural sea. Rather than crashing through the breakers, though, the aether-ship was lurching drunkenly over them, gliding a few feet above the pitted surface, hurled by the arcane science of its Kharadron-wrought engines. Light knifed through the seams in its iron hull, splitting Morbium's endless dark.

Every now and then she heard Gotrek cry out, his voice rising up from beneath her like the howl of a wounded leviathan. Trachos was down in the engine room with him, battling to harness the aether-gold Gotrek was channelling, but Maleneth was glad to be nowhere near them. There were alternating bouts of anger, confusion and excitement in the Slayer's voice. He sounded even more unstable than usual. Even though he was hidden from her, his presence was unmissable – beams of golden light were shining up through the deck plating. It looked like the ship had a piece of the sun stowed in its bilges.

At the end of another deck she could see Prince Volant, standing unaided at the wheel, legs apart as he struggled to keep his footing. Lhosia was at his side, tied to the gunwale and cradling one of the Unburied. She was crying out instructions to the prince, and he responded by wrenching the levers and handles that surrounded the huge brass wheel.

'What did I do to deserve this?' muttered Maleneth.

Murder the one person who ever cared for you?

Despite her nausea, Maleneth laughed. '*Cared* for me? Cared for my blood, you mean. And only in the way a cat cares for a mouse.'

You never understood me, Witchblade.

'I understood you as well as I needed.'

And look where it got you.

'It's got me within reach of that rune. And once I have it, no one in Azyrheim will say a word against me. I'll be the hero of the Order. The hero of the age! Sigmar himself will want to meet me.'

You're no closer to getting your hands on that thing. I've told you the key, but you're too ignorant to listen.

'The key? What key? And why would I listen to you? What possible reason could you have to help me?'

Anger crept into her mistress' voice. *Khaine. You're as dim-witted as the Slayer. What do you think will happen to me if you die down here?*

Maleneth rarely heard anything other than derision from the blood amulet. There was something intriguing about this new, furious tone. She started to pay attention. 'You're already dead. What does it matter to you if I live or die?'

Whatever this is, it is not death, Witchblade. Do you think this is just your subconscious speaking to you? Do you think I'm merely a fragment of your mind?

Maleneth shrugged. 'The thought had occurred.'

Her mistress' anger grew as she was forced to speak so plainly. *Idiot girl. You have captured a facet of my soul. While you live I retain a portion of life. A wretched morsel, admittedly, and attached to your disastrous existence, but it is all I have.*

Maleneth cradled the amulet in her hand, studying the dark liquid at its heart, smiling. 'Yes, the most suitable torment I could think of. Letting a piece of you live on, powerless, watching me ascend to the heights you dreamed of.'

Play your facile games, Witchblade, but if you do not steal that rune from the Slayer, neither of us will leave Shyish.

'Then cease your prattling and stop talking in riddles. If you really want to help me, if you really do have an idea, share it.' She took the blood vial from the amulet and dangled it over the rolling deck. 'If my games are so facile, perhaps I will abandon them? Perhaps I will rob you of your chance to watch my ascension?'

Put that back! I will tell you what I saw.

'You will.' Maleneth smiled, rolling the vial between her fingers, revelling in the power she held over her former betrayer. 'And you will do it quickly.'

Khaine curse you. I will make you pay. I will–

'You will dribble across this deck and be forgotten. Unless you speak up quickly.'

Very well! I will speak so plainly even you might understand. Do you remember watching the priestess commune with her ancestor?

Maleneth nodded.

What did she say?

Maleneth laughed. 'She warned us to keep away because she would be so "fragile".'

Exactly – her body grew brittle and she warned you not to touch her. And the padlock she wears around her neck. Can you remember what happened to that?

'Nothing. *Nothing* happened to it.'

Precisely. Her flesh was transformed. She grew brittle and weak, but her necklace was unchanged. What if the Slayer were transformed in such a way? He would be so brittle and weak he could be smashed like porcelain.

Maleneth slumped back against the gunwale, her pulse racing. 'Of course. And the rune would be left intact.'

It's ur-gold. Tempered by that duardin rune master back in Aqshy. And Gotrek's not truly a fyreslayer. He has no interest in their god. That rune does not belong in his body. If you destroyed his flesh, the Rune of Blackhammer would be left in the broken shards.

'And how would we move this ship if Gotrek was dead?'

Think! You only need the rune to channel the ship's power. You don't need the oaf.

Maleneth shook her head, still dubious. '*Why* are you helping me?'

You're all I have, you fool. If I don't help you, you will die down here and I will be... I will be nothing.

There was genuine emotion in the voice. Maleneth could not believe her mistress was telling the absolute truth, but perhaps it was part of the truth. And the idea was a good one. She laughed. 'And how do you suggest I convince Gotrek Gurnisson to worship moths and hug corpses?'

Even in a mind as barren as yours, some of my training must have taken root. Think. I have given you the key. Find a way to use it.

Maleneth shook her head. 'He would never–'

She gasped. 'Khaine.' All across the deck, Gotrek's rune-light blazed brighter, dazzling her again.

'Valaya's teeth!' howled the Slayer. It sounded like he was in pain.

Maleneth was blinded for several unpleasant minutes. She tried crawling into a foetal position to ease the nausea, but that made her feel like she was one of the cadavers in the cocoons. She tried standing to see if that was any better, just as Gotrek let out another howl.

A few seconds later, Maleneth breathed a sigh of relief. The aether-ship was slowing down. The spinning motion of the decks grew slower and slower until, with a final, metallic screech of gears, the whole thing ground to a halt.

After all the noise and movement that had preceded it, the quiet was eerie. Everyone on the deck glanced around in confusion.

Maleneth stood on trembling legs and looked out across the waves. There was nothing but the peaks and troughs of the Eventide. 'Lord Aurun?' she called out. 'What is this? Why have we stopped?'

The knight shook his head, frowning as he looked up towards Lhosia and Prince Volant.

The prince strode across the deck and stamped on the hatch to the engine room. 'Slayer! What happened?'

There was no answer.

Maleneth muttered a curse and untied herself, then staggered across to the hatch. 'Let me speak to him,' she said, opening it and climbing down the ladder.

The engines were still sparking with rune-light, and she spied Trachos way down in the bilges, at the bottom of a second ladder. She continued down and rushed over to him. The air was hazy with bitter-smelling smoke, and it took her a moment to spot Gotrek, sprawled against the engines. His muscle-bloated frame was shimmering with energy. He looked like a star chart, covered in lines and intersections, all centred on the rune.

'Grimnir's taking me,' he grunted. 'And I'll not stand for it!' Dozens of cables dangled from his chest where Trachos had attached him to the ship's engines. 'I'm not a bloody fuel pipe!'

Trachos shook his head. 'The Master Rune is the only way to channel the aether-gold. And without aether-gold we have no way to move this ship.'

Prince Volant had climbed down after Maleneth. He leant through the acrid fumes. 'You swore an oath. Are you breaking your word?'

Gotrek struggled to his feet and glared up at Volant. 'I'm no oathbreaker. I'll get your moth eggs home.' He looked down at the rune. 'But there has to be a better way.'

He jostled the cables and scowled at Trachos. 'This rune is a vampire, manling. Think of something else.' Rune-fire flashed across his beard as he talked. 'Another hour of this and there'll be nothing left of me.'

Trachos rattled the broken cables. 'These are ruined. We need your rune.'

Now. Now's your chance!

The voice spoke with such vehemence that Maleneth half expected the others to hear it.

She looked from the raging Slayer to Trachos and then to Lhosia, who was halfway down the ladder, watching the exchange. She thought hard about what her mistress had said. If she could convince the Slayer to commune with the corpses, he would be vulnerable, and the rune would be within her grasp.

'Is there a way…?' she began, her voice faltering, unsure what she was going to say.

Everyone turned to stare at her.

She looked up at Lhosia. 'Did you say the Unburied power your fortresses?'

Lhosia nodded.

'I wonder...' She shrugged, ready to be ridiculed. 'Could they help us use Gotrek's rune in some *other* way? If your ancestors could see it – if they could understand its nature – could they release its power without causing Gotrek to be changed like this? If they could channel the power from the rune, it could still work as a conduit for the aether-gold.'

Volant shook his head, but Lhosia peered at Gotrek with interest.

'I do not understand the nature of that rune, but the Unburied understand most things. Some were alive when the Kharadron sold us the *Spindrift*. One way or another, I'm sure they could help.' She looked back up towards the deck. 'If Gotrek were willing to join me in communion with the Unburied...'

Gotrek backed away, his eye flashing. 'Join you? You want to join me to those *things*? Not a chance.' He started to climb up the ladder, and the others followed.

'You would only need to sit with me to join the communion,' said Lhosia as she emerged onto the deck.

'No.' Gotrek was stomping around, glaring at the cocoons.

'We need to do *something*,' said Lord Aurun, staring out across the sea. 'Look.'

They all peered into the darkness.

'What is that?' asked Maleneth. With the rune-light gone, it was hard to see far across the waves. 'Is the sea moving?'

Prince Volant muttered a curse and shook his head. 'Archers!' he cried. 'Ready your bows!' He turned to the scythe-wielding knights gathered around them. 'Prepare to be boarded.'

Maleneth crossed the deck and leant out over the rail until her eyes made sense of the movement. Thousands of ghouls were rushing over the Eventide, scrambling up the dusty waves and sprinting towards the ship.

There was a rattle of armour as the knights drew scythes and raised shields while the archers rushed into position.

Try him again. Force him.

Maleneth rushed over to Gotrek, who was glowering at the approaching horde.

'Look how many there are,' she whispered, leaning close.

'I can take them.' He rolled his shoulders with a cracking sound and raised his axe.

At what cost? prompted the voice in her head.

'At what cost?' she echoed, waving a knife at the massing shadows. 'What will be left of you when the fighting is done? You'll have to call on every ounce of the rune's power.'

He glared at her, then down at the rune with even more anger.

'Think about it,' she said. 'If these Unburied know half as much as the priestess thinks they do, they may be able to find a way for you to use the rune's power without giving yourself to Grimnir. Wouldn't that answer all of your problems?'

Lhosia was standing a few feet away, watching the exchange. 'I believe they could help,' she said.

'Get this ship moving!' roared Prince Volant, striding across the deck to where his steed was waiting. 'I will hold them as long as I can.'

'You're going out there alone?' Gotrek looked impressed.

Volant nodded as he mounted the skeleton drake. 'I won't lose these souls to those animals.'

The creature spread its skinless wings and pounded them, hanging over the ship as the prince stared down at Gotrek. Volant kicked his steed into motion and rocketed off into the darkness, hurtling towards the approaching horde.

Gotrek watched him go in silence. The rage slipped from his

gnarled features, and Maleneth was surprised to see how the prince's words had moved him.

He respects him, she realised. She looked at the knights waiting around the ship in stoic silence, prepared to die for their ancestors. *He likes them.*

Light flashed in the darkness as Prince Volant reached the first wave of ghouls. He scythed trails of amethyst through the night, lashing out at the teeming figures beneath him.

'Archers!' cried Lord Aurun from a few feet further up the deck. 'On my order!'

There was a clatter of arrows being nocked.

Gotrek gave Maleneth one last glare, then turned to Lhosia and nodded. 'Do it quickly. Before I change my mind.'

Stand ready. Watch for him changing. The Stormcast Eternal will try to protect him if he realises what you're doing.

Trachos was nearby, watching Gotrek and Lhosia in silence.

Maleneth was about to suggest he head below decks to examine the engines, but then she forgot all about him, entranced by the bizarre transformation taking place.

Lhosia had sunk one hand into the cocoon and begun singing. The rag-like covering started to glow, revealing twitching shapes beneath as Lhosia placed her other hand on Gotrek's rune.

As Lhosia murmured her song, Gotrek's weathered muscles started to lose their chestnut colour, turning the same ash-white as the cocoon.

'Grungni's oath,' he whispered, his skin becoming a white carapace.

'Keep still,' murmured Lhosia. 'And close your eyes.'

Maleneth had been so amazed by the transformation that she had momentarily forgotten why she had engineered the whole fiasco. She stepped closer, gripping her knives, pleased to see that Trachos was too busy staring at Gotrek to notice what she was doing.

She flinched as a dreadful shriek rang through the night.

Trachos whirled around and the Erebid soldiers staggered, lowering their weapons. Only Lhosia seemed unaffected, so far gone in her ritual that she was oblivious to the noise. Gotrek cursed, but remained still.

Now!

Maleneth ignored her mistress, looking out across the sea for the source of the horrific screech.

There was a flash of purple light, and Volant's steed hurtled beneath a looming shadow.

The shadow let out another scream, even louder than the first.

Pain seared through Maleneth's skull. It was like knives jamming into her head.

Aurun ordered to his men to loose their arrows, but the archers were reeling in pain and their shots hit nothing but air.

Gotrek growled, tormented by the sound but unable to cover his ears. As he snarled, the rune in his chest pulsed back into life, scattering glimmers of light between Lhosia's fingers and sparking in his eye.

'What's happening?' gasped Maleneth as rune-light flashed through Lhosia's robes, down her arm and into the cocoon.

The figure within flashed like kindling and Lhosia gasped.

The anger faded from Gotrek's eye as he stared down the deck.

'I see them,' he muttered, sounding dazed.

Now!

Maleneth ignored the voice in her head. She had followed Gotrek's gaze and seen something incredible. Across the ship, every one of the cocoons was lighting up, mirroring the one in Lhosia's arms and burning with rune-light. The light rippled across the metal deck and shimmered down the pipes that ran under the gunwales.

Something juddered beneath Maleneth's feet, then settled into a steady rumble.

'The aether-gold,' said Trachos, hurrying back to the hatch and vanishing below decks.

Maleneth gasped in agony as the screech sliced into her head again.

Prince Volant was directly overhead, thirty feet or so above the ship's dome, locked in battle with a grotesque mockery of his own steed – an undead horror, its wings trailing shreds of dead skin and its jaws ripped back in a fixed snarl. This was the source of the dreadful shrieking. The creatures clawed and snapped as Volant lashed out with his scythe.

Out on the Eventide, the ghouls were slipping and tumbling across the waves, and some had reached the *Spindrift*. The ship was drifting so low that the creatures were able to bound up its hull and clamber over the railings.

The Gravesward raised their shields as slavering wretches slammed into them.

Aurun leapt into the fray, howling orders. Scythes flashed, scattering limbs and sending ghouls toppling from the ship.

'It's moving!' cried Maleneth, dodging a headless mordant as it slapped onto the deck. She looked around in wonder as the Unburied burned brighter and the ship screeched into motion, turning around its central dome.

Prince Volant crowed in triumph, bathed in arcane light as he beheaded the screaming monster. It thrashed its vast, bat-like wings, then flipped backwards, crashing into the crowds of ghouls.

The prince swooped across the deck. 'Lash yourselves to the ship! Tie yourselves down!'

As the *Spindrift* picked up speed, lots of the monsters fell back onto the waves below, but some were still loose on the deck.

While the soldiers obeyed the prince and began tying themselves to masts and gunwales, Lord Aurun strode across the decks, hacking furiously at the ghouls and hurling them over the railings.

Maleneth dashed to his side, opening the throat of a mordant that was about to pounce on him from behind. Aurun turned in time to see her rip the blade out and kick the gasping creature over the railings. He nodded in thanks before striding past her to return the favour, slicing his scythe through a ghoul that was about to leap on Maleneth.

They weaved across the deck, protecting the Erebid as the ship gained speed, juddering and rolling so violently that Maleneth felt as though she were drunk, reeling and staggering as she fought.

'Bravely done, aelf,' gasped Lord Aurun as he stumbled past her, making for the dome. 'Now tie yourself to something!'

She fell backwards, the motion of the aether-ship wrong-footing her, sending her plummeting through the air towards the Eventide.

A hand locked around her wrist, jolting her arm painfully in its socket as someone hauled her back onto the deck, lashing her quickly to the ship before it lurched again.

'You're making a habit of this,' she gasped when she realised who her saviour was.

Trachos nodded as he checked the ropes he had used to secure her. 'I'll take that as a thank you.'

His turn of phrase was so natural she laughed in surprise. 'Was that a *joke?*'

He made a sound that might have been a laugh.

'What happened to you?' She tried to peer through the eye-holes in his helmet. Hearing Trachos speak so normally seemed even more miraculous than the power ripping through Gotrek and Lhosia.

When he had finished checking his knots, Trachos sat back against the railings, shaking his head. 'Your plan is working. The Unburied are somehow directing the rune-fire down into the engines. Aether-gold is flowing freely through the engine.'

Maleneth shook her head in disbelief. The last thing she had expected was that her absurd plan would work. She gripped the railings as the decks turned faster around the dome.

Trachos looked over to where the bone-white Slayer was still sitting with the priestess, surrounded by a nimbus of aetheric currents. Unlike everyone else on board, they were calm, not tied down in any way, fixed to the spot by the energy burning through them, linking their brittle shells to the cocoons lying around the ship.

'He…' said Trachos, shaking his head as if unable to complete his thought.

'Gotrek?' Maleneth frowned. '*He* what?'

Trachos sounded confused. 'I was forged in the light of Sigendil, by the will of the God-King. Sorcery has no power over me. And yet I feel the Slayer has changed me in some way.'

'*Something* has changed. You sound almost intelligible.'

'The Slayer had faith in me,' he muttered. 'When I did not.'

Maleneth laughed in disbelief. 'I have never understood humans, Stormcast Eternals even less so. You sound like those dispossessed duardin who wanted to pray to him.'

'I raised the gatehouse,' Trachos replied gruffly. 'I freed those cocoons, when the Erebid thought it was impossible. I made this vessel move.' He looked up at the spinning stars. 'I felt Sigmar's power working through me again, as surely as I did when I was first forged in Azyr.'

Maleneth leant closer to him, lowering her voice. 'So?'

He laughed. The sound did not seem at home, coming from his battle-scored faceplate. 'I think, perhaps, I am starting to make peace with my god. And it would not have happened without the Slayer.' He looked back at Gotrek. 'What *is* he, Witchblade?'

Maleneth was about to mock his reverent tone, but as she glanced at Gotrek, hurling the *Spindrift* through the dark, haloed by the souls of the Unburied, the words snagged in her throat.

CHAPTER TWENTY

THE LINGERING KEEP

Maleneth was shocked to realise that she had fallen asleep. The motion of the *Spindrift* had settled into a steady, loping rhythm, and she had gone untold days without rest, but she still cursed as she woke, grabbing her knives and glancing around for attackers.

Trachos was at her side, his massive, battered armour shielding her from the wind. Beyond the ship the darkness was absolute, but Gotrek and Lhosia were still engulfed in a dazzling corona, scattering splashes of purple and gold over the Eventide.

The grinding of the engines was unchanged, but there was a new sound rising, an oceanic roar that Maleneth guessed was the reason she had awoken.

'What is that?' she asked, but as the decks completed another rotation, her question was answered. Up ahead, just a few miles away from the prow of the *Spindrift*, was a colossal fortress. It was the largest structure she had seen since arriving in Shyish, and it was built in the same style as the Barren Points – a tangled briar of iron and bone, curving and bur-like with looping, knotted towers. It burned purple on the horizon, like a sinking violet sun.

'The capital,' replied Trachos. His voice had regained some of the automaton-like coldness. 'They call it the Lingering Keep.'

'That noise.' She frowned. 'Is that cheering?'

He nodded and pointed past the prow.

A few hundred feet ahead of the ship, Prince Volant was flying through the flashing lights, leading his honour guard of mounted knights. His scythe was held victoriously over his head, and the crowds on the city walls had raised their voices in tribute.

'You'd think he'd won a war,' she sneered. 'Rather than organising a hasty retreat.'

'He has returned to them. Perhaps they did not expect him to.' Trachos pointed at the cocoons on the deck. 'And he has returned with these.'

They both fell quiet as they watched the city rushing towards them, taking a moment to study the strangeness of the place. As its sharp, thorny details grew clearer, Maleneth realised just how vast it was. It was almost on the scale of the free cities built by her own order. There was a curved, tusk-like tower right at its centre, many hundreds of feet tall, soaring over the rest of the barb-like structures, glittering with narrow arrow-slit windows. 'Prince Volant's palace, I presume,' she said, pointing it out.

'No. I heard Lord Aurun talking while you were asleep. That tower is called the Halls of Separation. That's where the Erebid need to take their ancestors.' Again, he surprised Maleneth with how normal he sounded. 'How unique those buildings are. I have never seen such strange architecture. I wonder if in all of Shyish there are two underworlds that look the same. We all have such a different idea of what lies beyond the grave.'

'There will be no grave for you.' She raised her knife in the air with a dramatic flourish. 'You live on! Stormcast Eternal! Unfettered by mortality! A light in the darkness! Burning for all eternity!'

He studied her from behind his battered faceplate. 'You're mocking me.'

Maleneth lowered her blade and shook her head. 'I *was*, but you're too damned earnest for it to be any fun.'

He maintained his stare. 'I had a normal life. I was a mortal man before Sigmar chose me to join his Stormhosts. I was destined to live, hate, love and die just like everyone else.' He looked at the approaching city. 'Who knows, perhaps this would have been *my* afterlife? I do not even recall what nation I belonged to before I became…' He tapped his armour. 'Before I was remade in Sigmar's image. But whatever fate was allotted to me has been taken. I serve the God-King. And nothing else matters.'

Maleneth shrugged. 'What more could you want? You serve your god through strength and courage. You spill blood in his name. You rid the realms of his enemies. Isn't that enough?'

'As long as I can remember whose blood to spill.' He shook his head. 'My god is not like yours, aelf. Khaine requires you to give him blood and power. He has no interest beyond that. The God-King does not seek power merely for its own sake.'

She sneered. 'You really have been reborn, haven't you? Have you forgotten what happened to you last time you were in Shyish? Are you so sure Sigmar's creations are as perfect and divine as all that? Are you really so different from me?' She leant closer. 'Why did Sigmar send hammer-wielding killers into the realms? Was it to broker peace? Was it to negotiate a truce? No. He sent you to wreak murder and ruin. Your god is no different from mine. Every time you crush another skull, Sigmar smiles, Lord Ordinator. Every drop of blood is a tribute.'

'You're wrong. Sigmar sent his Stormhosts to free mankind from the yoke of its oppressors. To save it from tyranny.'

'And what about when you were killing those unarmed families, Trachos? Were you freeing them from tyranny?' Maleneth's voice was full of scorn, but she realised, to her surprise, that she was genuinely interested to hear his answer.

Trachos nodded. 'I *have* strayed close to the precipice. But now I see that there is hope, even with this tiny ember of humanity I have left, I can–'

The cheers suddenly grew in fervour, drowning Trachos out, and she saw that they had nearly reached the city walls.

'What?' she said, wanting to hear what Trachos had to say, but it seemed he could not hear her over the din.

They both stood up and watched over the railings as the rotations of the *Spindrift* began to slow.

The light around Gotrek and the priestess faded, giving the pair a less divine appearance.

Your chance is almost gone, said Maleneth's former mistress. *In a few more minutes he will be flesh and blood again. You'll have to move now if you want to get that rune.*

He's surrounded by soldiers, Maleneth thought. *And he's in the process of saving all of our lives. Do you really expect me to plant a knife in him now?*

She untied herself and climbed stiffly to her feet, slapping her cramped limbs and stretching her back until the *Spindrift* was steady enough for her to cross the deck and approach the Slayer.

Trachos clanked after her.

You'll have no chance with the Stormcast Eternal watching. Get him away. Trick him into going below decks.

Maleneth ignored the voice, staring at Gotrek. His eye was closed and, like Lhosia, he was sitting completely still. His skin was still pale and shell-like, and he looked more like a statue than a living being. Robbed of his erratic, surly manner and bombastic voice, he seemed an entirely different proposition. Traces of light still played around him, and she could almost imagine that the people of Morbium were cheering for him rather than their prince. They certainly would be if they knew what he had done.

Something is happening here, she thought. *Something is happening with this Slayer. He is not like anything I have encountered before.*

Fool. Stop being pathetic! Look! His skin is almost normal again. Do it now.

It's more than just the rune, she decided. *He is destined for something. Whatever he thinks of gods, I think one of them has sent him here. He must have some kind of divine patron. How else could he have faced everything he has faced, with so little planning or logic, and still be alive? He's brutish and thoughtless and has no ounce of finesse, but nothing touches him. How can that be? Something is* propelling *him through these trials, directing him and loading him with power. And if I killed him here, now, I would never know what it was – or what Gotrek is. What he's here for.*

Blood of Khaine! What are you talking about? He's not propelled by a god – he's propelled by stupidity. There's no divinity in that sweating lump. Look at him! You said it yourself – he's a talking hog, too ignorant to recognise the danger he keeps throwing himself in. The only thing he's here for is to destroy himself in the most vainglorious way possible. There is nothing to be gained by letting him live. Kill him now, while you have the chance. Give him the doom he wants, or you will die here. With these vile people. And so will I.

Maleneth shook her head.

Gotrek opened his eye, blinking and confused, looking as if he had spent a night drinking. He caught sight of Maleneth and Trachos, watching him in dazed wonder.

'Grungni's balls. Why are you looking at me like that?'

Lhosia opened her eyes at the sound of his voice and gazed at the lights, fading quickly around the deck as the *Spindrift* slowed.

'It worked,' she said, glancing over the prow at the city as she lifted her hand from Gotrek's rune.

Gotrek stood, rolled his shoulders and sniffed, making a long, liquid rattling sound. 'What next, lass?' He stomped over to the railing and looked out at the prince and the walls of the Lingering Keep. 'Where do we need to take these things before your prince will consider them saved?'

Lhosia gently removed her hand from the cocoon, and across the ship, the lights began to fade. 'Incredible,' she whispered. 'I've never seen anything like it. They were *all* present. Every one of the Unburied. There were a thousand souls on this ship.'

'Priestess!' bellowed Gotrek, waving her over to the railings and nodding to the city. 'What now?'

Lord Aurun staggered towards them, flanked by Gravesward. He was covered in cuts and bruises, but his eyes were bright.

'Now the prince will perform his rite.' He gestured at the cocoons. 'With the Unburied assembled in the Lingering Keep, he will be able to save them.' He smiled at Lhosia. 'The prince told me you and he will harness the light of a magic stone. He said you will rebuild the Iron Shroud and put an end to this invasion.'

The wonder faded from Lhosia's eyes. 'Would that it were that simple, old friend. The prince has a powerful relic called the Cerement Stone. He believes that with the Unburied in the Lingering Keep, he and I will be able to channel their power into the stone and create a new ward, strong enough to protect them. We will be able to keep them safe from the mordants. It will be a *kind* of Iron Shroud, but not one that will protect the whole princedom.' She looked back the way they had come, at the vast darkness that had once been lit by the prominents. 'Nothing can be done for the rest of Morbium.'

'But if we are locked away in the capital, what will become of us?' said Aurun. 'Wouldn't we starve?'

'The prince has not shared all the details with me.' She shook her head, looking grim. 'He said nothing of our survival, only of the Unburied.'

Aurun frowned as the ship's momentum carried them over the final approach to the city and the ship rumbled to a halt. It bumped to a stop alongside a broad wynd that led to a set of enormous gates forged to resemble folded wings, mirroring the shield designs of the Gravesward. The highway teemed with refugees, hundreds of exhausted-looking people hauling carts and sacks towards the city. Many of them were wounded, and they all looked emaciated, but they were cheering Prince Volant with even more gusto than the soldiers on the battlements.

The soldiers on the boat leapt to action, hurling ropes to the wynd, where gaunt-faced refugees grabbed them and tied the aether-ship to the metal road.

Lord Aurun led the way down a gangplank, proud and victorious, waving to people like a monarch as the rest of the ship's passengers trailed after him.

Gotrek was right beside Aurun, looking eagerly up at the city gates as Maleneth and Trachos hurried after him.

The Gravesward formed an avenue of shields for them to march down, and as Prince Volant soared overhead, over the city walls, Aurun and the others marched through the gates, entering a square crowded with hundreds more refugees and soldiers.

The noise was incredible. The people saw the cocoons and cheered even louder, crying, 'Morbium Eternal!'

Prince Volant landed in the centre of the square, his bone steed clattering against the flagstones. He dropped from his saddle, attempting to look triumphant but unable to completely hide the fact that he was injured. He moved in awkward, sudden lurches, but waved his men away when they rushed to help.

'I have kept the oath of the Morn-Princes!' he cried, looming over the crowd. 'I will never abandon our past!' He waved his scythe at the cocoons, which were being carried into the square. 'We *will* endure!'

The crowd hurled his words back at him.

'Incredible,' whispered Maleneth to Gotrek. 'They've lost their entire kingdom and now they're cheering a half-dead prince.'

Gotrek glared at her. 'They kept their oath. That means nothing to an aelf, but it means a lot to them. I thought these realms were peopled solely by treacherous thagi and cack-handed morons. But these people are prepared to risk everything for the honour of their ancestors.' He took a deep breath, threw back his shoulders and punched his chest. 'It does me good, aelf. It does me good to see this. Perhaps not *all* of the old ways have been forgotten.'

They joined the crowd around Prince Volant as he continued his speech, describing the battles he had fought to save the Unburied as more and more people crushed into the square.

'They look worse than their pet corpses,' muttered Maleneth. 'And what do they think will happen when the ghouls get here?'

Gotrek was about to answer when a loud clattering sound announced the approach of more soldiers. A column of Gravesward entered the square, riding beneath an arch and heading straight for the prince. They were mounted on wingless versions of the prince's skeleton steed, and their armour showed no signs of battle, shimmering with a dull lustre in the light that spilled through the streets. There was a carriage at the head of the column that looked like a mobile ossuary – an elaborate construction of sharpened bones led by four bleached, fleshless horses. As the carriage reached Volant, a knight climbed down. He wore a wreath of iron rose petals and held himself with the casual, languid bearing of an aristocrat.

'Your majesty!' the noble called out across the noise of the crowd. 'The Unburied prophesied your return, but it is wonderful to see you so soon.'

Prince Volant laughed. 'Soon?' He gazed out across the crowd, studying the crowded streets. 'We must talk, Captain Ridens.'

The captain nodded and gestured to a nearby building. 'The chapter house, your majesty. We will have privacy in there.'

The knights made another colonnade of shields, and they passed through the crowds and approached a tall, narrow building that looked quite different from those around it. Most of the architecture that lined the square was built of the same bone-like contortions as the rest of the city, but this building was a slab of ink-black stone and its design was simple and unadorned. The only decoration was a pair of folded white moth wings on the door.

The captain led the way inside, closely followed by Prince Volant, who had to stoop under the doorframe, High Priestess Lhosia, Gotrek, Maleneth, Trachos and finally Lord Aurun and a detachment of Gravesward. Aurun ordered some of his men to stand watch outside, then slammed the door.

The entrance was long, narrow and lined with crackling torches. It led into a wide circular chamber with a domed roof and twelve alcoves spread equally around its circumference. In each alcove was a white shield, forged in the shape of a wing and carved with small lines of text.

There was a circular stone table at the centre of the room, and Prince Volant strode across to lean over it, fists pressed to the stone and head bowed. He was breathing heavily.

'Your majesty,' said Lord Aurun, hurrying towards him. 'We must tend to your wounds. Let me send for an apothecary.'

Volant removed his black-and-white helmet and dropped it onto the table with a clang, then waved Aurun away. 'Later.' He glanced at one of the soldiers. 'Food. And water.'

The knight nodded and hurried away as Volant turned towards the captain. 'Tell me everything.'

He nodded, speaking quickly. 'The garrisons from the prominents have been deployed across the city walls, as you instructed.'

'How many?'

'Nearly four thousand, your highness.'

'How many archers?'

The captain hesitated. 'There are four thousand men in total, your majesty. Roughly two thousand Gravesward. The rest are archers, assorted foot soldiers and militia.'

Volant stared at him for a moment. He sighed and nodded. 'And the Unburied?'

'Other than those you have just brought from the Barren Points, every surviving cocoon has been taken to the Halls of Separation, as you instructed.'

Volant nodded again. 'The host that follows in our footsteps is larger than anything we anticipated. Four thousand soldiers will not suffice.'

The captain paled, but before he could reply, the prince continued.

'But neither would fifty thousand. Our only hope is to hold the walls until I and the high priestess have completed the rite. With the power of the Unburied gathered together in a single location, we can use the Cerement Stone to guarantee their future.'

The captain nodded. 'We have positioned the men exactly as you ordered, your majesty.'

'I will see for myself before I leave the walls.' Volant grimaced and pressed a hand to his side, closing his eyes. Then he noticed that the captain was looking awkwardly at him. 'Anything else?'

The captain nodded. 'Something peculiar happened at the Sariphi Docks. The relics...' He frowned, struggling to explain himself. 'The relics began moving. And making noises.'

'Relics? Which relics?'

'The aether-ships, Morn-Prince – the ironclads and frigates. They were shaking and rattling, shedding light from their hulls.

Some of them moved with such force that they damaged the nearby buildings.'

Volant glanced at Gotrek and Lhosia.

Gotrek shrugged and looked at Trachos. 'Blame the manling.'

The captain had not looked at Gotrek or Trachos properly until that moment. He now stared at them in surprise.

'Your companions, your majesty. Are they the cause of the problems at the docks?'

Trachos shrugged. 'The old Kharadron devices form a network across your whole princedom. In triggering the duardin mechanisms at the Barren Points, it's possible I have also triggered engines here.'

'Triggered them?' said the captain. 'What do you mean?'

'If that's everything, I will inspect the walls,' said Volant, ignoring the captain's question and waving to the door.

'One minute.' Gotrek held up his hand, and Prince Volant halted. 'We had a deal. I saved your corpse eggs. Now it's time to keep your side of the bargain.'

'Nothing is saved yet,' replied the prince. 'The mordants will be here within hours. We need to hold these walls until the high priestess and I have performed our rite, or the Unburied will be destroyed along with everything else.'

Gotrek narrowed his eye. 'Get them to the capital. That was the deal. You owe me a god.'

'You swore to *save* them,' said Volant, speaking softly despite Gotrek's bullish tone.

Maleneth noticed that the prince spoke to the Slayer very differently to the way he addressed the captain. The impatience was gone. He was talking to Gotrek as an equal.

'You have shown bravery and skill beyond anything I would expect to see in a non-Erebid. And there is power in you that goes beyond my understanding. I thought you were insane when you spoke of challenging Nagash, but now...' Volant shrugged. 'Now I think you might just be destined for something greater than the rest of us, Gotrek Gurnisson.'

'That's as maybe,' he muttered, 'but I did not come here to fight your wars.'

Volant shook his head. 'I am not asking you to fight our wars. I would ask only this – lend me your axe and your courage one last time. Today will either rob us of thousands of years of tradition or see us victorious, preserving the dignity of our elders as the rest of Shyish falls to ruin. If you will help my knights hold the city walls, I can go with Lhosia to the Halls of Separation and make my forefathers proud, either by my triumph or by my glorious death.'

Gotrek looked at the shields mounted in the alcoves and the poems carved into them. There was a long, tense moment as he seemed to forget about his surroundings. 'I lost everything,' he said finally, his voice low. 'And now I'm stuck in this shoddy, mannish age.' He scowled at Maleneth. 'Surrounded by people who care nothing for tradition and respect.' He met the prince's eye and nodded. 'It would do me good to fight for something again. To fight alongside someone who wishes to preserve rather than change.' Gotrek nodded. 'I'll hold the wall for you, Morn-Prince.'

He stepped closer and tapped his axe on the prince's armour. 'But know this. I will also hold you to your oath. When those cocoons are safe, you send me to Nagash.' He spat on the floor. 'Or you will have something worse than ghouls to worry about.'

Prince Volant nodded. 'We have an understanding.'

CHAPTER TWENTY-ONE

THE GHOUL KING

The Morn-Prince ordered Lord Aurun to accompany Lhosia and the Unburied to the Halls of Separation, promising to join them shortly, then led Gotrek to the battlements above the city gates. As Maleneth and Trachos followed, they received shocked glances from the soldiers who lined the steps. Maleneth smiled at them, conscious of how white and hungry her grin would look in her bloodstained face. She was probably the first aelf they had ever seen. She was keen to make the right impression.

'We spied the mordants even before we saw you approaching,' said Captain Ridens as they climbed the stairs inside one of the thorn-like towers that lined the walls. 'Every survivor who reached us brought news of them, explaining that the prominents had been taken.' He grimaced, shaking his head. 'They described terrible things, all of them. But it was not until two days ago that we started to see what they were talking about.'

They reached the top of the tower and stepped out onto the curtain wall. A chill wind lashed against Maleneth, and ranks of soldiers backed away, bowing, as they made space for the prince to approach the wall.

He stared out into the darkness. 'What do you mean? I can't see any mordants out there.'

The captain nodded to some soldiers further down the wall, standing beside a catapult the size of a house. They leapt into action, lighting tapers and fastening bundles of dried wood to the weapon. There was a rattle of whirring cogs as the catapult sent an arc of fire towards the stars. It landed with an explosion of sparks, half a mile from the city, splashing light over the Eventide.

Maleneth hissed in disgust. Lit up briefly by the explosion were lines of ghouls. She had seen plenty of the creatures by this point, so it was not their crooked, hunched bodies that shocked her, nor the gore dripping from their wasted arms. It was their lack of movement. Every ghoul she had seen was frenzied, but the light had revealed lines of motionless flesh-eaters. They had gathered in ranks, like a normal, reasonable army. Seeing them like that, standing with such a vile pretence of sanity, was worse than watching them leap and claw.

'How long have they been like that?' she said as the light faded, leaving her with a disturbing after-image.

Captain Ridens looked at Prince Volant, who nodded.

'For five days.'

'They've been standing there for five days?' Maleneth laughed in disbelief. 'Doing nothing?'

The captain nodded. 'Survivors from the other prominents say this is unusual – that the mordants are not usually so well ordered.'

'Damn right,' she muttered. 'What *is* this?' she asked Gotrek. 'What are they doing?'

The Slayer shrugged. 'Looks like they're waiting for a command.'

'A command from whom? And how would they follow an order even if it came? They have no minds.'

Prince Volant replied without taking his gaze from the darkness. 'The histories talk of such behaviour. It is not unheard of. Mordants have been known to act with reason in the presence of a...' He hesitated, looking for the right word. 'A leader of some kind.'

'A leader?' Maleneth was incredulous. 'You saw them. They're like wolves fighting over a carcass. They can't recognise leadership skills. They couldn't distinguish a leader from a thigh bone.'

The prince looked past her to Trachos. The Stormcast Eternal had taken out his square-framed spyglass and was adjusting its nest of lenses, flipping clasps and turning rows of polished brass cogs. He held the device up to one of the eyeholes in his helmet.

'Can you see in the dark with that machine?' asked Volant, but Trachos did not answer. He stood in silence for several seconds, looking in different directions, until he spotted something and gave a grunt of recognition.

He handed the device to Gotrek and pointed out past the wynd that led to the gates.

Gotrek looked where Trachos was indicating and laughed. 'Well, would you look at that. *He's* impressively ugly.'

Maleneth snatched the spyglass from him and stared through the lens. By some cunning artifice of its Azyrite makers, the device was able to penetrate the pitch dark. It was not true vision but a ghostly approximation of sight. Lines of ghouls simmered into view, as if they were painted in smoke, faint, ephemeral and grotesque.

'What do you mean?' she asked. 'Who's ugly?' She flinched, forgetting that she was looking into the distance as a revolting shape filled the eyepiece. It was a monstrous, snub-faced creature, like the one Prince Volant had battled over the *Spindrift*, but this one was saddled and ridden by one of the large species of ghouls. The rider was as corpse-grey and withered as all the other mordants, but where they hunched and lurched, this one affected an attitude of regal disdain, reins held loosely in one listless hand and its chin raised in haughty indifference. Of all the flesh-eaters she had seen since reaching Shyish, this was the first one that Maleneth had found truly shocking. Its flesh had the same rotten, rag-like texture as the others, and its eyes were the same blank, oversized orbs, but unlike all the rest, this creature was dressed in scraps of armour and carried a rusty longsword on its back. As it shifted in its saddle, Maleneth realised that the ghoul was even wearing a dented circle of metal on its gleaming pate.

'It thinks it's still a man,' she said, with a mixture of amusement and unease. There was something unnerving about seeing such a debased creature assuming the air of a noble warrior.

'There are more of them,' she laughed as she spotted other riders circling the one with the crown. There were half a dozen or so, all with the same bat-like steeds and the same absurd facade of regal bearing. Some of them carried shields and pennants, as though they were proud knights, and one of them was riding side-saddle, as though it were a noblewoman heading out on a hunt with her courtiers and servants.

Prince Volant held out his hand and she handed the device up to him. 'I have not seen them behave like this before,' he said after studying the strange figures. 'What does it mean?' He looked at Captain Ridens. 'Have you seen this? Mordants behaving like nobles?'

Captain Ridens seemed unnerved every time Volant so much as glanced his way. At this question he looked distinctly panicked. 'Your majesty,' he mumbled. 'I do not understand the question.'

Volant handed Ridens the spyglass and directed him to the riders circling above the army.

Ridens paled. 'Those things were not there last time we fired the flares, Morn-Prince. They must have been following close behind you. I have heard…' He lowered the spyglass and looked up at the prince. 'The survivors all have something terrible to tell.

Some spoke of a ruler of the mordants, leading them into battle as if they were rational, human soldiers.'

Maleneth frowned up at the prince. 'Did you say ghouls have been known to act with reason in the presence of a "leader"?'

Volant nodded. 'According to the histories.'

Gotrek grinned. 'Then this might be even more interesting than the last scrap. At the Barren Points they were like drunks trying to find their own feet, but if they fight like actual soldiers, in those kinds of numbers…'

'It might not matter,' said Trachos, still staring out into the darkness.

'What do you mean?' asked Maleneth.

'Lift the spyglass a little higher. Look past the ghouls.'

Volant did as Trachos suggested. 'Nothing,' he said after a moment. 'Storm clouds. Nothing else.'

Maleneth stared at Trachos with a feeling of grim realisation. 'Storm clouds?'

He nodded. 'Bone rain. Coming fast.'

CHAPTER TWENTY-TWO

SHELTER FROM THE STORM

The streets of the Lingering Keep were already chaotic before Prince Volant sounded the alert. When he ordered everyone to take cover, there was a stampede. Screams rang out through the city. People clawed at doors and dived through windows. There was a desperate battle to find shelter as thunderheads rushed through the night. There were some in the city who had seen the results of the bone rain, and fear spread like a plague, leaving people as frantic and deranged as the monsters gathering beyond the walls.

Even those who had not seen it before could tell this was no natural storm. Mountainous clouds boiled into view, flickering with amethyst and enveloping the wynds, hurtling towards the gates that had only been slammed minutes earlier as the last few arrivals scrambled into the Lingering Keep.

Maleneth sprinted through the madness, dodging mobs of panicked refugees. She had almost crossed the square when she realised Gotrek was way behind her, walking casually from the walls, his axe slung nonchalantly over his shoulder.

'Slayer!' she yelled.

Trachos was at her side, and they both stopped to wait for him.

Volant and his captain were at the centre of a crossroads, yelling orders to the soldiers and trying to marshal the crowds into some kind of order. There was such a panic that the Gravesward had to form ranks and raise shields, driving people back to avoid a crush.

'There are empty houses and temples in the eastern quarter!' shouted Volant, climbing onto his steed and launching it over the crowd. Its wings dragged clouds of dust as Volant tried to redirect the people. He waved his scythe. 'Head that way!'

The mob was too deranged to respond, so Volant spoke to the skeleton drake and it opened its jaws in a roar so loud it cut over the noise of the approaching storm.

Finally some of the people paid attention, allowing the Gravesward to shepherd them away, relieving the bottleneck at the crossroads, but new crowds surged into the square from other directions and the situation was soon even worse.

'The storm will hit in minutes,' said Trachos. He and Maleneth had stepped out of the flow of bodies, climbing up a flight of colonnaded steps that led to a set of doors. The Stormcast Eternal was looking through his spyglass at the clouds. 'These people are not going to make it.'

Gotrek shoved his way through the mob and stomped up the steps. He looked sullen. 'Nagash is scared. That's what this is all about. He's doing everything he can to stop me reaching him. He's swamping this city in skull-chewers so the Morn-Prince can't send me to him.' He glared at the carnage in the square. 'And it's not going to work.'

'I can never decide whether to be impressed or amused by you,' said Maleneth. She waved one of her knives at the scene below – thousands of desperate, fear-maddened people, clambering over each other as a cataclysmic storm gathered overhead. It looked like an apocalypse. 'Does nothing here give you pause? Is there nothing about this situation that makes you think you might *not* be destined to reach Nagash?'

Gotrek laughed. 'Bloody aelves. So quick to accept defeat. That was always your problem. Comes of being knock-kneed poetry readers.'

He looked up at Trachos. 'We need to reach these Halls of Separation everyone keeps blathering on about. That's where the prince sent the ghost eggs. We'll go there and stand watch over the doors. I'll take on every ghoul in the realms if I have to, until the priestess has finished her spell, but I'd rather guard a door than a city.'

Maleneth pointed at the tusk-shaped spire looming over the city. 'The Halls of Separation are miles away, and Trachos just told you the storm will hit in minutes. You have the legs of a pot-bellied pig. How exactly do you intend to outrun those clouds?'

Gotrek shrugged. 'The manling will work something out.'

Trachos stared at him. Then he nodded and stood a little taller.

Maleneth rolled her eyes. 'How does this lump-headed brute have such an effect on people? How has *he* made you believe in yourself again, Trachos? How can your faith have been renewed by a god-hating savage?'

Trachos ignored her, peering around at the architecture. 'This is an advanced civilisation, by the look of the buildings.' He waved at an ornate arch reaching over their heads. 'They have preserved things most realms lost in the Age of Chaos. These techniques must date back to the time before Chaos, when Sigmar still walked the realms. I see his hand in every–'

'Sigmar?' guffawed Gotrek. 'You can't lay everything at the feet of the hammer-dunce! These people have learned some half-decent engineering skills, and that can only have come from dwarfs. Or at least those pale shadows of dwarfs you call duardin.'

Screams broke out not far from where they were talking as the Gravesward began using their scythes on the crowd, cutting people down in an attempt to save others who were being crushed by the mob. As the crowd heaved in a new direction, bone carriages splintered and toppled and fleshless horses panicked, trampling through the mayhem, their black plumes bobbing as they tried to find a way out.

'*Minutes* away, you said,' reminded Maleneth, waving at the looming clouds. 'Perhaps now isn't the time to discuss engineering?'

Trachos was still facing Gotrek. 'If the Erebid built their city on duardin principles, how would they have dealt with sanitation?'

Gotrek shrugged. 'Latrines. Sewers.'

'Have you lost your final shreds of sanity?' muttered Maleneth.

But Gotrek was grinning. 'Sewers – of course.'

Trachos studied the facade of the building they had climbed up to. 'That ironwork looks like waste pipes.' He leant out from the steps and looked down to the corner of the building. 'We could follow that outlet and see where it leads.'

'You want to crawl through the sewers?' asked Maleneth. 'For miles?'

'Nowhere is safer than underground,' replied Gotrek. 'Besides, which would you prefer, muck or bone rain?'

Trachos led them back down the steps, muttering and glancing back at the walls of the building as he tried to follow the route of the pipes.

At the bottom of the stairs they hit the crowd. Maleneth grimaced as people crashed into her, but the bulk of a Slayer and a Stormcast Eternal was enough to smash through the crush. Trachos waved them on, heading round to the corner of the building.

As they left the main flow of people, clouds began sailing over the walls.

Some of the soldiers managed to force their way down from the battlements, but others took cover in towers and archways, looking as though they were preparing to battle the weather.

'Here,' said Trachos, hurrying down an alleyway at the side of the building. He reached a metal hatch and stamped on it with his boot, creating a loud, reverberating clang.

Gotrek grinned. 'Good work, manling!' He climbed up onto an overturned cart and looked over the heaving crowds.

'Morn-Prince!' he howled, but there was no sign of Volant.

The noise of the crowds and the growing storm drowned out even the Slayer's booming tones.

'Gotrek!' cried Trachos as he levered the hatch open and revealed a flight of stone steps leading down into the darkness. 'We have to go now.'

'Where *is* that blessed prince?' snarled Gotrek, his cheeks flushing with anger. 'He needs to order these people into the sewers or they'll all be massacred. Morn-Prince!' he bellowed, his eye sparking, but there was no reply.

Maleneth ducked past Trachos and climbed down the steps, descending into the darkness. Glimmers of white shimmered over the walls. 'It's now or never,' she said, looking back at Trachos.

'Morn-Prince!' cried Gotrek a third time. The gold sparks in his eye were mirrored by a flash from the rune in his chest, and his words tore through the city, charged with the power of the rune, ringing out with such fury that people staggered.

The sneer fell from Maleneth's face. Gotrek's cry sounded like the voice of a god.

The mayhem ceased. Everyone in the square turned to face him.

'The sewers, you imbeciles!' Gotrek's face was purple. 'Get underground!'

People stared at the Slayer, clearly shocked, then did as he ordered, sprinting for drain hatches and sewers.

A few seconds later a bright rattling sound filled the city as the downpour arrived, crashing over the walls like waves of broken teeth.

Gotrek leapt down from the cart and raced towards Maleneth and Trachos with hundreds of terrified people following him, all trying to escape the deluge.

'Go!' cried Gotrek, pounding down the steps and disappearing into the darkness. There was a loud splash as he disappeared from sight.

Maleneth grimaced at the thick stench that rushed up in his wake. 'Smells as bad as him,' she muttered, hurrying down the steps.

CHAPTER TWENTY-THREE

THE ASCENSION OF KING GALAN

'The Wolf is with us!' cried King Galan as he felt his steed changing beneath him, its bones snapping and elongating and its muscles swelling. He could feel the undeniable power of his lord as the horse became a sinewy armoured drake, with vast taloned wings and powerful reptilian jaws. The creature pounded its wings and lifted him from the road, up over sun-drenched wheat fields. On his back he could feel the weight of his ancient longsword, Rancour. He had sworn not to draw it until he had the leader of the rebels kneeling before him. The sword had been blessed by Shadow Priests on the eve of the war, impregnated with the might of the Wolf, but he would not fritter its sorcery on any old warrior – he would unleash it with great ceremony on the head of his would-be usurper, with the Hounds of Dinann witnessing his righteous fury.

Nia and Lord Melvas were with him, their steeds elevated by the same miracle as his own. Other lords of the Dinann followed quickly after, laughing in wonder as their horses' hooves became claws and their flanks sprouted wings. They left the road and began racing through the air, trailing tails through the early dawn as their riders raised spears and howled.

The same miracle had occurred at each of the previous battles, but Galan still felt his pulse racing as he looked down at his army, charging into battle below him.

'One last time!' cried Nia, grinning at him from a few feet away.

'One last time!' he laughed, gripping his spear as he rushed towards the battlements.

The traitors were so awed by the miracle of the Wolf that Galan landed on the walls to find them already abandoned. The rogues who had seized the castle were scrambling for cover, tumbling down the steps and fleeing across the courtyard.

Some of them had managed to injure themselves in their desperation to escape, and as King Galan rode down the walls, he reached a group of bloodied, terrified wretches who tried to crawl away at his approach.

'I offered you mercy at every turn,' he said, pointing his spear at one of the gibbering wrecks, who was slipping and stumbling towards him, shaking his head.

The soldier muttered and cursed, unable to meet his eye, and Galan finally understood what was happening. He could not believe he had not suspected it before. The glorious victories, miracles like the drakes, the terror in the eyes of his victims – they all pointed to one thing: he was *ascending*. The oldest of all the prophecies had come to pass – the prophecy of the Wolf Lord. This was why the Shadow Priests had imbued Rancour with such power. This must be why his later years had been so quiet and lacking in glory. The Great Wolf had been waiting for this moment to raise him up and show him the glory that had always been his due.

Nia's drake landed beside him on the wall, and she leant out from her saddle, slamming her spear into the man's chest. He staggered away, dazed, then fell as she wrenched her weapon free. 'Not much of a fight,' she said with a smile, glancing around at the few wounded soldiers left on the walls. They were all flinching and cowering, as though attacked by invisible foes.

'I'm changing, Nia,' Galan said, his voice trembling with the glory of his revelation.

She looked at him in shock. Then she clearly saw the pride and power in his face, and her smile broadened. 'As are we all, my love.'

She drove her horse on down the wall, drawing her longsword and cutting down everyone in her path as the other lords landed, looking around in wonder at the abandoned battlements.

'There is still work to do!' cried Galan, pointing his spear down into the courtyard and the streets beyond. There were hundreds of wounded and fleeing soldiers. Lots were running into buildings to hide, but many were crawling into sewers, fleeing underground like rats. 'The traitors refused every entreaty to peace. Show no mercy!'

He clicked his heels and his drake leapt from the wall, hurtling down towards the crowds. Figures scattered as he landed, not even trying to defend themselves.

'What is this?' called Nia, landing near him. 'They battled so hard to hold the outlying keeps, and now, now that we reach the capital, they have no fight in them.'

Galan sat back in his saddle, watching the slaughter. 'They know they've lost.' He looked around the castle. 'It's even bigger than I expected.'

She raised an eyebrow. 'Maybe this is a more suitable place to rule from?'

'No,' replied Galan. 'I will make an example of this city. I will leave no brick standing. I will raze it to the ground. And if anyone considers challenging my rule again, they will only need to look here to see what their fate will be.'

He pointed to a bright, gleaming needle of white stone. 'Make for the central keep. The ringleaders will be there.'

Galan turned to the lords who were landing in the courtyard behind him. 'Open the gates, assemble the men. Gather the war machines. Bring this city down.'

CHAPTER TWENTY-FOUR

SACRAMENT OF BLOOD

Trachos' light flashed over barrel-vaulted ceilings, revealing the incredible age of the sewers. The stones had been rounded and smoothed by the centuries, slumping and swelling in places, as though bloated by tumours. It looked like they were crawling through diseased innards.

The foetid river running down the tunnel was knee-deep on Maleneth, but that meant Gotrek was wading up to his thighs. The water had no chance of slowing the Slayer though. While Trachos called out directions, a brass compass in one hand and his blazing sceptre in the other, Gotrek raced through the filth, vaulting pipes and leaping over the remains of old cave-ins.

'This is more like it!' he shouted, his greataxe slung across his back as he rushed through the darkness. He slapped the wall. 'Good, solid work. I could be back in the Eight Peaks.'

Trachos looked to Maleneth for an explanation.

She shrugged. 'He shares your enthusiasm for drains. How nice.'

'The north pipe,' said Trachos, casting light down another tunnel.

Gotrek nodded, humming cheerfully to himself as he splashed off in that direction.

'How long will this take?' Maleneth asked, catching up with Trachos.

'It looks like the main sewer runs from the central tower out to the city walls. We should be able to take a more direct route than if we were above ground. We might be there in less than an hour.'

She was about to reply when the tunnels juddered. Dust and brick fell from overhead, throwing up splashes of muck and clouds of flies, and Maleneth would have fallen if Trachos hadn't grabbed her arm.

'Prince of Murder,' she said. 'What was that?'

He shook his head. 'Maybe Nagash's storms are powerful enough to shake city walls?'

'I don't think so. It didn't seem like that in Klemp. I think that's the flesh-eaters entering the city.'

He strode on through the sewer, hurrying after the disappearing shape of Gotrek. 'Ghouls? How could they shake walls?'

'Siege engines?'

Trachos shook his head. 'You've seen them. How would they have the skill to use war machines?'

'Remember that giant?' she said, racing after him. 'The thing that Gotrek fought in the Barren Points? Perhaps they have creatures like that up there?'

He glanced at her, then nodded. 'We need to move faster.'

They ran as fast as they could through the effluence, but after a few minutes there was another tremor, then another, and Maleneth found herself struggling to keep up with Gotrek.

'What if he succeeds?' she gasped, swatting flies away.

'What?'

'What if we make it to the tower and Gotrek holds back the ghouls until the prince performs his spell?'

He shrugged. 'We have to hope that Lhosia and Prince Volant are right – that her rite will protect this city.'

'They said it would protect the *Unburied*. That's not quite the same thing.'

'What option do we have?'

'None, but that's not really what I meant, anyway. If this works how Gotrek hopes it will – if the Erebid really *do* send him to Nagash – what will you do then?'

Trachos glanced at her. 'I will…' He hurried on, shaking his head. 'I will go with him.'

'Really?' She nodded to Gotrek. His broad, hulking shape was clearly picked out in Trachos' light, and they could hear him humming cheerfully to himself and laughing at jokes he was muttering under his breath. 'You'd follow *that* to the Lord of Undeath?'

'Whenever you speak of him, your voice is full of such bile.'

She laughed. 'Of course. Look at him. Who wouldn't find him ridi–'

'But…' Trachos looked at her again. 'Since the Barren Points, I hear something else in your voice too.'

'What?'

'You have seen the same thing I have seen. The Slayer is not just some wandering brigand. He's important. He *means* something. He's here for a reason. The priestess saw it too. And so does the Morn-Prince. Gotrek has more than his own doom riding on those tattooed shoulders.'

She sneered, but could not find it in herself to disagree.

'What will *you* do if he succeeds?' asked Trachos. 'If they send him to Nagash, will you just stay here?'

'I don't know!' she snapped. 'None of my options seem particularly enticing at the moment.'

She was about to change the subject when an explosion rocked through the sewer, bathing her in amethyst light.

They fell into the muck, unbalanced by a tremor even more violent than the preceding ones.

Maleneth thrashed under the water for a moment, then lurched from the filth, cursing and spitting.

Gotrek was up ahead, shrugging off rubble and looking up at an opening that had appeared in the ceiling. A column of purple light was shining down through the hole and it framed the Slayer, picking him out of the darkness.

'Trachos,' hissed Maleneth, realising that his torchlight had faded.

She whirled around, scattering flies and water. The light from overhead was enough to reveal him, trapped beneath the surface of the water, pinned in place by a huge section of pipe that had been dislodged by the blast.

'Can you breathe underwater?' she muttered, rushing back towards him, realising how little she knew about Sigmar's stormborn warriors.

She could see him straining in the murk, trying to heave the shattered masonry off his chest.

Let the dullard die, said the voice in her head. ***Good riddance.***

To Maleneth's surprise, she found that she was not willing to leave Trachos behind. Something about their conversations had intrigued her. And she felt that they were unfinished. Besides, she had a feeling that Trachos might still prove to be the key to getting the rune back to Azyr.

She grabbed the fallen pipe, trying to heave it away. It was impossible – she could not shift it an inch, even with Trachos shoving from the other side. Bubbles rushed from his armour and he thrashed furiously.

'Gotrek!' she cried. The Slayer had backed away to the far side of the hole in the ceiling and there were now shapes in the column of light that separated her from him – pale, glittering shards clattering down through the hole.

'Bone rain,' she muttered.

It was hard to see Gotrek clearly through the downpour, but she could tell he was shaking his head, powerless to reach her.

She looked the other way, back down the tunnel, and saw pale purple light coming from that direction too. 'Another hole,' she muttered. 'The whole place is coming down.'

Trachos twisted violently under the water, straining and bucking against the pipe.

She grabbed it again and pulled with all her strength, but it was hopeless.

'Khaine,' she wheezed, backing away and shaking her head. As she watched Trachos drowning, an unexpected fury washed through her. If she had engineered his death, she might have seen matters differently, but the idea of him being taken against her will was infuriating. 'We *need* you,' she muttered, trying again to shift the stone.

Light flickered over the walls and flashed in her eyes. She thought for a moment that another hole had opened in the ceiling, but it was Trachos' torch, shining beneath the surface of the water and throwing rippling lights across the arched ceiling.

'Gotrek!' she shouted again, but she knew it was useless. If the Slayer passed through that curtain of rain, he would be cut apart like anyone else.

Splashes echoed down the tunnel and she turned to see a hunched, loping shape lurching into view. Even in silhouette, she could recognise the wiry, twisted frame of a ghoul.

She cursed and backed away from Trachos, whipping her knives from her belt as more ghouls rushed from the shadows, their pus-yellow eyes flashing in the light of Trachos' torch.

She could see the Stormcast Eternal watching her from underwater as his struggles grew weaker.

'What can I do?' she said, taking another step away from him as the crowd of ghouls thundered through the sewer, twitching and grunting as they splashed through the effluence. There were dozens of them, just minutes away, and even more dropping into view behind.

'Well?' she demanded. 'Any advice?'

You should have killed the Slayer. Then you wouldn't be stuck down here with your back to the bone rain and flesh-eaters about to rip your lungs open.

'Thanks,' she said. 'Very helpful.'

She looked up the tunnel again. Gotrek had gone, carrying on without them. It made sense. The Slayer had never made any pretence of friendship. If he had ever had friends they had died a long time ago. But, absurdly, she still felt an odd sense of betrayal. In the months that she had travelled with the Slayer, she had begun to feel as though their fates were somehow entwined.

'I'm a fool,' she muttered. The first of the ghouls was only a minute or two away. She could see its black, jagged teeth drooling saliva as it tried to fix its febrile gaze on her.

Give us a death to be proud of. There was none of the usual venom in her mistress' voice. She sounded unusually calm. *Show Khaine we deserve a place at his side. These things bleed. Cut prayers into them.*

A cruel smile stretched across Maleneth's face. There were far too many ghouls for her to win this fight. There was no need to play it safe. Her mistress was right – she may as well abandon herself to the glory of the kill. She could revel in the bloodshed and devote herself, body and soul, to the Lord of Murder.

'In mine hand is the power and the might,' she whispered, dropping into a battle stance. 'None may withstand me. By the Will of Khaine I will bathe in the blood of mine enemies.'

Not far from where she was standing, Trachos finally became still, but Maleneth had already forgotten him. There was nothing left in her mind but the moves of a lethal dance.

She lashed out as the first ghoul reached her, spinning on her heel in an elegant pirouette to open its throat and send it crashing into the water.

A bright umbrella of blood engulfed her, and she sighed with pleasure before sidestepping the next ghoul, hammering her knives into its back and ripping it apart with an ecstatic howl.

The kills merged into a fluid ballet of hacks and lunges. Maleneth flipped and rolled, singing to Khaine as she opened throats in his name. Her mistress howled along with every cut.

CHAPTER TWENTY-FIVE

A TEST OF FAITH

King Galan rode hard through blood-filled streets, howling orders as the city toppled around him. Ancient towers and sprawling manses were pulled to the ground, and as the traitors fled in panic, his men cut them down. It was brutal and merciless, a massacre the like of which he had never witnessed before. For a moment, he wondered if he had gone too far. Had he become the kind of tyrant he had always sworn to oppose?

Nia saw the hesitation in his eye. 'This is the only way,' she gasped, plunging her spear into another back and wrenching her drake round to face him. 'When people hear of this victory they must quake. They must be horrified and appalled by the fate of these people.'

Galan nodded. They had discussed this many times on the road to the capital. He was old. And without an heir. If people believed they could turn on the crown without fear of death, the kingdom would not survive another year. This was his last chance to show what became of anyone who tried to claim independence. And yet... As his soldiers tore down statues and performed far worse atrocities in his name, his battle lust left him. 'To the tower,' he said, pointing his spear at the building that dominated the whole city. 'Once I find the ringleader and introduce him to Rancour, in front of the whole city, our message will be clear. And then we can finally rest.'

He ducked as, in the next street, a huge temple collapsed, pulverised by one of his war engines, sending a writhing tower of dust up into the hazy summer heat. A powerful sense of purpose rushed through him. The wounded rebels were all fleeing to the tower at the centre of the city. Once he reached that building, he would ascend. He was sure of it. He would breach that central keep and butcher everyone inside, and then the Great Wolf would crown him not just king, but immortal Wolf Lord.

He glanced at Nia, grinning despite the carnage boiling all around him. And Nia would be his eternal queen. This was why they had come – not just to quell a foolish rebellion, but to reach this point and be elevated to a new life.

He grabbed Nia's arm. 'I can feel him riding with us.' He pointed his spear at the tower, and his voice trembled. 'He's in there, I know it. Today, we will walk at his side!'

She stared at him, her eyes glistening.

And they rode on, killing with more fury than ever before.

CHAPTER TWENTY-SIX

A PATH THROUGH THE DARKNESS

Maleneth lost herself to the ritual of sacred murder. She abandoned every thought of Sigmar and the Order and thought only of Khaine, moving with more speed, cruelty and elegance than she ever had before. Bodies piled up around her, scored with holy sigils and drained of blood, until finally, inevitably, the sheer volume of them began to overwhelm her. As the piles of dead collapsed towards her, she stumbled, banged against the sewer wall and fell cursing to her knees in the water.

A ghoul locked its bony hand around her neck, but she sliced through the wrist, cutting the hand free and staggering clear as the mordant lunged after her, oblivious to the blood rushing from its arm.

As Maleneth backed away, cutting down more ghouls, she trod on something hard and cold under the water.

It was Trachos' sceptre, shining through the murk.

Still fighting, she crouched and grabbed the golden rod.

The ghouls stumbled, dazzled by Azyrite sorcery. The thing was covered in runes and dials, like all of Trachos' equipment, but Maleneth did not attempt to decipher its workings – she simply used it as a club, smashing it into the face of the next ghoul to reach her and scattering beams of frigid light through its shattered skull.

The sceptre proved a useful weapon, but the memory of Trachos dulled some of her fervour. She glanced over at the fallen pipe. His turquoise armour was still visible, but he was no longer moving.

Khaine's hunger still pounded through her veins, but another thought was now vying for her attention. An idea had occurred to her. She vaulted a ghoul and splashed down near Trachos.

She jammed the sceptre into the water, forcing it under the fallen pipe. Then she stood on it, using her weight to try to lever the masonry off Trachos.

The sceptre was made of the same unyielding alloy as Trachos' armour, and it took her weight, lifting the pipe up from the water.

Maleneth balanced on it like an acrobat, ducking and swaying as she fought, then fell back as Trachos rose like a river god, swinging his hammers furiously and driving the ghouls back.

'Don't expect my help every time you fall over,' she gasped, dodging to Trachos' side and fighting with her back to his.

He laughed, but it turned into a series of hacking, liquid coughs. He managed to keep fighting, but he looked like he could barely stand.

'Gotrek?' he managed to gasp.

She shook her head.

He snarled in frustration, lashing out at the ghouls with growing strength. 'He needs you!'

'What?' In the confusion of the fighting, she wondered if she had misheard him.

'Gotrek needs you,' said Trachos. 'You're his sanity.'

She laughed. 'You dunce. I've been looking for a way to get rid of that oaf since the first day I met him.'

'Then why are you still with him?'

Maleneth thought of how she had failed to kill the Slayer on the *Spindrift*, when it would have been so easy.

Trachos pointed at the sceptre Maleneth had left sticking out from beneath the fallen pipe. 'I have an idea,' he coughed, blood spraying from his helmet. 'On the count of three.'

'On the count of three what?'

'Jump.'

They were now so completely surrounded by ghouls that she could no longer see the walls of the tunnel. 'Where?'

He started counting.

'Wait!' Maleneth cast around for a place to leap, but he ignored her, and as he reached three she jumped, landing feet first on a ghoul's shoulders and knocking it back into the others.

Trachos moved at the same moment, but rather than jumping clear, he dropped down onto the sceptre wedged beneath the pipe.

The metal held even under his weight, and it levered the remains of the pipe from the wall. Bricks and mortar smashed into the tunnel, along with a deafening torrent of water.

Maleneth fell back, knocked from her feet. She scrambled to right herself, but jumping clear had kept her from being washed away by the sudden influx of water.

Bodies and stones thudded into her, and as the water rose, she thought she might suffer the same fate she had just spared Trachos.

She tumbled backwards, coughing and cursing, then managed to leap from the stinking water and get back on her feet.

'What in the name of Khaine are you doing?' she cried as she saw Trachos a few feet away, the sceptre in one hand, a hammer in his other.

He punched his hammer into a knot of ghouls and nodded to the opening he had made.

'It will rejoin the main tunnel further up.'

Maleneth glanced at the quickly rising water. 'So will our corpses.'

She leapt past him, diving into the tunnel. She had only moved a few feet when she realised that Trachos was not with her. She twisted to look back over her shoulder.

Trachos had staggered away from her, hammering his way into the centre of the ghouls.

'Go!' he cried, glancing towards her as the ghouls boiled over him, tearing at his armour. Cracks of light appeared in his neck brace – tiny fingers of lightning that danced across his armour, scorching the air and flinging shadows across the walls.

'Now!' he yelled, a furious warning in his voice, as he hurled his sceptre towards her.

She caught the sceptre, but instead of fleeing, she scrambled back down the pipe towards him. The water was already up to her waist and the walls were juddering, filling the sewers with a worrying groaning sound.

'What are you doing?' demanded Trachos, smashing more ghouls back into the water.

She glared at him. 'It's your fault I'm down here. You're going to lead me out.'

'It's not safe to be near me,' he grunted, grabbing the neck brace of his battleplate, causing more sparks to slash through the gloom. 'I'm damaged.'

'Who isn't?' She threw his sceptre back to him. 'Lead me out.' The water was now up to her chest. '*You're* no Slayer. Doom-seeking doesn't suit you. Stop looking for a glorious death. I'll never get out of this wretched place without you to lead me. It's a damned labyrinth. Without you and your machines, I'll wander down here forever.'

He hissed a curse and used the sceptre to punch through the ghouls, pushing back towards the hole he had torn in the wall.

'Follow me!' he said as he clambered up into the pipe.

The mordants tried to rush after them, but after Maleneth had killed the first few, the way became clogged with twitching bodies. Dozens more tried to cram into the pipe, but they were so frenzied they only compounded the problem, jamming it with thrashing limbs.

'This way!' called Trachos, wading on through the water, his torchlight flickering over wet, mossy bricks.

As she hurried after him, she noticed something. 'The water's rising in here too!'

He nodded without pausing to look back. 'The whole system is flooding. Something is destroying the city.'

Water was spraying from overhead, and every now and then came a resounding boom that caused the structure to shudder as though it had been punched.

'Is this thing going to come down?'

Trachos nodded, pausing at a crossroads and pointing his sceptre down each route, shining blue light into the darkness as he tried to decide which way to go. 'Something is smashing through it.'

He took out a small, golden box and flipped back the lid to reveal whirling needles in a polished wooden frame. He stared at them until they stopped spinning and all pointed in the same direction, then snapped the box shut and waded on through the water.

They had not gone more than a few steps when there was another boom, much closer this time, and a shuddering crash as the ceiling behind them gave way, filling the tunnel with bricks and clouds of dust. When the dust cleared, Maleneth saw that the way back was completely blocked by fallen rubble.

The water was now almost as high as it had been out in the main sewer. Maleneth was waist-deep in filth.

'Don't worry,' said Trachos, carrying on. 'My aetherlabe was clear – there is an exit up here that will lead back to a larger pipe.'

He rushed on towards a rusty, circular door with an iron wheel for a handle, similar to the doors on the *Spindrift*. He grabbed the wheel and tried to turn it, but the mechanism started to crumble in his grip, shedding lumps of rusty metal.

The water was up to Maleneth's chest. She moved to Trachos' side and grabbed the wheel, lending the Stormcast Eternal all her strength.

More rusty metal came away, but there was no sign of the thing turning.

The tunnel was shaken by another booming blow, and the sound was now so loud that there was no mistaking the truth – something big was headed their way.

Trachos handed her his sceptre and took something else from his belt. It looked like a sapphire encased in silver, and as he raised it over his head, light shimmered in the heart of the stone. With his other hand, he unclasped his helmet and removed it, letting his white plaits tumble down his breastplate.

Maleneth gasped at the sight of his face. It was even more brutal than the last time she had seen it – the mass of old scars had been joined by a new kind of injury. In several places, the rough mahogany of his skin had changed, covered now by a tracery of silver capillaries that glittered and flashed as he moved. There were pulses of light blinking across his cheeks and jaw where the silver threads were most numerous.

'What's happening to you?' she said, but Trachos did not seem to hear. His eyes were closed, and he pressed the blue gemstone to his forehead.

The walls shook again. 'Whatever that is, it's close,' she muttered.

Trachos was mouthing words. He took the stone away from his face and shook his head, looking at Maleneth. 'This is the only way.' He returned the stone to his belt and turned back to the rusted door. 'There is no other route back to the main sewer.'

The water was up to Maleneth's chin by this point, and she cursed. The wheel that opened the door was now completely submerged. She ducked under the surface and tried to grab it, but her hands could not even grip it in the filthy water.

'What now?' she gasped as she stood back up.

Trachos shook his head, looking at the wall of rubble behind them. 'We could try digging.'

She laughed, stepping on some broken bricks and hauling herself a little further away from the quickly rising water.

The walls shook with so much fury that she fell. From underwater she saw Trachos stagger backwards, away from the rusty door, bathed in light and trying to shield his un-armoured face.

She leapt back up out of the water and came face to face with a demented, blood-splattered snarl.

'What are you two playing at?' yelled Gotrek, framed by the door he had just destroyed. 'I have a god to slay.'

CHAPTER TWENTY-SEVEN

THE FLESH-EATER COURT

'I'm touched that you came back for us,' said Maleneth as the Slayer dragged her through the remains of the door.

Gotrek ignored her, grimacing at the sparking silver veins shimmering across Trachos' face. 'Grungni's teeth. No wonder you wear a hat.'

Trachos looked puzzled, reaching up to touch his cheek.

Maleneth staggered on up the pipe, struggling to keep her head above water. 'Can we compare wounds later?'

For a while they were swimming more than walking, but eventually they reached another intersection and tumbled back down into the main sewer, sliding and bouncing over the rubble until they landed with a crash at the bottom of the main concourse.

The water was only about a foot deep, and they sat there for a while panting and coughing. Even the Slayer seemed tired, leaning back against a broken support strut and massaging his massive forearms.

'If you two stop dawdling we might reach that tower before the whole city comes down.' He waved his axe at the various openings that led off the main pipe. 'I hope for your sake that you know which way to go, manling.'

Trachos was studying his reflection in the surface of his helmet and muttering to himself.

'It won't get any less ugly,' said Gotrek. 'Can you get us to the tower or not?'

Trachos fixed his helmet back in place and nodded. 'You only needed to keep going straight on. I told you, the main sewer leads from the tower.'

Gotrek shrugged and climbed to his feet. 'Let's get moving then.'

'But you already knew that,' said Maleneth. 'Trachos told us the route when we first came down here.' She gave the Slayer a wry smile. 'You were still in the main tunnel. You weren't lost. You didn't *need* to come back for us. I think you missed us.'

Gotrek glared at her, then stomped off up the tunnel. 'I just wanted to make sure I didn't wander around down here till doomsday.'

Maleneth winced as she stood and stumbled after him. Every inch of her was bruised and cut, and she could not remember the last time she had eaten.

'Aelves,' snorted Gotrek. 'No stamina.'

She shook her head in disbelief. 'Every time I start to think you might be *slightly* interesting, you open your mouth. Then I remember that you're an irascible infant trapped in the body of an ale-infused boar.'

Gotrek snorted and spat. 'What's an irascible?'

'Don't play the fool,' she muttered. 'You're absurd enough.'

'It's stopped again!' called Trachos.

They looked back down the pipe and saw that he had halted near one of the holes spilling light down from the streets above.

'The bone rain has stopped,' he said, shining his torch across the opening.

'What of it?' said Gotrek, walking back to him. 'You said the sewers were the most direct way.'

'But they're flooding.' Trachos waved his light over the water rising all around them. 'It's not as high yet as it was in the smaller tunnels, but it will be soon. And this whole structure is unstable. Whatever has been shaking the city has dislodged the foundations.'

He waded to the far side of the tunnel and shoved a fallen column.

Gotrek and Maleneth backed away as the masonry toppled towards them, smashing against the edge of the opening above and creating a crumbling ramp back up to the street.

Gotrek barged past her and clambered up the column. 'Keep up, aelf. You don't want pretty boy fishing this rune out of my corpse while you're still swimming with turds.'

She gripped her knives tighter as she climbed up after him, amazed to think that she had actually been pleased to see his face a few minutes ago.

They emerged to a scene of such desolation that it halted them in their tracks.

The storm had been brief but apocalyptic. Roofs had collapsed and windows had shattered, and scattered across the streets in every direction, people were crawling through the wreckage, clutching wounds or sobbing over the corpses of their kin.

Even Gotrek looked shocked. The tower at the city's heart was burning brighter than ever, bathing everything in the amethyst pall of death magic, and the desolation was terrible to look at.

Gotrek grimaced at the wounded and the dying. 'The prince could have got them underground quicker. This could have been avoided.' He nodded at the tower. 'Looks like something big is happening in there.' He rushed across the street, clambering over wrecked carts and carriages and ignoring the pitiful figures heaped around him.

As Maleneth and Trachos staggered after him, he dropped down into an empty street and hurried past the facade of what looked to be a temple, wrought of the same pale, bone-like curves as the other buildings they had seen. There were broad, sweeping steps leading up to it, and dozens of wounded people were sprawled across them, obviously struck down before they had managed to reach the temple doors.

Maleneth and Trachos tried to keep pace with Gotrek, but they were both carrying dozens of injuries, and by the time they dropped down into the street, he was far in the distance, running down a broad, empty boulevard that led to the foot of the tower.

People were sprawled all around them, groaning in pain and fear, both soldiers and civilians, cut apart and defenceless – and ghouls were rushing towards them from every direction.

'This is a deliberate tactic,' Maleneth said, shaking her head, surprised she had not realised sooner. 'Their leader must be some kind of sorcerer. He hurls this bone rain at his enemies, and then, by the time the mordants arrive, there's nothing left to fight.'

One of the ghouls was just a few feet away, and as she passed, it leapt at her. She dodged easily, lashing out with her knives as the spitting wretch stumbled on, spilling its blood across the dusty road.

As the ghoul thudded to the ground, dozens more lurched towards her, grunting and grabbing pieces of wreckage.

Trachos hammered two into oblivion, humming as he fought, and Maleneth cut down more, but there were already hundreds spilling from the streets, tearing at each other in their frenzy to feed.

Maleneth and Trachos ran on along the one remaining path through the mob and reached the approach to the tower.

Gotrek was almost at the doors, silhouetted by the light leaking through the walls, when something odd happened.

The ghouls backed away, moving in unison, as though responding to a silent command.

Maleneth staggered to a halt, confused. 'What are they doing?' The ghouls were acting as if they had regained control of their senses, shuffling together and even trying to form regimented lines, like an army of drunks attempting to look sober for a parade. 'Are they ghouls or not?'

Trachos waved her on. 'It doesn't matter – we need to reach that tower. Volant will be waiting in the Halls of Separation.'

Maleneth shook her head as she studied the crowds. 'It's like they're still human.' She gave Trachos a warning look. 'Surely you, of all people, want to know what you're killing?'

He slowed to a halt and looked around. 'They're flesh-eaters.'

The ghouls were still hunched, aberrant horrors, convulsing and snatching, but they were trying to form orderly lines and none of them were making any attempt to attack. They had made a living colonnade down the length of the boulevard, and dozens more were joining their ranks every second. Maleneth guessed that there must already be a few hundred.

Gotrek halted and looked back at the grotesque parade while Maleneth and Trachos jogged towards him.

'What are they playing at?' he demanded as they reached him. 'Why are they doing this?'

They both shook their heads and stared back down the boulevard. There was now a vast crowd of the flesh-eaters, huddled together in a strange semblance of order. Many of them still wore shreds of clothing, and some might have almost passed for normal if not for their blank eyes and awkward, jerking limbs.

'Maybe that's why,' said Trachos, pointing his sceptre towards the city walls.

Maleneth stared into the distant gloom and saw what looked like a flock of birds soaring over the rooftops, heading straight for them. She quickly realised the truth. They were the huge, bat-like things they had seen through Trachos' spyglass on the city walls. She heard their dreadful, screeching cry echoing through the streets.

'Khaine's blood,' she hissed. 'Not these things again.'

'No,' said Gotrek, jabbing his axe at the winged monsters. 'They are not the same.' He laughed as they flew closer and were lit up by the light of the tower. 'These are noble steeds.'

The riders were straight-backed and proud, their chins raised, and banners trailed from their saddles. Some wore pieces of broken barrel on their heads, like crowns, and some carried pieces of wreckage on their arms, as though they were shields. But their flesh was as ravaged as the figures lined up to greet them, and their bodies were just as gnarled and misshapen.

'It's the Ghoul King!' roared Gotrek, grinning. 'How regal he looks on his giant, dead bat.'

Maleneth waved a knife at the expectant crowds of ghouls lined up in front of them. 'What would happen to these legions of flesh-eaters if you killed their noble leader?'

Gotrek raised an eyebrow. 'Interesting idea.'

'We need to enter the tower,' said Trachos. 'Gotrek has sworn to guard the Unburied until the prince and Lhosia have performed their spell.'

Maleneth shook her head. 'A spell that will save the Unburied, but not necessarily us. They were notably vague on that point.' She pointed at the surrounding streets. Ghouls were shuffling closer from every direction, lining up with the others. 'Can you see how many of these things there are? And look over there.' She pointed further out into the city, back the way they had come. Columns of figures were marching beneath the Ghoul King, countless hundreds of mordants arriving from the Eventide.

Gotrek sucked at his beard, frowning, considering her words.

Then the light in the tower pulsed with renewed energy, scattering beams across the underside of the clouds, and a bell rang out, dull and tuneless, like the one they had heard when they first reached the borders of Morbium.

They all turned to look at the building. It was like a coiled white tusk, peppered with circular windows. The smooth, honeycombed walls were made of polished bone, and as the light grew, the tower looked like a shimmering flame.

'Something's happening up there!' cried Gotrek, scowling. 'They've bloody started without me.' He waved his axe at the army gathering behind them. 'There will be plenty of time to deal with these morons.' With that he turned and raced through the doors of the tower.

Maleneth and Trachos followed him into an atrium, slamming the doors shut behind them. The smooth, undulating walls of the tower contained no floors, only a single spiral staircase at its centre, surrounded by a wide, open, circular space. The staircase climbed to a central platform hundreds of feet above, and the walls were hung with thousands of white, wing-shaped shields, all covered in lines of poetry. There was something eerie about such an enormous space, devoid of rooms or furniture and bathed in purple light, and Maleneth paused for a moment, shaking her head. She felt as though she was in a dream.

The light was coming from about halfway up the walls, where the shields were replaced by hundreds of cocoons that nestled in the curves, burning with inner light. After the noise and violence of the last few days, Maleneth was shocked to find that the tower was quiet. Other than the echoes of the bell, there was a strange, peaceful hush. The screeching of the terrorgheists had been silenced as soon as they shut the doors. It was as though they had stepped into another realm.

She looked out through the nearest window and saw that the

ruined city was still there, along with the crowds of ghouls, but their din had been silenced.

'Witchblade,' said Trachos, rushing past her and heading up the stairs.

She snapped out of her reverie and saw that the Slayer was climbing up into the light, moving fast.

Maleneth ran over to the staircase. The spiral was broad and shallow, but circling at such a pace still made her dizzy after a few minutes of running, and the building was so huge that she felt as though she was making no progress, turning without climbing in a soundless void.

The bell rang out again. Inside the tower it was deafening, and Maleneth cursed, clamping her hands over her ears as the sound reverberated through her skull.

Just as the ringing seemed to be fading, the wall of the tower caved in, slabs of bone and metal tumbling across the steps.

Maleneth dropped into a crouch as a terrorgheist screamed into view, thrashing its wings and hurling broken masonry across the staircase.

There was a ghoul on the monster's back, wearing a crown and a preposterous air of nobility. The rider carried a rusted, crooked spear, and it pointed the ridiculous weapon at Gotrek, who was still racing up the steps, not far from the circular platform at the top of the tower.

A second terrorgheist smashed through the walls, causing more of the building to topple and revealing the rows of rooftops outside.

The creatures were enormous and revolting, skin trailing from their bones in ragged shreds and rotten intestines snaking behind them as they turned. They both had the same pug-nosed, bat-like faces, and at a signal from the Ghoul King they screamed in unison.

Maleneth howled, but her voice was lost beneath the screeching of the terrorgheists.

Trachos had halted a few steps further up. He was shaking in pain, and the sparks around his helmet had grown worse, dancing across his pauldrons and down his chest armour.

She managed to climb up towards him, still crying out as the terrorgheists whirled around them, screeching and pounding their wings.

Trachos was struggling to stand, but she grabbed his arm and hauled him to his feet. He leant on her shoulder, almost crushing her with his armoured bulk, before righting himself and starting to limp up the stairs.

Something hurtled out from the upper steps and slammed into one of the terrorgheists. The creature pounded its wings, trying to maintain its position as its rider stood in the saddle, straining to see what had hit its steed.

'Gotrek,' mouthed Maleneth, guessing the nature of the projectile even before she saw the Slayer clamber up the terrorgheist's neck, grin furiously and slam his axe into its skull.

CHAPTER TWENTY-EIGHT

RANCOUR

'Nia!' cried King Galan as the traitor beheaded her steed.

Her drake slumped beneath her and plunged towards distant flagstones.

Galan kicked his mount forwards, steering it after her. He hurtled past the steps at the centre of the tower, struggling to hold his reins.

Nia's steed trailed crimson as it looped and fell, but he could still see his queen, hanging onto its ridged back. The traitor was there too – squat and heavy and gripping an axe almost as tall as he was. His head was shaven apart from a central strip greased with so much animal fat that the hair stood up in a flame-like crest. He was climbing over the dead animal even as it fell, still trying to reach Nia, drawing back his axe to strike again.

'No!' howled Galan, driving his drake towards the ground as he tried to ready his spear and take aim.

His steed swooped low and slammed into Nia's drake seconds before it landed, sending all of them tumbling across the floor. Galan was hurled from his mount and thudded into the wall, losing his spear as he hit the stones.

He sat there for a moment, too dazed to move, staring up at the hollow tower, trying to remember who he was. There was a circular window nearby that looked out onto the wide boulevard. His men were gathering outside, preparing to attack, and the sight of them filled Galan with pride. They had fought their way through the city with ease, and their chins were raised in triumph as they rode towards him, colours flying in the breeze. Behind them, his war machines were laying waste to the city, pulverising everything.

'Galan!' cried Nia.

She was lying a dozen feet away, at the foot of the stairs, pinned beneath her dead drake and struggling to breathe.

He groaned at the sight of her, unable to hide his shock. She had been crushed. There was blood rushing from her armour and her hips were twisted at a revoltingly unnatural angle.

'Galan?' she called again.

The traitor with the mohawk was on the other side of the stairs, looking equally dazed, massaging his face as he used his axe to lever himself back onto his feet.

Galan rushed over to Nia and tried to shift the dead drake. It was impossible. The beast was the size of a full-grown oak.

Nia reached up to him, no fear in her voice, only frustration. 'Damn it.' She strained to move. 'Can you move it?'

He wanted to scream and pull away. To see his love like this was more painful than anything he could have ever imagined. But he knelt next to her, forcing himself to meet her feverish gaze.

'Why do you look at me like that?' she croaked, struggling to breathe. The colour was draining quickly from her face as the pool of blood spread around her. She nodded, slowly, and settled back against the floor.

Galan could think of nothing to say. A numbness seized him at the thought of life without her.

She gripped his arm, smiling through her pain. 'We have almost done it, Galan. We are almost there. *You* are almost there.'

There was a thud of boots as the Hounds of Dinann entered the tower and dismounted. Their triumphant expressions faded when they saw Galan holding their dying queen. They stumbled to a halt, lowering their spears.

'Melvas and the others are here,' he said, struggling to speak. 'Rest for a while, and I will come back for you when the traitors are dead. Then we will fetch the healers to–'

She silenced him with a horrific smile. 'No lies. I see the truth in your eyes. No healer can help me now. But I'm not afraid of death, Galan. This is all I ever wanted. To die in battle, with you by my side. I would rather this than any number of–' Her words were interrupted by a violent coughing fit.

'I could never have been a king without you,' he said.

She tried to nod, but the coughing grew worse until she was choking. Her grip on his arm tightened and she pressed her already blue lips against his skin, giving him a last, long kiss. Then she lay back, still smiling as her final breath rattled from her chest.

Galan stared at her, his own breath stalling in his lungs. He gently touched her silver wedding ring, tracing the runes, remembering the day he had put it on her hand.

Then he saw someone striding towards him across the atrium.

Fury jolted through him, forcing him to take the breath he had been holding back. It was the barbarian with the crest of golden hair – the muscle-bound savage who had murdered his queen.

Galan forgot his grief and lurched to his feet. He did not care who the strange-looking warrior was. Nia's murder would not go unavenged. He reached over his shoulder and found, to his relief, that Rancour was still there. He drew the longsword and gripped it in both hands, feeling its sorcery pulsing through its handle. Then he rushed at the barbarian.

'King of the ghouls!' cried the savage, laughing as he saw Galan coming towards him. 'Finally we meet!'

It was only now that he was so close that Galan saw how short the warrior was. He had an absurdly muscular frame, but his head only came level with Galan's chest. Galan had never encountered a duardin before, but he was educated enough to know that this must be one.

'On your knees, murderer,' he cried, drawing Rancour back to strike.

The duardin laughed again, clearly unimpressed. 'Are you trying to talk? With half your neck missing?'

Galan faltered, unsure what the barbarian was talking about. He touched his neck, but found no wounds.

'Tricks won't save you,' he hissed.

He hefted the ensorcelled blade with all the strength he could muster, aiming for the duardin's mocking grin.

The savage parried, but as the sword struck the axe, sorcery erupted from Rancour's blade, hurling him backwards in a storm of darkness, as though he were buried under gauzy black sheets.

The duardin cried out in annoyance as he tried to fight his way through the darkness. He swung his axe furiously, causing a flame to shimmer in the metal, but the harder he fought, the more dense the darkness grew, tightening around him like a net.

'Curse you!' he roared, staggering from side to side, unable to free himself.

Galan circled him, relishing the moment.

Then he came to a halt, noticing something strange. There was a golden face embedded in the duardin's chest, and as the warrior struggled to escape Rancour's sorcery, the metal mask pulsed with inner fire, glowing like an enormous ember.

As the duardin reeled back and forth, howling in outrage, Galan stepped quietly towards him, drawing back Rancour, feeling its seething power. The blade was charged with the might of the Great Wolf. It was blessed with sorcery so powerful it would cut through anything – even the golden rune.

But as the rune-light flooded into Galan's eyes, he felt a strange sensation. It was as though the breeze were blowing through his neck rather than against it. He remembered the duardin's strange insult and reached up to touch his throat. His fingers brushed wet, torn meat.

Cold dread gripped him, as though he were waking from a dream, but he still could not tear his gaze from the rune in the duardin's chest. The light burned through his mind, twisting his thoughts, giving him the most peculiar sensation that he was not who he thought he was.

Pain exploded in Galan's chest as a blade jutted out from between his ribs.

'No need to look so grave,' whispered a sardonic voice in his ear.

He staggered forwards, and his attacker wrenched the blade sideways as he fell, tearing his flesh apart.

Galan hit the floor in a fountain of blood and looked back to see a sneering aelf standing over him, whipcord thin and clad in barbed, blood-splattered leathers.

He tried to rise, but she put her boot on his chest, holding him down and waving a disapproving finger. He collapsed back onto the floor, dizzy with blood loss.

The aelf strolled away with the sprightly, elegant steps of a dancer, heading over to the duardin.

From where Galan was lying, he could see Nia's dead drake and the soldiers who had entered the tower. Only, they weren't soldiers at all. They were something else – grey, twisted horrors, with torn flesh and leering, lipless mouths. Rather than watching over their fallen queen, they were hunched over her steed, tearing hungrily at its flank, ripping its muscles, filling their mouths with blood.

He could just see Nia's outstretched hand, mottled and grey, like rotten meat. Then he saw the wedding ring, glinting on her bloodless finger.

With his last breath, he whispered her name.

CHAPTER TWENTY-NINE

FEEDING FRENZY

'Bloody wizards,' muttered Gotrek as the darkness dropped away from him. He stamped on the shadows that tumbled across the floor and writhed away from him. Within seconds, they had all faded and he was left glowering at the flagstones. He caught sight of Maleneth, still holding her knife with the dead ghoul at her feet.

'Saved by an *aelf*,' he groaned.

She laughed at his ingratitude. 'Ah, but you're a charmer, Gotrek Gurnisson – humble and eloquent in equal measure. You always know just the right thing to say. Truly, you are a credit to your species.'

He glared at her, embers dancing in his furnace-like eye.

Maleneth tensed and gripped her knives.

Then a broad grin spread across Gotrek's face. 'You're almost funny,' he laughed. 'For a backstabbing aelf.'

She bowed with an exaggerated flourish. 'I can but try.'

One of the ghouls reared up from the dead horse, its throat jammed with meat and blood rushing down its skin. It reached out towards them, groaning hungrily, but before it could take a step, another mordant dragged it to the floor and began eating it, snarling and gasping as it ripped flesh with its teeth.

Maleneth and Gotrek watched, bemused, as the ghouls all turned on each other in a snorting, growling kill-frenzy. They seemed oblivious to anything but the body nearest to them, and they quickly devolved into a heap of thrashing limbs and clawing fingers.

Through the windows, Maleneth could see the ghouls gathered outside in the boulevard, and they were all behaving the same way. They abandoned all pretence of being an army and turned on each other, lunging at whoever was nearest. Even the terrorgheists had joined the carnage, diving from the rooftops and devouring creatures they had previously fought alongside. 'What in the name of Khaine are they doing?'

Gotrek watched the carnage, shaking his head. 'Even ghouls usually manage to attack someone other than themselves.'

'You killed their leader,' called Trachos from the stairs above. 'These things have no minds of their own. They were only acting with a purpose because of that.' He waved his sceptre at the Ghoul King's corpse. 'You have achieved what the prince asked of you.'

'What do you mean?' said Gotrek. He nodded at the cocoons up in the rafters of the tower. 'They're not saved yet.'

'You have saved them from the ghouls. The flesh-eaters will be so busy devouring each other, the Erebid will have no problem slaughtering them when Prince Volant summons them back out of the sewers.'

Gotrek glanced at Maleneth, and she gave him another exaggerated curtsy, delighting in the fact that she had done his job for him.

'All that remains now is for Volant and Lhosia to perform the rite they spoke of,' she said. 'To fire up their magic stone and protect the Erebid from future invasions.'

Gotrek looked up towards the top of the tower. The hexagonal platform in its eaves was shining so brightly he had to shield his eye. 'Let's get up there before they get so excited they forget what they promised me.'

CHAPTER THIRTY

DEATHWISE

As they reached the building's upper levels, they found themselves surrounded by Unburied. Maleneth remembered what Lhosia had said about each cocoon carrying hundreds, even thousands of souls, and she marvelled when she saw that the walls were covered in countless hundreds of them. They were all cradled in niches of smooth bone, like seeds in an enormous white pod, and the nearer they were to the platform, the brighter they shone. As she ran, Maleneth felt as though she were racing into the heart of a star with giant embers tumbling all around her, burning as they fell. The platform was made of the same pale, translucent material as everything else, and shadowy figures were walking across the surface, passing back and forth above her head.

They were still several minutes away from the platform when Maleneth cried out in alarm and stumbled to a halt.

'Keep moving, aelf!' snapped Gotrek, glancing back at her. As soon as he saw what had happened to her, he stopped too.

'What are you doing?' he demanded.

'Doing? I did nothing!' she said, staring at her arms. Her skin was naturally pale, but it had been transformed, turned into the same bone-like substance as the walls. Even her clothes had changed to the same material. 'This is what happened to you!' she cried, pointing at the rows of cocoons. 'When you joined yourself to those things. It's happening to you now! Look!'

Gotrek exclaimed in annoyance. His leathery, tattooed muscles now resembled dusty alabaster, as did the plate of armour on his shoulder. He stared at his palm, grimacing at the change in his flesh.

'Don't move!' called Trachos.

'Don't move? What do you mean, don't move? We need to get up there.' Gotrek turned to continue up the stairs.

'Remember what the priestess told you,' said Trachos. 'You're fragile in that state. Tread carefully.'

Gotrek halted and looked back. 'And what about you?'

Trachos' armour was now the same chalky white as everything else. He shook his head, staring at his arms.

'Ha!' crowed Maleneth. 'Not so eternal after all. Tread carefully yourself!'

The figures overhead suddenly rushed to one side of the platform, and the cocoons on the walls pulsed even brighter.

'Sod this,' grunted Gotrek, and carried on up the stairs, but he was moving noticeably slower.

The final stretch of steps opened into a fan shape as they led onto the platform. Gotrek, Trachos and Maleneth walked out into the light together, shielding their eyes as they stepped onto the smooth, powdery floor, gripping their weapons. It occurred to Maleneth that they were moving like old comrades in arms, standing side by side, trusting each other implicitly. As soon as she noticed this, she sidestepped away from the other two, muttering in annoyance.

As Maleneth grew accustomed to the light, she saw that her

skin had regained its normal appearance. The others were the same. The transformation that had overtaken them on the stairs had ceased as soon as they stepped up onto the dais.

There were a dozen people assembled on the platform. To her left was Lord Aurun, flanked by six knights of the Gravesward. He looked like he was about to be crowned – chin raised, shoulders back and eyes gleaming with pride.

In the centre of the platform were High Priestess Lhosia, three other priests and the towering shape of Prince Volant. The priests were standing in a circle around the prince, arms raised and hands clasped, and Volant was kneeling. It looked like he was holding an exploding star. Thousands of white moths fluttered around his hands, forming a ball of teeming, flashing wings.

Gotrek opened his mouth, but before he could speak, Prince Volant's voice rang out through the lights. His words were cracked with pain but still sure and proud.

'Deathwise we fly, rescued from life and cradled by sod. From the tombs of fell-handed forefathers, red-scarred and charred, death-tongued and hale, we bring faith, we bring hope, we bring eternity.'

Maleneth wanted to announce their arrival, but the air was so heavy with sorcery that she dared not speak for fear of triggering some kind of transformation.

Lhosia echoed Volant's invocation, and then the prince spoke again. His voice was lower this time, and more resonant, echoing through the shadows. 'Deathwise we fly, rescued from life and cradled by sod. From the tombs of fell-handed forefathers, red-scarred and charred, death-tongued and hale, we bring treasurelings. We bring gifts. We bring offerings to the deep, deepest dark.'

This time the words had a dramatic effect. The cocoons in the walls pulsed, then grew dark. There was a pair of small braziers positioned at the top of the steps, and if it weren't for their flames, the whole platform would have been plunged into darkness.

'Those are not the words,' said Lhosia, backing away, breaking the circle and staring up at the prince. 'What are you doing?'

When Lhosia had loosed her grip, some of the moths had flown away, scattering over the platform and fluttering up, into the spire of the tower.

Volant looked up through the clouds of whirling insects, his face grim.

CHAPTER THIRTY-ONE

THE CEREMENT STONE

The prince was not wearing his helmet, and as he turned to face Gotrek, his eyes creased into a slight smile.

'You made it.' He ignored the confused-looking priests and walked over to the Slayer. 'I hoped you would, but the odds were long. You are a unique individual, Gotrek Gurnisson. A rare find.'

Lhosia was staring at the dark cocoons on the walls, looking increasingly more outraged. 'What are you doing, Morn-Prince? Why did you alter the rite?'

'You hoped I would make it?' said Gotrek. 'What are you talking about?'

Volant watched Gotrek with glazed, lifeless eyes. He looked like he was intoxicated. 'You hold the gods in the contempt they deserve.' He waved a dismissive hand at everyone else on the platform. 'When you said you had come to bring your fury down on Nagash, it made my heart sing, Gotrek. We are of a similar mind, you and I. And you have done great work, bringing these souls here.' He pointed at the small patch of darkness hanging in the centre of the moths. 'I could never have managed this without you.'

Lhosia and the other Erebid stared at the prince, mystified, as he continued.

'This offering guarantees the future of the Erebid.'

Gotrek shook his head. 'Offering?'

Volant looked sadly at Lhosia. 'We've kept our ancestors hidden for all these centuries. But now we are undone. The Lord of Undeath has harnessed a power beyond anything he has wielded before. We can no longer just cling to our prayers and hope to outrun the tide.'

'What have you done?' asked Lhosia quietly.

'I have gathered hundreds of divine souls,' said Volant, glancing at the dark shape in the centre of the moths. 'Souls that have eluded Nagash for centuries.'

Lord Aurun glared at the Morn-Prince, gripping his scythe with such fury that his arms were shaking.

Maleneth looked at where Volant had been kneeling and saw a shimmer of purple in the ball of moths. It was a gemstone, faceted and dark.

'Do you mean that the Cerement Stone will *preserve* the Unburied?' said Lhosia.

Prince Volant shook his head, suddenly seeming tired. He massaged his scalp as he paced across the dais, distorting the intricate tattoos on his face. 'Nothing preserves life except power. I see that now. For a long time I thought there might be another way, but now I see that the only way to gain freedom from the gods is to *buy* it. Prayers, devotions, ancestor worship… It's all meaningless. But offerings win the favour of any god. And thanks to this duardin, the Cerement Stone has captured more souls than I could ever have hoped. And now it will send them to Nagash.'

'Nagash?' gasped Lhosia, glancing over at Lord Aurun, her face drained of colour.

'Seize him!' howled Lord Aurun, pointing his scythe at the sorcerer. 'He's a *traitor!*'

Aurun and the Gravesward rushed forwards, weapons raised, but Prince Volant shook his head despairingly at them. Just as they were about to reach him, he lashed out with his scythe, slicing through armour and hurling his attackers across the dais.

The knights stumbled and fell, clutching their throats and chests. There was a loud clattering as scythes and shields bounced across the floor.

Aurun leapt to his feet and attacked again, but Volant clubbed him down, towering over the knight and pummelling him with the haft of his scythe.

The prince looked around at the gasping knights, then nodded and addressed Gotrek again.

'This tower is linked to Nagash's own citadel, and I have now linked it to the Cerement Stone as well. I have all the souls I need to complete the ritual – I can now do as I promised and send you with them. You can finally confront your past.'

'What?' Gotrek shook his head. 'Why? Why would you send your ancestors to Nagash? After everything you people said about your forebears.'

The prince's expression darkened. 'Morbium is gone!' He waved dismissively at Lord Aurun. 'No one else here has the sense to see it, but I realised the truth weeks ago. *Months* ago. And I have been living with it ever since, knowing that everything we have worked for all these centuries has come to nothing. Knowing that every one of the prominents will sink beneath the Eventide. It shamed me, Gotrek Gurnisson!' His voice cracked. 'I was going to be the one Morn-Prince who failed to preserve his bloodline. The one ruler of Morbium who let memories be lost! The Great Necromancer was going to take everything! Every trace of our past.

'At first I thought there might be a way to find an offering *outside* Morbium. I employed shrivers to scour the princedoms, looking for a gift that would be fit for a god – some way to buy our safety. But it was hopeless. What single individual would satisfy Nagash? I needed more. Only the Unburied would appease the Great Necromancer. These souls that have eluded him for so long.'

'Kurin?' laughed Maleneth. 'He was working for you?' She looked triumphantly at Gotrek. 'I told you that conjuror in Klemp was a fraud. He was fishing for victims to send to Nagash. I bet he was delighted when he heard you say you *wanted* to go to him!'

Gotrek glared at her, but Volant did not hear Maleneth's words, too intent on justifying his actions to the Slayer.

'Once the rite is complete,' he continued, 'Nagash will take ownership of the Unburied. The Cerement Stone will send every one of them to him. The Lingering Keep will sink beneath the waves like all the other prominents, and every soul will go to the necromancer. Then I will be–'

'Nagash's servant,' said Gotrek, his lip curling in disgust.

'I serve *no one!*' snapped Volant, finally losing his veneer of calm. All around the dais, the Gravesward were clambering to their feet, clutching wounds, but the prince ignored them.

'For now,' he said, his voice still taut, 'Nagash has the upper hand. But let a few centuries pass, and Sigmar will hold sway, or maybe some other god that has yet to emerge from the aethervoid. Who knows? What matters is that as the gods rise and fall, the bloodline of the Morn-Princes will endure. With the souls of the Unburied I have bought myself safe passage. I have bought a chance for at least one of the Erebid to escape the Nadir. I will survive, and begin again.'

Lhosia hissed a curse and moved to attack, but her acolytes held her back as Volant raised his scythe, saving her from being cut down.

Gotrek looked thoughtfully at the struggling figures on the dais, considering the prince's words. 'If you're sending these souls to Nagash to buy yourself peace, why would you send me? I'm not after peace. I'm not some willing victim. I came for vengeance.'

Volant shrugged. 'And I believe you might find it.' He peered down at Gotrek. 'Your soul has been altered. You are more than mortal but better than a god.' He shook his head. 'I have no idea what you are, but perhaps you *will* destroy Nagash. Perhaps that is why you were brought to these realms – to end all these schisms and power plays. I'm sending these souls to buy freedom from tyranny, but if you destroy Nagash, there will *be* no tyranny.'

'And if I fail to destroy him?'

'Then I have presented the arch-necromancer with an even greater present than I promised. Your soul would be the jewel in his crown. What matters is that I will be far away, taking my bloodline beyond the reach of arrogant, self-absorbed gods.'

Trachos unclasped his hammers from his belt and tensed, ready to attack, but then paused and looked at Gotrek, as if waiting to see how the Slayer would respond.

Is Gotrek our leader now? wondered Maleneth. *Is that what we have come to?* The idea appalled her. *Do we just follow him whatever he decides to do?* She was struggling to understand why, but both she and Trachos seemed to be in Gotrek's thrall.

Strike him down then! Stick a knife in that fat neck. Try another poison.

Maleneth shook her head. There was such a powerful, momentous feeling in the air that she could not bear the idea of ending this scene before it had been played out. She had to know what would become of the Slayer. And of the Erebid.

'People have been promising they'll get me to Nagash since I arrived in this wretched hole,' snarled Gotrek. 'So far it's come to nothing.'

Volant waved Gotrek over to the cloud of moths and pointed to the gem at its centre. 'Place your hand on the Cerement Stone. I am about to finish the ritual – the stone will send you to Nagashizzar. You will see Nagash *today*. Have your vengeance, Gotrek, or answers, or whatever it is you seek.'

Gotrek stepped closer, reaching out to touch the stone.

'Gotrek!' cried Trachos, finally breaking his silence. 'This man is a–'

Volant whispered and amethyst light leapt from the stone, blazing around his scythe. 'This stone is part of me!' he shouted. 'I'm bound to it, and it to me.' He swung the blade, hurling purple flame. 'Together, we are invincible!'

Trachos staggered, clutching his gorget, bathed in light. He dropped to his knees with a clang, sparks tumbling down his chest. As he struggled, the purple lights grew brighter, eating into his armour, causing him to convulse and kick.

Maleneth shook her head. For a long time she would have gladly watched the Stormcast Eternal die, but not at the hands of this pompous prince. There was nothing she hated more than someone who lied better than she did.

'Gotrek,' she said, but before she could get any more words out, Volant lashed out again, hurling more light. Pain knifed into her throat, and she dropped to the floor beside Trachos, unable to breathe.

Gotrek glanced back at her, his expression blank. As she clawed at her throat, feeling the strength drain from her limbs, the Slayer studied Prince Volant. For what seemed like an age, Gotrek looked from Volant to the stone and the people dying on the dais.

'I have been in these realms for months,' he said finally. 'And I had given up hope of finding anyone who thinks like me.'

Maleneth felt a rush of hopelessness as Gotrek placed his hand on Volant's shoulder. 'And now, in this lightless pit, I see that I was wrong to despair. Not everyone in these realms is as stupid as I thought.'

Maleneth's vision grew dark as her oxygen-starved brain lost hold on reality. She pictured scenes from her past, from the Khainite Murder Temples where she had learned to pray through violence, and the halls of the Azyrite scholars, where she had first understood the power of Sigmar's Stormhosts. The scenes merged and coalesced as her consciousness slipped away.

Gotrek smiled at Prince Volant.

Then he smashed the Cerement Stone with his axe, hurling crimson shards through the air.

Volant roared and reeled across the platform, clutching his face.

Moths whirled around Gotrek's axe, flashing against the fyresteel.

The walls lit up as the cocoons pulsed back into life.

Maleneth managed to gasp a choking breath as the flames dropped away from her.

With fragments of the Cerement Stone still tinkling across the floor, Gotrek strolled after the howling prince.

'I thought these realms were blind to the things that really matter,' he said, 'but the people of Morbium have proved me wrong. They value tradition. They respect their ancestors. They record every detail of their past. They *believe* in something. They believe hard enough to fight and to die for it.'

Lhosia, Trachos and the others were still gasping for breath and trying to sit as Gotrek reached Volant and pointed his axe at him. 'And they deserve better than to be betrayed by their own lord.' He glanced at Maleneth. 'I was wrong. Whatever I've lost, there *are* still things worth fighting for. Even here.'

Volant had fallen to his knees, and cracks had spread over his face. He looked like he was about to be sick. 'I placed all of my power in that stone.' His voice was a strangled hiss. He glared at Gotrek. 'You will rue the day you–'

His words were cut off, along with his head, as Lhosia's scythe slammed through his throat.

CHAPTER THIRTY-TWO

A THING OF VALUE

Gotrek stood brooding over Volant's shattered remains, passion burning in his one good eye. The prince looked like a broken vase, hundreds of pale shards, each showing a jumbled glimpse of his face.

All around the dais, people were climbing to their feet, gasping and coughing and struggling for breath.

Maleneth gave Trachos her hand, and Lhosia's acolytes rushed to steady the priestess as she staggered away from the prince's corpse, staring at her bloody scythe.

Lord Aurun and the Gravesward grabbed their weapons and dusted down their armour.

'You could have gone with him to Nagash.' Maleneth was, once again, baffled by the Slayer's behaviour. 'You could have fulfilled your destiny. You could have met your doom.'

Gotrek nodded, staring at Volant's splintered corpse, his expression grim. 'Aye.'

Trachos walked across the platform and stood next to the Slayer. His breath was wheezing inside his helmet and he was clutching the rent in his neck armour, but he managed to stand straight and there was no sign of the tremors that had troubled him before.

'I thought you and the prince were of one mind,' sneered Maleneth. 'I thought you would see yourself in him.'

In the harsh light of the Unburied, Gotrek's face looked more weathered and beaten than ever. 'I did. I did see myself in him. And I did not like what I saw.'

'What do you mean?' asked Trachos.

Gotrek shrugged. 'He cared for nothing but his own future. He was deluding himself that he was fighting for his race, but he was just a coward. I might not have been so sure.' He turned towards Lord Aurun and Lhosia. 'If I had not seen your bravery.' He placed his hand over the rune in his scarred chest. 'The gods haven't tainted everything. Not yet. So perhaps I was sent here to…' He shook his head. 'Perhaps I came here to do *more* than die?'

They all fell quiet again as Gotrek wrestled with his thoughts. Even Maleneth felt reluctant to interrupt.

'What about your old friend?' she said after a while. 'Felix, was it? He wanted you to come here, didn't he? And face Nagash.'

Gotrek scowled. 'Maybe the wizard in Klemp was tricking me? He did have the look of a charlatan. Or perhaps Felix wanted me to come here to stop Prince Volant.' He lowered his voice. 'Besides, the manling is dead. Long dead. Which makes me a gullible fool.'

Lhosia spoke up, looking at Gotrek with newfound respect. 'You saved the Unburied. You saved all of us. But what will we do now?' She was addressing him like a subordinate requesting orders. 'The city is still conquered. If everything Volant told us is a lie, then there is *no* rite that will save them. There is no new Iron Shroud.' She looked at the shards of Cerement Stone. 'The mordants are everywhere, and we have no way to escape them.'

'Then we make our stand here,' said Lord Aurun in strident tones. 'We will not abandon a single soul. We will hold this tower until our dying breaths. The Lingering Keep is not lost while we live.'

The Gravesward clanged their scythes against their breastplates, but Lhosia looked doubtful.

'Think,' said Aurun. 'Most of our men should have reached the sewers before the rain hit. I can muster them. However many mordants there are out there, they will have a hard fight making it up these stairs with a thousand archers firing down on them and a shield wall waiting at the top.'

One of the knights saluted. 'I will sound the horns, my lord.'

'Wait,' said Gotrek, halting the knight before he reached the stairs. He looked at Aurun. 'The halls of my ancestors were filled with the corpses of warriors who died defending their homes. It is an honourable way to die.'

Aurun tilted his head in a slight bow. 'You have given us another chance, Slayer. Whatever the odds, we will fight on.'

Gotrek nodded. 'You are brave, and honourable, but…' He shook his head, frowning. 'Perhaps, like me, you can do more than just die with honour? I never expected to find anything of worth in these realms. *People* of worth. And now that I have found a thing of value, I wonder if there is a way to preserve it.'

Aurun shook his head. 'We will not abandon our ancestors.'

'Nor should you. But perhaps you could abandon something else.'

Gotrek was staring into the middle distance, his expression rigid. 'I come from a proud race. As proud as your own. And in our pride, we refused to change. We refused to move on.' He glanced at the rune in his chest. 'And we died. All that pride, all that wisdom, sacrificed for bricks and mortar.' He waved at the building around them. 'For towers like this. To honour the past is good, and right, Lord Aurun, but to be enslaved by it is another matter.'

'What are you suggesting?' asked Lhosia.

Gotrek pointed with his axe at the rows of cocoons that lined the tower walls. 'Your duty is to the Unburied, not this city. And the Unburied can be moved. You could die here, fighting until the end – and by Grungni I would honour your memory for doing it – or you could take them away and find a new place to live, find a new *way* to live.'

'How?' demanded Aurun. 'Where could we go?'

Gotrek shrugged and waved at the ruins outside, smoking and crowded with feasting ghouls. 'What could be worse than this? And now Nagash has thrown your borders open to the other princedoms, there will be plenty more ghouls coming your way. Along with any other army that happens to be passing.'

Maleneth shook her head. 'Even if we could fight our way to the gates, the wynds would be crawling with mordants. How could we go anywhere?'

Gotrek looked at Trachos and raised an eyebrow.

'Yes.' Trachos' voice was hoarse but confident. 'I can do it.'

'Do *what?*' demanded Maleneth, irritated that they seemed to be sharing secrets.

Gotrek turned back to Aurun. 'When we first reached the city, we spoke to someone in the chapter house – a captain. He spoke of strange happenings at the docks.'

'Captain Ridens, yes. He said something had triggered the old Kharadron engines. The aether-ships. He said they lit up.' Aurun looked at Trachos. 'You said you might be responsible.'

Trachos nodded. 'At the Barren Points I ignited power lines that run beneath the whole of the Eventide. They date back to whenever the princedom was first colonised.'

'So the aether-ships are working again?' said Lhosia. 'Could you pilot them?'

'They might be working. Some of them, at least.'

Lhosia gripped Gotrek's arm. 'Then we could cross the Eventide. With the Iron Shroud gone, we would be free to cross the underworlds. With you to help us, we could find a new home, another corner of Shyish, far from the mordants.'

Gotrek gave a grim laugh. 'I've seen this realm. You won't like it. But there are other places.' He nodded towards Maleneth and Trachos. 'Places where people like this hold sway rather than Nagash.'

Lhosia shook her head. 'But could we reach the docks?' She looked out through a window. Seen from so high, the city was like an ant's nest, teeming with life as mordants flooded from every direction.

'Have you noticed that none of them are attacking us?' said Maleneth. 'Since *I* killed their king, I mean.'

Trachos nodded. 'They are leaderless. They are no longer an army.'

'They'll still try to chew your face off,' grunted Gotrek, 'but they're quite busy killing each other. We should be able to cut a path through them once you muster your men.'

'Lhosia, is there any reason the Unburied can't be moved?' Lord Aurun said.

She seemed dazed by the direction of the conversation, but she shook her head, waving to her acolytes. 'We could perform the necessary rituals. It would take a few hours, but it can be done.'

'Then perhaps we could save them,' muttered Aurun.

Gotrek stretched, rolling his massive shoulders and arching his back, causing the face in his chest to glint in the torchlight. 'I gave you my word I'd save them.' He clanged the haft of his axe on the floor and unleashed one of his terrifying grins. 'And I keep my bloody oaths.'

For someone who professed no interest in religion, Maleneth was constantly surprised by Gotrek's unshakeable faith. He believed resolutely in his own indestructibility. He wore self-belief like a suit of inch-thick plate.

He marched back out into the city like he was taking an evening stroll with nothing more pressing on his mind than finding a tavern. There were hundreds of ghouls crowded into the boulevard, thousands more in the surrounding streets, and he was blind to all of them, leaving the Gravesward to cut them down as he chatted calmly to Lord Aurun, asking for directions to the docks and discussing options for a destination. As they walked and talked, Maleneth noticed how animated Aurun was becoming – despite everything that had happened, despite the destruction all around him, he seemed excited. Gotrek had no trace of diplomacy, no tact, no desire to be political, but he had turned the Erebid noble into an eager convert and given him hope in the face of ruin.

Behind them, Erebid priests hauled their ancestors into the streets, abandoning centuries of religion on the word of a one-eyed duardin with an ale-matted beard and a face that looked dredged from a wreck.

'How does he do it?' muttered Maleneth.

Trachos was a few paces behind her, readying his hammers as the ghouls started to gather, sniffing the air and slavering. 'He's headed somewhere,' he said. 'It's written in his face.'

'To his grave,' she said, but she could not make her cynicism ring true. She knew what Trachos meant. Everyone else was limping through life, but Gotrek was charging.

She drew her knives and grinned, wading into the fight.

CHAPTER THIRTY-THREE

GHOST SHIPS

Gotrek staggered down to the quayside, wiping sweat from his face and laughing. He glanced back at Trachos, who was a few paces behind him, cleaning blood from his hammers. 'On my oath, manling, what a sight. That's the most glorious thing I've seen since falling into these wretched hells.'

Trachos looked up from his hammers and nodded in agreement.

Arrayed before them, glimmering in the darkness, were six vast edifices – colossal duardin faces, wrought of metal and wearing coats of faded, peeling paint. The figureheads towered over Gotrek, grander even than the one on the *Spindrift* and just as ferocious – savage, battle-hungry goliaths, roaring in silence, lit up by the fires of the burning city. They were of a different design to the *Spindrift*. They looked more like traditional ships, but were forged of iron and brass and topped by enormous metal spheres. Runes were painted across the hulls and mechanical weapons bristled from every gunwale.

Gotrek placed his hand on the first prow he reached, patting the ancient riveted metal with a low, resonant clang. 'I don't have much time for the Kharadron, but this *is* impressive. Proper, sturdy engineering. Almost reminds me of honest, well-crafted dwarf work. It will do me good to travel this way.'

Lhosia followed him to the ship, and over the next ten minutes, hundreds more people poured down onto the quayside – civilians and priests, flanked by lines of Gravesward, fleeing from the carnage behind them. The Lingering Keep was aflame. As buildings had collapsed, destroyed by the confused, rampaging ghouls, fires broke out, whipping through the corpse-filled streets and engulfing the city's temples and townhouses. The tower where Prince Volant had died had collapsed not long after the Gravesward removed the Unburied. The whole structure had been weakened by the terrorgheists, and there was now a column of whirling dust and embers where it had once stood.

Lord Aurun had seemed reinvigorated since Gotrek suggested leaving the city. He had taken command of Prince Volant's armies without a moment's thought, ordering them to form a defensive perimeter around the docks until the city's surviving civilians had made it down to the quayside. The bone rain had massacred many of the refugees, and the ghouls had killed even more, but there were still thousands of people left to swarm around the ancient ships, filling the air with a panicked clamour, laden with belongings and, in the case of the priests, cradling the cocoons that held the Unburied.

'Not much of a fight, eh?' said Gotrek as Lord Aurun made his way through the crowds.

Aurun nodded. 'They seem more interested in destroying each other than attacking us.'

'They are only the beginning,' said Trachos, his tone bleak. 'I have seen this happen in other underworlds. First come the creatures you call mordants, and then, once the kingdom is in tatters, the spirit hosts arrive, led by Nagash's own generals.'

Aurun looked back at the flames. 'I understand. The princedom is gone. I knew that the moment I heard Prince Volant's lies. It is time to begin again.'

Lhosia gazed up at the vast, furious face that loomed over them. 'But can we really leave? What will you do? How do we make them sail again?'

Trachos headed over to a ladder that reached up the side of the hull. 'If these ships still have aether-gold on board, as the *Spindrift* did, we should only have one problem.'

He started to climb, his sigmarite boots hammering on the ladder's metal rungs.

Gotrek nodded, looking pleased with himself. Then he frowned, staring up at Trachos. '*What* problem?'

Maleneth might have been imagining it, but she thought she heard a trace of humour in Trachos' reply.

'The conduits. They will most likely have corroded, as they did on the *Spindrift*. We'll need some way to channel the fuel.' He hesitated. 'A powerful piece of ur-gold would do it.'

Gotrek looked at his chest rune with a furious expression, preparing to howl an insult at Trachos.

Maleneth started to laugh.

Your Celestial Highnesses,

Forgive the break in communication, but after leaving Klemp, the Slayer's quest to find Nagash took a strange turn that led me beyond the reach of even the most dedicated Azyrite agents. I will spare you the details, at least until I return to Azyr, but suffice to say, I am still in Gotrek's company, as is the Stormcast Eternal, Lord Ordinator Trachos. We have finished our delightful sojourn in the Amethyst Princedoms and are now on the road to a stormkeep recommended by Trachos. It is a large fortress known as Hammerskáld, where I hope to find a messenger who can carry this missive to you. I find it hard to explain exactly how this has come to pass, but we will reach Hammerskáld travelling in a fleet of ancient Kharadron aether-ships, with a dispossessed nation trailing in our wake. The entire population of a forgotten underworld has adopted Gotrek as their holy saviour. Since leaving their homeland, many of their priests have painted stripes on their heads in mimicry of his greasy mohawk, and soldiers have hammered their weapons into new shapes in an attempt to make them resemble the Slayer's axe. It is singularly the most absurd thing I have ever seen – pale-faced waifs, in their hundreds, attempting to emulate the heavy tread of an inebriated duardin.

By all the gods of all the realms, I swear that I have no idea how such a thing is possible. But along with the absurdity of it, I sense something else. It is hard to explain, but I sense a significance to all of this that I cannot quite explain in words. I imagine you now think me as deluded as the refugees, but if you could see him, hauling an entire diaspora through these ruined hells, you might understand. He has an inexplicable magnetism. He attracts people as easily as he attracts flies. They are drawn to him, caught in his trajectory, convinced he can help even though he is so clearly unable to help himself.

He takes no pleasure in it, mind. Where others would delight in such adoration, Gotrek considers it an inconvenience, hurling abuse at his followers, demanding they leave him in peace and stop asking him so many questions. If it weren't for the alcohol they keep offering him, I think he would have jumped overboard days ago. He has clearly come to regret his newfound altruism. I imagine we will leave Hammerskáld without this fervid host in tow.

But I digress. The Master Rune is still safe, but I feel no closer to convincing the Slayer that he should return with me to Azyr. I had hoped he might do so as soon as we reach Hammerskáld, but I am troubled to report that he is now in the grips of a new obsession. Despite the dreadful ordeals we endured in the princedoms, he seems to have quite abandoned his mission to face Nagash. He now assures me that he can 'fix' the Mortal Realms if he can lay his hands on an axe he once owned. Apparently, the enormous fyreslayer greataxe he currently wields is not impressive enough. He says it hinders his ability to teach the realms any 'bloody sense', so he has set himself the challenge of retrieving a weapon that probably never existed beyond the addled confines of his own ale-steeped brain.

I am painfully aware that my return to Azyr is terribly overdue, your highnesses. And I imagine that you have despaired of me ever bringing you the rune. Perhaps you have even sent other agents of the Order to replace me and complete the job. But I will give you this warning – the Slayer will not be fooled, bought or strong-armed. For all his hatred of gods, he is the closest thing I have ever met to one. I have still to decide if he is a tragic simpleton or the greatest hero of the age, but whatever he is, I am closer to understanding him than anyone else alive. And I am therefore your best chance of harnessing the rune for Sigmar's crusade. For Khaine and the God-King, I swear I will find a way to claim this elusive prize. And, while doing so, I shall also endeavour to solve the infuriating enigma of Gotrek Gurnisson.

Your most loyal and faithful votary,
Maleneth Witchblade

ABOUT THE AUTHOR

Darius Hinks is the author of the Warhammer 40,000 novels *Blackstone Fortress*, *Blackstone Fortress: Ascension* and the accompanying audio drama *The Beast Inside*. He also wrote three novels in the Mephiston series: *Mephiston: Blood of Sanguinius*, *Mephiston: Revenant Crusade* and *Mephiston: City of Light*, as well as the Space Marine Battles novella *Sanctus*. His work for Age of Sigmar includes *Dominion*, *Hammers of Sigmar*, *Warqueen* and the Gotrek Gurnisson novels *Ghoulslayer* and *Gitslayer*. For Warhammer, he wrote *Warrior Priest*, which won the David Gemmel Morningstar Award for best newcomer, as well as the Orion trilogy, *Sigvald* and several novellas.

YOUR NEXT READ

BEASTGRAVE
by C L Werner

In the untamed wilds of Ghur, darkness is rising. Rival warbands battle over the dread Beastgrave. Will Beastlord Ghroth prevail or can Branchwraith Kyra and her dryads stop his foul plans?

For these stories and more, go to **blacklibrary.com**, **games-workshop.com**, Games Workshop and Warhammer stores, all good book stores or visit one of the thousands of independent retailers worldwide, which can be found at **games-workshop.com/storefinder**

An Extract from
Beastgrave
by C L Werner

The stink of burning flesh slammed against Ludvik's senses and drove the last wisps of sleep from his head. He was roused from exhausted slumber by the blaring of the watchtower's trumpet, and the foul stench was enough to snap him into full awareness. No mistake, no idiot's jest. Calamity had befallen Locmalo, and every inhabitant of the town was being called to action.

As he rushed from the earthen barracks he shared with twenty other men, Ludvik saw flames leaping up into the night. They threw eerie shadows across the clustered timber buildings. Several of the structures were alight, with fire flashing from their windows and doorways. Plumes of smoke rushed up from beneath crumbling sod roofs – long grey fingers that spilled upwards into the sky.

More than the roar of the flames and the blare of the trumpet assailed Ludvik's ears. Screams rang out from the burning homes. He saw a ragged figure emerge from Marek the cooper's house. The fire-wrapt shape took a few stumbling steps and collapsed in the muddy street. Steam sizzled off the dying frontiersman's smouldering clothes.

Ludvik's first instinct was to run for the nearest well and seize one of the buckets laid there against the threat of fire. As he turned to do so, another sound impressed itself on his awareness. A sound more frightful than the shrieks of people trapped in burning houses. Inhuman howls and bestial war-whoops rose from beyond the log palisade that encircled Locmalo. Ludvik felt cold horror rush through him. He knew the sort of creatures that made that savage din, just as he knew the doom that now reached out for the settlement. A doom the humans had long thought to defy.

The children of the forest had come. Come to punish this invasion into their domain. Come to sweep away the creep of civilisation into the wild places and stamp out the human trespassers.

Ludvik's hand fell to the long-bladed hunter's knife that was always strapped to his arm. The frontiersmen had learned to their cost to never be without some means of protection, even when in the safety of their own beds. He had seen Udalrich's body. He had been murdered in the night by a stealthy prowler. The inhuman killer had cut him open to eat his liver, all without waking the other dozen men in the barracks.

'They have broken through the outer wall!' The shout carried down from the frantic sentinel up in the watchtower between blasts on the trumpet. The reaction of the men around Ludvik was a mixture of despair and anger. For himself, he felt only a kind of sickness in his belly, a sour churning of the soup he had for supper.

Two palisades defended Locmalo – an outer and an inner fence of sharpened logs. Between these was a cleared pasture where the people grazed their herds. Ludvik himself had two cows out there, animals he had purchased with the pelts he had captured through the autumn. It was his first step towards becoming independent, establishing himself so he would not have to brave the forest and the beasts that yet lurked beneath its boughs.

Ludvik heard the agonised wailing of the cattle. The attackers were in the pasture and slaughtering the livestock. For a moment, all he could think of was his own loss. Then a cold chill swept through him. If the attackers found a way through or over the inner wall, it would be men not kine that would be massacred.

Ludvik ran towards the walls. He saw the beadle with a cartload of spears handing weapons to anyone who came near him. Men and women, old and young, anyone with the strength and heart to carry a bow or swing an axe, were hurrying to the palisade to take up the fight. Ludvik hurried to the beadle and snatched a spear from the cart. He took only a heartbeat to judge its quality before he was moving again. The muddy streets of Locmalo were a bedlam of fright and confusion. As the defenders ran towards the walls, fiery objects came hurtling down into the settlement. Ludvik saw one of them splash in a puddle of mud. It was an old skull stuffed with dried dung and sealed with pitch. He saw the crude glyphs daubed on the skull in streaks of blood. He trembled. Their enemies had called upon witchcraft to aid the attack.

More of the skulls came flying over the wall. They burned with an ugly orange glow as they sailed through the air. One of them struck the roof of the tannery. It shattered like an eggshell and splashed its contents across the roof and the nearby walls. Timbers were instantly set alight. Ludvik felt there was an unholiness about the way the flames spread. The fire's hunger was more than natural.

'To the wall! To the wall!' The command was shouted by Squire Dytryk himself. He stood near the main gate, Locmalo's five militiamen arrayed around him in a compact bloc. Only one of the soldiers wore his armour. The others had been stirred from their sleep with barely enough time to grab helmets and shields. The squire himself only had a bearskin robe on, though he'd picked up his sword before dashing out into the street.

'To the wall!'

The cry was taken up. The direction gave the defenders focus, something to fixate upon before fear and confusion could break their resolve. Ludvik joined the line of spears that formed about the base of the wall. He jabbed upwards at the dark shapes trying to climb the palisade. He felt grim satisfaction when a horned figure fell back into the shadows and a thin rivulet of blood trickled down the shaft of his spear.

A few hunters with bows moved among the spearmen, adding their arrows into the mix. Ludvik wished he had gone back for his own bow as he watched his comrades ply their deadly skill. Whenever an enemy presented itself, an arrow would speed towards it. Even when they missed, the threat from the archers was enough to make the attacker drop back.

Behind the line of spears, those settlers with axes and swords clutched their weapons with anxious fingers. As much as Ludvik envied the hunters with their bows, he was thankful he had at least a spear to drive the attackers back. If all he had was an axe or his knife, he'd be forced to stand idle with the others. Watching and waiting. Dreading the moment when he would be called into the fight. The moment the beastkin forced their way into Locmalo.

Ghroth watched the fires rise, their glow illuminating the inner palisade. The herdchief wiped the string of saliva that dripped from his fangs. The smell of cooking human was almost intoxicating, far more than the scent of slaughtered cattle. It did not take much to goad the brays and ungors of his warherd into charging the wall. The real test of his authority was getting the larger gors to restrain themselves. Few beastkin understood patience or had the discipline to plan for the future, however immediate it might be.

Ghroth was one of those few. His craftiness and his ability to delay gratification, were what set him apart. It was why he had supplanted the old herdchief, waiting until after a vicious fight with the tree-fiends of Thornwyld before challenging him for his position. He wore the horns of his rival, bound around his left hand like a spiked gauntlet. It was a reminder to the rest of the beastkin of his strength. When the warren of humans was crushed under his hooves, that too would serve as a reminder to the warherd. It would be a display of his wisdom. An example of his power.

The ungors and brays threw themselves at the walls. Smaller and slighter than the more bestial gors like Ghroth, their lack of bulk was something of a benefit to them as they tried to clamber up the logs. Covered in fur, with hoofed feet and nubby horns, these beastkin were closer to humans in appearance than others in the warherd. The brays in particular had manlike faces and builds – Ghroth even employed them to decoy humans in the forest by making them think the brays were men like themselves.

With their present task, there was no question of the brays being mistaken for humans. The frontiersmen were attacking anything that tried to get over the walls. At the edge of panic, their desperate efforts were fending off the beastmen. Many of the ungors fell into the pasture with ugly gashes and cuts. A few of the brays collapsed with arrows through their chests.

'Small horns never get in.' The comment came as a sullen growl from the armoured brute that stood beside Ghroth. A full head taller than the herdchief, Kruksh had adorned his black-furred girth with metal plate looted from dead humans and orruks. Even his goat-like face was banded with strips of mail. The grotesque greenskin cleaver he carried would have been impossible for most gors to wield.

Ghroth glared into the bestigor's beady yellow eyes. Kruksh

grunted in contempt. There was no cunning in his gaze, only the impertinent confidence of a creature that relied solely upon his brawn. 'Small horns not need get in,' Ghroth stated. He gestured at the injured ungors and at the tips of the spears that could be seen waving behind the wall. 'Small horns fight. Show where manflesh fight. See where manflesh strong.' He gave Kruksh a piercing look, trying to find some awareness there. 'See where manflesh strong, see where manflesh weak.'

Kruksh slapped his chest and snorted. 'All manflesh weak,' he asserted.

Ghroth bared his fangs at the implied insult. He raised his arm, ensuring Kruksh could see the sharpened horns of the old herdchief. The bestigor lowered his head and averted his eyes. There was no challenge there. At least not yet. Ghroth resisted the impulse to tear out Kruksh's throat. Right now killing the humans was more important. Besides, it was more practical to kill a rival in front of the entire warherd. That way all of the beastkin would know their place.

The sharp tang of smouldering dung made Ghroth turn. He watched a pair of ungors run towards the palisade with smoking skulls in their hands. Loops of dried gut were wound about the skulls and, as the beastmen drew close to the wall, they swung the weird missiles in an arc. When the arc reached the right speed, the ungors let go and sent the skulls flying over the wall. A moment later there was a loud whoosh and flames erupted from the settlement.

Ghroth stalked over to where the ungors had received their macabre weapons. His nostrils flared in revulsion at the unnatural scent of the creature crouched beside a stack of skulls. Useful as magic might be to the warherd, none of the beastkin liked to be near something as steeped in the arcane reek as the shaman Sorgaas. The cloaked mystic was daubing glyphs on the skulls with the severed head of a serpent. He dipped the reptile's blunt nose into a bowl of blood and painted the sorcerous signs on the bones. Normally the smell of blood would excite Ghroth, but the shaman's activity had corrupted the scent, made it somehow rancid.

'More flame for manflesh,' Ghroth growled, trying to make the words more of a command than a question. He was chief of his warherd – even the giant bullgors obeyed him – but he still felt a tremor of fear when the smell of Sorgaas was in his nose.

The shaman looked up from his labour, the hood of his cloak drawing back to expose a lupine muzzle covered in blue-black fur. A single horn rose from above his nose, branching out into two sharp points. The entirety of the horn was stained with glyphs, and talismans dangled from its bifurcated tips. Cold eyes, yellow and slitted like those of a serpent, stared up at Ghroth. Sorgaas lifted a hand that was scaly, with black talons at the tip of each finger, utterly unlike the slender gloved member that held the snake's head.

'All will burn,' Sorgaas said. He turned his talons towards the pile of skulls. 'Magic enough for all of these. This is why I tell you to wait.' He thrust his claw skyward and pointed at the stars. 'Now is the time when my magic is strong. Now is when the gods of men are weak.'

Ghroth glowered at the shaman. 'Ghroth herdchief,' he stated. 'Victory mine.'

Sorgaas tapped the snake's head against the skull he was painting. 'Yes, and these will bring you victory. You will be a mighty herdlord. If you listen.' The ophidian eyes strayed from Ghroth and focused on the two ungors who had come creeping back to retrieve more of the fiery skulls.

Ghroth followed the direction of the shaman's gaze. The ungors cringed away from him. He grunted his satisfaction and motioned for the beastmen to continue. Whatever awe they might feel for their shaman, they did not forget it was their herdchief who ruled.

'Burn the manflesh,' Ghroth snarled. 'They know fire. They know fear.' He turned and looked at the palisade, drawing the smell of humans from the wind. 'They know death,' he declared. 'Good feast for warherd.'

Ghroth studied the way the ungors and brays were driven back. He fought against the impulse to simply charge the fortification. There had been other attacks against the humans before, attacks that had failed because the beastkin did not restrain their bloodlust. Ghroth would show the warherd. He would show them why he was their leader. This attack would not fail.

The packs of ungors and brays rushed the walls, pressing the defenders to divert fighters to oppose them. The gate itself was only lightly challenged, just enough so that the humans would not become suspicious. If they were too wary they would try to reinforce it, but if they could be gulled into believing the warherd was threatening the whole of the palisade it would cause them to move where the danger was greatest.

After a few moments of study, Ghroth turned to Sorgaas. 'Give signal,' he told the shaman.

Sorgaas set down the snake head and rose to his feet. He clasped his mismatched hands together, pressing them tight against his chest. The slithery eyes rolled back, the pupils vanishing beneath the orbits of his skull. An eerie chill gripped Ghroth as dark energies were drawn into the mystic's body. The dangling talismans clattered against the bifurcated horn as Sorgaas shivered.

'*Urugu*,' Sorgaas suddenly shouted. He thrust both arms into the air and from between his hands a stream of green light flared up into the night.